SUMMER at

FORSAKEN LAKE

MICHAEL D. BEIL

A Yearling Book

Text copyright © 2012 by Michael D. Beil
Cover art copyright © 2012 by Greg Call
Illustrations copyright © 2012 by Maggie Kneen

All rights reserved. Published in the United States by Yearling, an imprint of Random House Children's Books, a division of Random House, Inc., New York.
Originally published in hardcover in the United States by Alfred A. Knopf, an imprint of Random House Children's Books, New York, in 2012. Yearling and the jumping horse design are registered trademarks of Random House, Inc.

Visit us on the Web! randomhouse.com/kids
Educators and librarians, for a variety of teaching tools, visit us at RHTeachersLibrarians.com

The Library of Congress has cataloged the hardcover edition
of this work as follows:
Beil, Michael D.
Summer at Forsaken Lake / by Michael D. Beil.
p. cm.
Summary: Twelve-year-old Nicholas and his ten-year-old, twin sisters, Hetty and Haley, spend the summer with their Great-Uncle Nick at Forsaken Lake, where he and their new friend Charlie investigate the truth about an accident involving their families many years before.
ISBN 978-0-375-86742-2 (trade) — ISBN 978-0-375-96742-9 (lib. bdg.) —
ISBN 978-0-375-89791-7 (ebook)
[1. Summer—Fiction. 2. Families—Fiction. 3. Lakes—Fiction.
4. Great-uncles—Fiction. 5. Ohio—Fiction. 6. Mystery and detective stories.] I. Title.
PZ7.B38823495Su 2012 [Fic]—dc23 2011023511

ISBN 978-0-375-86496-4 (pbk.)

Printed in the United States of America
10 9 8 7 6 5 4 3
First Yearling Edition 2013

To the memory of James and Dorothy Yargo

June 20
Dear Dad,

   The train just crossed into Pennsylvania, and the conductor told us that it's still a LONG way to Erie. So far, it isn't too bad, even if the whole train does smell like somebody threw up. Not that different from the subway in New York, I guess.

   Thanks for the extra money—pretty sneaky sticking it inside a book. You probably thought I wouldn't find it until August, but Treasure Island looked a lot more interesting than the books I HAVE to read this summer, so I started it while we were waiting at Penn Station. I'm still not sure what I'll have to spend money on in Deming, Ohio. Mom says there's no movies and no fast food for miles. Oh well, I'm sure I'll figure out something.

   The twins threw this huge fit last night, and said they weren't going to get on the train. Mom finally got them to settle down by promising them that if they behaved all summer with Uncle Nick, she'll get them a puppy in the fall. I should throw a tantrum—maybe she'll send me away to boarding school and I won't have to put up with the twins anymore. To tell you the truth, I wish I were on the plane with you to Cameroon instead of on this smelly train, even

1

though I looked up "meningitis" last night and it sounds kind of scary. Be careful, okay?

Love,
Nicholas

PS I forgot to tell you: I got two hits and turned two double plays in our last game of the season. We lost anyway.

CHAPTER ONE

Goblin tugged at her mooring, darting back and forth, her bow pitching high in the air and then dropping violently with every frothy, white-tipped wave. Her rope halyards—used to hoist the sails—slapped against the varnished wooden mast, and a corner of sail that had worked loose flapped noisily in the steadily building breeze. The leaves of the sugar maple tree in the front yard, so brilliantly green a few minutes earlier, turned their dull undersides upward, a million mirrors reflecting the angry gray sky above. Farther out on the lake, the whitecaps were already beaten down by a curtain of rain being pulled across the lake and toward the house and porch where Nicholas Mettleson sat.

Goblin tugged at her mooring, darting back and forth, her bow pitching high in the air and then dropping violently with every frothy, white-tipped wave.

His uncle—great-uncle, actually—had promised to take him and his twin sisters sailing today, but now that would have to wait. The worst of the squall—the heavy wind and the thunder and lightning—would pass by quickly, but the forecast called for the rain to continue most of the day. Nicholas was only a little bit disappointed, though. After all, it was just the third day of summer vacation; there would be plenty of time to learn to sail in the next two and a half months.

A few minutes later, Nicholas's great-uncle Nick, a steaming mug of coffee in hand, came out onto the porch through the screen door, followed by his gray-muzzled dog, Pistol. "Mind if we join you? Looks like a doozy. No better place for watching a good thunderstorm."

Nicholas smiled at him and scooted to the end of the wooden porch swing, where he felt the mist on his face as the rain blew through the screening. "Do you think *Goblin* will be all right?" he asked. "It's really bouncing around out there."

"Oh, don't worry about her. She'll be fine—ridden out worse lots of times. Much worse." The chains supporting the swing squeaked as Nick and his young namesake settled in to watch the storm with Pistol curled up on the seat between them.

"Did you really build it, er, *her*?" Nicholas asked. He had been sailing only once before—in a much smaller boat at summer camp upstate two years earlier—and was still getting used to the idea that the twenty-eight-foot

Goblin was a *she*, not an *it*. He was also trying to figure out how Nick, who, as a young man, had lost most of his left arm in a farming accident, could possibly have hand-built a boat as beautiful as *Goblin*.

"From keel to masthead," Nick said proudly. "I'll show you some pictures later if you like. Built her in the barn out back."

Just then, a jagged blue flash of lightning lit up the darkened sky, and they both braced for the loud *crack* that followed.

"That was *close*," Nicholas said, a touch of worry in his voice.

"Mrs. Phillips's television antenna," said Nick. "Gets it most every time. Sticks up about a hundred and ten feet. All so she can watch those soap operas. Never had much use for television myself. There's a little one around here somewhere, if you kids get desperate. Course, reception isn't much out here. Last time I checked, I think I picked up two stations in Erie."

"Aren't you afraid the lightning will hit *Goblin?*" Nicholas asked.

"Oh, I'm sure it has—more than once. No harm—she's properly grounded. The current goes from the mast right down through the keel and out."

"What if you were holding on to the mast when it hit?"

"Can't say as I'd recommend that, Nicholas. You'd

probably look a lot like one of those neon signs in Times Square."

Nicholas laughed. *Maybe this won't be such a boring summer after all.* Before Nick picked them up at the train station in Erie, Nicholas had met his uncle a grand total of three times: twice at weddings, and once for the funeral of Nick's wife, Lillie, who had died two years earlier. When his dad first suggested sending him and his twin sisters to Nick's house on Forsaken Lake for the whole summer, Nicholas was skeptical—especially after looking up the word "forsaken" in the dictionary and discovering that it meant "abandoned or desolate." On the inside, he was quite certain that he would hate it, but his dad seemed so excited about it that he hid his true feelings—or tried to. Even though he had never spent any time "in the country" himself, all his friends back in New York City assured him that it would be the most boring summer of his life.

"There's nothing to do in the country," said one.

"There's nowhere fun to go," said another.

"And everybody knows everything you do," said yet another. "So you can't do anything *fun* anyway."

Nicholas's father, Dr. Will Mettleson, painted a very different picture of life at the old Victorian house, just steps from the lake. Growing up, he spent several summers with Uncle Nick and Aunt Lillie, and loved every second. He learned to fish and sail and camp and how to build things with his own two hands, and he swore to Nicholas that he never once missed the city while he was there. And he promised Nicholas that if he hated it, he wouldn't have to go back the next summer.

But something else his father said really got Nicholas's curiosity moving at warp speed.

"That old house of Uncle Nick's, and the lake—they're both full of secrets. You just have to know where to look. You never know what you might find."

"Like what?" a wide-eyed Nicholas asked, forgetting his skepticism for a moment.

"Start in the tower room," his father said. "That's where I always slept. It has the best view; heck, it's the best room in the house. Maybe the nicest room on the whole lake. I've already checked with Uncle Nick—it's yours if you want it."

The tower room, he explained, jutted up through the middle of the house as if somebody had set a greenhouse on the roof, and could be reached only by climbing a tightly wound, vertigo-inducing spiral staircase. The windows gave it a spectacular view of the lake, and on summer nights when the air was perfectly still and it was too hot to sleep in the other bedrooms, a breeze blew through the gauzy, sun-bleached curtains, keeping the room comfortable. Inside, it was the ultimate in simplicity. A bed. A small dresser. A brass telescope on a tripod. In other words, the perfect room for the twelve-year-old Nicholas Mettleson.

Nick and Nicholas sat together, swinging slowly back and forth as they watched and listened to the storm barreling past them. The lake was calm again, its surface ruffled only by the rain that continued to fall, though not nearly as hard. With a sailing lesson out of the question for the time being, Nicholas decided it was a good time to start his exploration of the house—beginning with the tower room.

"I'm going upstairs for a while, to watch from my room," he said. "I'll bet it's like being right *in* the storm cloud."

Nick sent him off with a little wave. "Go. Enjoy. We'll go into town in a while. I need to pick up a few things. You can do a bit of exploring if you'd rather not go to the A&P."

Nicholas climbed the staircase, past the small, simply framed oil paintings that lined the walls, not noticing until he reached the last one that they were all signed *Lillie*. He didn't even know that his great-aunt had been a painter—and a pretty good one, he thought as he backed down the stairs to get a closer look at each. The paintings were a scrapbook of her life: the house and barn built by her great-grandfather in 1895; the lake in all four seasons; the yard, with its towering maples and poplars; and finally, Nick's pride and joy, *Goblin*—resting peacefully at her mooring in one painting, heeled over with spray flying over her bow in another. That one made Nicholas want to go sailing even more.

"Look, you can see all the way across the lake!"

"Whatcha lookin' at?" asked Hayley from the bottom of the stairs.

She and her twin sister, Hetty, had celebrated their tenth birthday a few days earlier. What with that momentous occasion and the long train ride from New York with only Nicholas for supervision, they saw themselves as *quite* grown up.

"Some pictures. I didn't know you were up. Did you have breakfast?" He was under strict orders to look after his sisters—to make sure they ate and went to bed on time and brushed their teeth.

"Of course we're up," said Hetty, joining Hayley. "How could anyone sleep through that awful thunder and lightning? I made toast. And Great-uncle Nick let us have coffee."

"You don't have to call him Great-uncle Nick, you know. Uncle Nick is fine. And you know you're not supposed to drink coffee—Mom said so."

"Can we come up?" Hetty asked. "We haven't seen the tower room yet."

"We've only been here a day," Nicholas said.

"Please? We won't bug you. Promise," said Hayley.

"All right. You've got five minutes."

They ran up the stairs, pushing past Nicholas and into the tower room, where they went straight to the windows that looked out over the lake.

"Oh, it's looovely," said Hayley, taking on a sophisticated air. "Look, you can see all the way across the lake!"

"You can do that from the porch, you idiot," sniped Nicholas.

"Don't be rude," Hetty said, pushing the curtain aside and pointing at *Goblin*. "I wonder why he named it *Goblin*. It's too pretty to be a goblin. Are we still going sailing today?"

"I doubt it. It's supposed to rain all day. He said we're going into town later to do some grocery shopping." Nicholas sat on the bed, leaning back against the headboard and noticing for the first time the two squarish oil paintings on the wall between the windows. The first was of the lake at night, the moon's reflection a diagonal slash across the rippled surface; in the distance, a sailboat—too small to be *Goblin*—seemed to be disappearing into the mist. The second, which looked as if it had been painted aboard the moored *Goblin*, showed the front of the house in the early evening, with golden light shining through the windows.

"Did you guys know that Aunt Lillie was an artist?" Nicholas asked.

"Duh. Of *course*," Hayley answered. "Mom and Dad used to have one just like this in their bedroom."

"Since when?"

"Since forever. It wasn't exactly like these—it just has the lake and the yard and some trees, I think."

"Where is it now?" Nicholas asked.

Hayley shrugged. "I dunno. I think Daddy took it with him after they—"

"Look! You can see someone in the tower room in this one!" Hetty cried.

"It looks like an old woman," said Hayley.

"She probably painted herself into the picture," Nicholas said, moving in for a closer look. "We saw a painting in school like that. Let me see."

The twins were right; there was a figure standing at the window, appearing to look back at the viewer, but the person's features were blurry, so it was impossible to tell who it was.

"Wait—there's someone else, sitting on the swing on the porch. That is definitely Uncle Nick," Nicholas said. Then he lifted the frame from the wall to look at the back of the canvas. "She painted this one in 1978. It's called *Evening Light*."

"What about the other one?" Hetty asked. "Wait, let me guess. *Moonlight Sail*."

"Not even close," Nicholas said, removing the painting from the wall. "It's called *2:53 A.M.*" He turned the painting over for another look. "That's definitely not *Goblin*. I wonder what boat it is."

He was about to rehang it when Hayley stopped him. "Wait. What's that?" She pointed at the wall where the painting had been hanging.

"What's what?" asked Nicholas. "Ohhh. That's weird."

Just below the nail on which the picture hung, a thin wire stuck out of a small hole in the wall, its end twisted into a loop. Nicholas put the end of his index finger in the loop and was about to give it a good tug when Hetty shouted, "Wait! What if it, you know, rings a bell that . . . summons evil?"

Nicholas couldn't help laughing at that. "Summons evil? Hetty, what have you been watching?"

She backed slowly away as he pulled steadily on the wire. It came out easily at first; then there was a bit more resistance.

"Stop! I heard something moving," Hayley said, feeling the wood paneling beneath the windowsill. "Right here, I think."

"I'm getting out of here," said Hetty, moving against the wall near the stairs.

"Do it again," Hayley insisted.

Nicholas pulled firmly again, this time not letting the wire slip back.

Hayley jumped when a section of the paneling sprang open, hinged at the bottom. "A secret compartment," she whispered.

"Cool," said Nicholas, kneeling down. "The wire connects to this latch."

"Wh-what's inside?" asked Hetty, edging closer, but still looking as if she expected Satan himself to pop out of the hole in the wall.

Nicholas waggled his eyebrows at his sisters. "There's only one way to find out." He felt around at the bottom for a few seconds, then reached farther back behind the wall, and farther, until . . . suddenly his arm was yanked by an unseen force, and he shouted, "Hey! Something grabbed my— Help!"

Hayley and Hetty screamed in perfect unison as Nicholas twisted and turned on the floor in apparent agony, his arm being pulled deeper and deeper.

"What should we do?" yelled Hayley, looking frantically at her twin.

But Hetty just screamed again.

"Gotcha!" shouted Nicholas, jumping to his feet.

Hayley and Hetty stood openmouthed for a full second before shouting, "Nicholas!"

"Man, you should have seen the looks on your faces," he said. "And by the way, thanks for all the help. Fat lot of good you two will be if I'm ever really in trouble."

"Everything all right up there?" a concerned-sounding Nick asked from the bottom of the stairs.

"We're fine, Uncle Nick," said Nicholas. "Just fooling around."

"He was being mean to us," Hetty tattled, sticking her tongue out at Nicholas.

"Well, be careful," said Nick. "Don't need anybody falling down these stairs and breaking their neck. Ruin your whole day. The rain's letting up, so we're heading into town in a few minutes."

"Okay, we'll be down in a second," Nicholas said.

He went back to the secret hiding place and reached in

once again. The twins kept away from him, arms crossed and half expecting him to try to trick them again. There was no trick, though. First, he pulled out a tattered spiral notebook, its front cover nearly torn off, and set it on the floor. The second item was more mysterious-looking. It was a round metal canister, gray-green in color, about six inches in diameter and half an inch thick. Someone had printed *The Seaweed Strangler* on one side with a black marker. Nicholas gently lifted the lid off and saw that a reel of movie film lay inside—the narrowest film he had ever seen. He unwound a few inches of the film and held it up to the light, but the pictures were so small he couldn't make anything out.

Meanwhile, Hayley picked up the notebook and flattened out the cover with her hand. "*The Seaweed Strangler*, by Will Mettleson," she read.

"Daddy wrote a story?" Hetty asked.

"Looks that way," Nicholas responded, glancing at the notebook. "But this is old movie film—from before video cameras were invented. I wonder if he . . ."

"What?" asked Hetty. "If he *what?*"

Nicholas turned to the twins. "I think maybe he made a *movie.*"

"Daddy? Made a movie?" said a doubtful-sounding Hayley.

"Can we watch it?" Hetty asked, getting more excited by the second.

"All right, kids, time to go," Nick shouted up at them.

"We'll be right down," Nicholas said, placing the film reel back in its canister and setting it and the notebook on the bed.

"I can't believe Daddy made a movie," said Hetty.

Nicholas smiled to himself, remembering his father's words: *You never know what you might find.*

* * *

One detail that Nicholas's father hadn't considered when planning his children's summer at the lake was Nick's attachment to his pickup truck, the only vehicle he had and the last remnant of his days as the owner of a small Ford dealership in Deming. It was a 1968 Ford—built long before the addition of backseats and other creature comforts. Nope, Betty (for that was her name—and no, Uncle Nick wasn't telling why) was a *truck*. Firm bench seat. AM radio. Manual transmission. (Nicholas marveled at Nick's one-armed driving technique.) Air-conditioning? In a truck? Who needs it when you have perfectly good windows that roll down . . . by cranking a little handle!

After the four of them squeezed into the cab, Pistol, a mix of beagle and who-knows-what-else, jumped in on Nicholas's lap before he could close the door.

"I guess Pistol's coming with us," Uncle Nick said. "You'll have to hold on to him if he sees any rabbits. He'll go right out the window after them."

Hayley and Hetty looked at their uncle doubtfully. "He wouldn't really," said Hetty.

Nick held up two fingers. "Done it twice already. The first time we were stopped, but the second we were going about twenty-five."

"Wh-what happened to him?" Hayley asked.

Nick shrugged. "Nothing much. Limped a little for a couple of days. He's a tough old son of a gun."

As they reached the end of the long gravel drive and pulled out onto Lake Road, Nicholas rolled his window up partway and slipped three fingers under Pistol's collar. Pistol turned to look at him, his tongue hanging from the left side of his mouth.

"Looks like you've met your match," Nick said.

Nicholas wasn't sure if that was meant for him or Pistol.

* * *

When they got to town, Nick and the twins went into the A&P, on Deming's town square, while Nicholas decided to follow Nick's advice and do a little exploring. He bought a can of soda at the corner gas station and then, remembering his promise to send his dad a letter or a postcard a week, stopped to browse through a rack of outdated postcards on the sidewalk in front of the drugstore. There were the usual pictures of the old railroad station, and the town square (with cars from the fifties and sixties parked in front of the diner), and a couple of aerial shots of the lake. They were ten for a dollar, so he picked out a dollar's worth, paid for them out of the money his dad had handed to him in the train station, and then started to walk up a side street with signs indicating that a school was nearby. Halfway down the block, a Little League baseball team was practicing in the yard behind a tired-looking school building. Except for a chain-link backstop, the field was bare; the outfield was covered in grass and weeds badly in need of cutting, and the infield was good old-fashioned dirt—which, on a rainy day like this one, meant good old-fashioned *mud*. Nicholas stopped and leaned against an oak tree next to the sidewalk to watch. On his team in New York, the Yorkville Yankees, he was a decent-fielding second baseman with a solid .285 batting average. But everyone knows that pitching wins baseball games, and the Yankees, sadly lacking in that department, ended the season in last place. Of course, if they had made the play-offs, he would probably still be in New York.

On the "mound"—actually a rubber floor mat from a car, set in the middle of the infield mud—a girl was getting ready to pitch. A long brown ponytail hung through the back of her cap, and she blew an enormous bubble with her gum as she listened to some instructions from the coach, who sat in a folding chair where the first-base-side dugout would be—if there *were* a dugout.

"Don't try to strike him out," he said of the chubby, red-cheeked boy waiting in the batter's box. "You can't strike *everybody* out, Charlie. Keep it low. Make him hit it on the ground."

She shrugged and blew another bubble. "I'll try."

The first pitch came in low, as the coach requested, and *considerably* harder than Nicholas expected. It landed safely in the catcher's mitt with a satisfying *pop* as the batter swung late.

On the sidewalk, Nicholas involuntarily puckered his lips into a silent whistle. If they'd had a pitcher like her on his team, maybe they would have won a few more games.

"C'mon, Crenshaw!" the coach yelled at the batter. "Look alive up there. You were late by a mile—and that wasn't even her best stuff."

Who is this kid?

She wiped her forehead with the back of her glove and stared in at poor overmatched Crenshaw. The second pitch was chest-high and even harder than the first, and he missed it, too.

"Not even close," the coach shouted at him. "Charlie, give him something to hit. This is supposed to be batting practice. The fielders are getting bored out there."

She turned to the shortstop, who sat cross-legged on an old duffel bag at the edge of the infield, and smiled. "Sorry, Zack."

He waved. "Hey, no problemo. Next time remind me to bring a video game or something."

Then she got set and threw a perfect strike—right down the middle of the plate—as Crenshaw swung fiercely, spinning and knocking himself down in the process. The ball smacked the catcher's mitt so hard that the catcher hopped up to his feet, shaking his hand in pain.

Nicholas hadn't intended to laugh out loud, but the sight of Crenshaw crumpled on the ground and the tiny catcher jumping up and down in pain made it impossible for him to contain that one loud *"Ha!"*

The pitcher glanced over at him and smiled. "You wanna try me, funny guy?"

Nicholas blushed a little, not saying anything and trying to blend into the oak tree. The rest of the infield joined in, taunting him to pick up a bat and show what he was made of.

"You're not afraid of a *girl*, are you?" the shortstop asked.

"Who is he, anyway?" asked the first baseman. "A spy from the Tigers?"

"Look at him—he looks like a wimp. I'll bet he can't even lift a bat," the second baseman teased.

Nicholas weighed his options. He could just walk—or run—away. Even though it seemed likely that he would never see any of them again, he knew that was a lousy choice. He had a pretty good idea of what he and his teammates would say to someone scurrying away in the same situation, and he couldn't bear the thought of hearing those insults.

He briefly considered faking an injury, telling them all he was recovering from a broken wrist, when he suddenly nodded at the pitcher. "Okay, why not?" he said. *What are you doing? Did you see that last pitch?*

"You sure about this, kid?" the coach asked. "You play ball?"

"Yeah, I can play. Not here—in New York," he said, picking through the scattered bats, looking for something his size.

"Oooohhh," the shortstop chided, assuming—in this case, correctly—that anyone from New York was from New York City. "A city kid. Show him how we do things around here, Charlie."

Nicholas finally selected a bat and wished that he'd worn a baseball cap so there would be something between his head and the disgusting batting helmet he pulled on. There was no way he was facing anybody who threw that hard without a helmet; that much he knew. Then he took his place in the batter's box, digging his feet into the sandy soil around home plate.

"You want my best stuff?" the pitcher asked.

"Definitely," Nicholas said, hoisting the bat over his shoulder. "When I get a hit off you, I don't want you to have any excuses."

Oh, that's good. Make her mad.

"That's fair," she said.

Nicholas, remembering something his coach told him about facing a pitcher for the first time, decided *not* to swing at the first pitch no matter how tempting it looked. He tensed as she went into her windup and let loose a fastball that was low and inside. It was a ball, but not by much. In four years of Little League in New York, he had never faced anyone who threw as hard as this ponytailed girl. He choked up on the bat a few inches and waited for the next pitch.

It was waist-high, on the inside half of the plate, the kind of pitch he usually laced over the shortstop's head into left field. Not this time, though. He swung his hardest, but he was late and the ball slammed into the mitt behind him. His lips did that involuntary whistle thing again. He stepped back to reevaluate, choking up another inch.

She was smiling at him from the mound, not a mean-spirited smile, but one that said, *I can't help myself—this is what I do.* And then she reared back and fired again. This time, Nicholas was ready, and he fouled the pitch off to the first-base side, forcing the coach to duck. He was still swinging late, but at least he made contact, which the girl acknowledged with a slight nod in his direction.

That foul ball gave Nicholas confidence, and he stepped up to the plate, wagging the bat over his shoulder, waiting for another chance. *I don't need a home run,* he thought. *A ground ball. A pop fly. Just don't strike out.*

On the mound, the girl took a deep breath and let go. The pitch was chest-high and well inside, and Nicholas instinctively jerked his head back—just in time to watch something extraordinary happen. A few feet before reaching him, the ball took a sharp left turn and gracefully crossed over the center of the plate, leaving him standing there openmouthed. A perfect big-league-quality curveball, unlike anything he'd ever seen in New York.

"Steee-rike three!" the catcher yelled.

"Yerrrr outta there!" the shortstop added unnecessarily.

Nicholas let the bat fall to the ground at his feet, which were still frozen in place. "Who *is* this kid?" he asked no one in particular.

"She's your worst nightmare, son," the coach answered. "A cute girl with a wicked curveball. Remember this name, kid: Charlotte Brennan. Charlie. You'll be hearing it again."

"You sure you don't wanna try one more time, city boy?" the girl asked. "C'mon. You're just getting warmed up." She seemed to want him to stick around, but Nicholas figured that was only because she wanted to humiliate him again.

He smiled and shook his head. "Maybe another time. I've gotta go." Overhead, the rumble of thunder confirmed that he was making the right decision.

"Well, I guess we'll see ya round," Charlie said, smiling back.

Charlie Brennan. Remember that name.

CHAPTER TWO

He got back to the truck just as the rain started to fall again, huge drops bouncing off the hood and roof with loud *ping*s. Uncle Nick, the twins, and Pistol were waiting for him, and they squeezed together to make room on the seat.

"Where did you go?" Hayley asked.

"Nowhere. Just down the street. Watching some kids play baseball."

"You should have played with them," Hetty said. "You're good at baseball."

"That right?" Nick asked.

"I'm okay," said Nicholas.

"We'll have to play some catch," said Nick. "If it ever stops raining."

Nicholas wasn't sure if his uncle was kidding or not. He looked at Nick's empty left sleeve, safety-pinned to the side of his shirt. "R-really?"

"What, you think I can't play catch with only one arm?"

"Um, no, I just, uh . . ."

Nick laughed. "It's okay, Nicholas. It's a fair assumption. I guess your dad never told you."

"Told me what?"

"Well, before I lost this," he started, glancing at his left shoulder, "I was a good ballplayer—shortstop. Played for the high school team, then a little American Legion ball—even had a tryout with the Pirates. Guess I wasn't quite *that* good. When I lost my arm, I didn't want to give up playing ball forever, so I taught myself how to pitch. I knew I'd never be much of a hitter again, and nobody expects the pitcher to be much of a hitter, you know what I mean? Learned how to kind of tuck the glove under my stump while I threw, and then get it back on my hand so I could field."

"That's incredible," Hetty said. "You're like a superhero."

"Ha! Not quite," Nick said. "But I *was* good enough to play for my old team out in Williamsfield. Pitched a no-hitter once. Still have the ball."

"A no-hitter!" Nicholas stared at him in wonder and puzzlement. *Why didn't Dad ever tell me any of this?*

"It was a long time ago. Nowadays, I help out with some of the local kids, that's about it. So, how about you? Wait, let me guess: catcher."

"Nope!" said Hetty. "Not even close!"

"Second base," said Nicholas.

"Good for you," said Nick. "Catching is too hard on the body anyway. The infield is the place to be." He paused as lightning streaked across the sky directly in front of them. "Sailing is definitely out for today, but we'll hit it bright and early tomorrow. Going to be a beautiful day. Right now, though, let's swing by the library and get you all library cards. If you're going to be here all summer, you're going to need one. They'll let you take out a couple of books today, and we can come back as often as you want. I'm a regular—I'm in there once a week at least. Today's going to be a good day to curl up with a good book, and I have just the one in mind for you girls. It's back at the house. And I'm sure I can dig up something for you, too, Nicholas. Between the library here and my own bookshelves, I think we can find some books about sailing that'll be helpful. You can't learn *everything* about sailing by reading about it, but you can start to learn some of the lingo, know what I mean?"

But Nicholas was already thinking of the strange discovery he'd made—the film and the notebook—and was looking forward to a little more exploring. "Um, you wouldn't happen to have a movie projector, would you?"

Nick turned to look at him, a quizzical expression on his face. "Now, that's a funny question. Why would you—"

"We found a movie in Nicholas's room," Hayley said, earning a dirty look from her brother. "In a secret compartment."

"You're not pulling my leg, are you?" Nick asked.

"Nope!" cried Hetty. "We really did. It's called *The Seaweed Strangler*! And we think Daddy made it."

"I'll be darned," said Nick, turning the truck into the drive. "You're right—your dad did make it. When he was about your age, Nicholas. I haven't thought about that movie in years. Figured it was long lost. Your dad never, uh, told you about it?"

"Seems like there's a lot of things he didn't tell me," Nicholas noted.

* * *

When Nick said they were going to "swing by" the library, Nicholas pictured a ten-minute visit. He figured that would be more than enough time to get a library card and maybe even pick up a book or two about baseball. But that was before he realized that the Deming Public Library

28

was much more than just a place to borrow books—it was bustling with activity, and Nicholas couldn't believe the flow of people in and out the front door.

"Hey, Janet," said Nick, pushing the three kids toward the librarian's desk. "Meet my nieces, Hayley and Hetty, and my nephew, Nicholas. They're going to be spending the summer with me, and they need some library cards."

Janet greeted them warmly, adding, "You're very lucky; Nick has the nicest place on the lake. It's my dream house."

"Kids, Janet here is the most powerful person in town," Nick said. "She has worked here for going on forty years, and not only does she know everyone in town, she can tell you what kind of books they all like, too. So, do you think you might find something for these three?"

"Let's see what we can do," Janet said. "Why don't we get you set up with cards first, and then we'll look around." She took a good long look at Nicholas, tilting her head slightly as if she recognized him. "You look familiar. Have you been in before?"

Nicholas shook his head. "Um, no. First time. Ever."

"He looks like his dad," said Nick. "*Just* like. He used to come in, too. Will Mettleson."

"Oh, of course. *Will*. I remember him; he liked books about sailing . . . and movies, I think. How about you, Nicholas? You look like a baseball player to me. We have a wonderful section devoted to sports. Are you a sailor, too?"

"Not yet," said Nicholas.

"But he will be soon," Nick said.

* * *

Dear Dad,

The first official postcard! I'm waiting at the library for the twins. Deming doesn't seem too bad, so far. My room + Nick's truck = awesome. He's like a rock star around here—everyone waves at him when he drives by.

Love,
Nicholas

PS The librarian thought she recognized me, but it was really you. People here remember everything. Scary.

* * *

Arriving at the house in the midst of another downpour, they made a mad dash for the door, with Pistol leading the way. After the groceries had been put away, Nick searched the bookshelves that lined an entire wall of the living room.

"Ah, here it is," he said, holding up a worn, much-loved hardcover. "*We Didn't Mean to Go to Sea*. Arthur

Ransome. A classic. You girls read this today, and you will truly be ready to go sailing tomorrow."

"Looks kind of old," Hayley said, flipping quickly through the pages.

"It is old. It's the book that made *me* a sailor. And if it worked for a knucklehead like me, I'm sure it can do the job on you two bright young ladies."

Hayley smiled at the flattery, but Hetty wrinkled her nose. "It looks kind of *long*. I'm not really a reader, like Hayley. I prefer TV."

"I see," said Nick. "Well, seein' as we don't really have TV out here—not what you're used to, anyway—why don't you give it a try. Maybe you and your sister can take turns reading it out loud."

"I guess so," Hetty said with a sigh. Hayley took the book from her and pulled her by the hand onto the porch.

With that task complete, Nick turned to Nicholas. "All right, your turn. I was going to find you some sailing books, too."

"And a projector, remember?" Nicholas said. "So we can watch the movie."

"Right. Almost forgot."

Nicholas thought he detected a little reluctance on his uncle's part, but he didn't say anything—he really wanted to see the movie.

"I know there's one around here somewhere. Your aunt Lillie tried to get me to clean out this closet for years. Now, getting it to work may be a whole 'nother kettle of worms. Cross your fingers that the bulb is still good." He opened a crowded, disorganized hall closet and started taking boxes down from the top shelf.

"Have you ever seen it—*The Seaweed Strangler*, I mean?" Nicholas asked.

Uncle Nick looked uncomfortable, like a witness who knew the answer to the question but, for some reason, didn't want to give it. "Well, uh, sure. The parts that are done. But it's been twenty-five years or more, and I don't remember much about it. Some . . . things . . . came up, and your dad never finished it. Seem to remember something about the final scenes not turning out right. He set the exposure wrong and they're too dark—can't see anything. Something like that. Those old cameras were kind of tricky. Ah, here we go," he said, setting the projector, enclosed in a sturdy steel case, on the table.

"Wow—they don't make 'em like that anymore," Nicholas remarked, feeling the heft of the thing.

A quick test run revealed it to be in perfect working order, but Nick talked Nicholas into waiting until after dark—which meant after nine o'clock—for the screening. "We can take a look at these home movies, too," he added, holding up a small reel of film that had been lying in the bottom of the case. "We'll have popcorn and make an evening of it."

* * *

With the twins happily passing *We Didn't Mean to Go to Sea* back and forth on the porch swing and Nick looking for an oilcan to stop one of the projector's wheels from squeaking, Nicholas climbed the stairs to the tower room. He threw himself onto the bed and opened the notebook with the torn cover. The first few pages appeared to be the random scribblings of ideas for the story and some calculations of the cost of buying and processing film, but then came a title page, repeating what appeared on the cover. Nicholas turned the page, finding the heading *Scene 1*, and started to read:

```
Long shot of the cove, early in the
morning. There should be some mist,
and the water should be perfectly
still.

Close shots of the trees around the
cove, birds, crayfish crawling on
sand.

Long shot of the cove. A rowboat
with one man in it slowly comes
into view. The boat stops and he
stands up, using binoculars to look
into the woods.

Medium shot of the woods. A small
branch moves, but you can't see
what is causing it.
```

Close shot of the man in the boat as he sets down binoculars and picks up a rifle. He aims at something in the woods and fires.

Extreme close-up of the Seaweed Strangler from the back. He turns to face the camera, and one side of his face is covered in blood. He roars and begins to run toward the camera.

Medium shot of the man starting to row like crazy.

Long shot of the cove. The Seaweed Strangler comes crashing out of the woods and into the water after the man. The man has a good head start and gets away.

Close shot of the Seaweed Strangler, standing waist-deep in the water, roaring at the man. Extreme close-up of his fangs.

Fade-out.

Nicholas closed the notebook and leaned his head back against the wall, struggling with the image of his dad, a doctor who spent two months a year in Africa working for Doctors Without Borders, as a teenager who was creative enough to make a movie. When he really thought about it, he couldn't even remember his father ever *reading* him a story, let alone making one up. Determined not to read the rest of the script until he saw the movie, Nicholas set the notebook on the floor by the bed and checked the secret hiding place in the wall for anything he might have missed earlier. The search turned up two more items. The first was nothing to get too excited about: an index card with the heading "Deming Public Library" and the title of a book, *Make Your Own Movie!* by Samuel Oswald.

The second, however, was *very* interesting.

It was a piece of paper, folded into a compact triangle, with a heart drawn around the name Will.

Nicholas had just unfolded it enough to read "Dear Will" when the twins interrupted him, their heads appearing simultaneously at the top of the stairs.

"Guess what, Nicholas," Hayley said.

"You forgot to knock," he replied, quickly refolding the letter and sticking it in his shirt pocket.

"You don't have a door, silly," said Hetty.

"Doesn't matter. Knock on the stairs before you come up."

Hayley sighed dramatically. "Oh, fine." She knocked on the stairs, but didn't wait for a response. "Guess what the name of the boat in this book is?" She held up *We Didn't Mean to Go to Sea*.

"I don't know," Nicholas said, annoyed.

"Guess!" the twins shouted at him.

"*Titanic*," he said.

"No. Come on, a real guess," Hetty pleaded.

"*Hetty?*"

"What?"

"No, that's my guess."

"What's your guess?"

"*Hetty.*"

"Nicholas!"

"No. *Hetty.*"

"You're impossible," said an exasperated Hetty. "It's *Goblin*."

"You know, like Uncle Nick's boat," Hayley added.

Nicholas stared at her. "Yeah, thanks. I think I got that. Let me see."

Hayley handed him the book, her place marked by the stub of her train ticket from New York. He leafed through a few pages, stopping at an illustration showing a cutaway view of a sailboat. "Wow—looks just like *Goblin*, too. What's this about, anyway?"

"Well, I'm pretty sure it's in England," Hetty started. "And there's this family on vacation, except for the dad, who's in the navy and is on his way back from China, I think."

Hayley took over. "The kids are out in a rowboat, and they end up helping Jim Brading get his boat—*Goblin*—tied up at the mooring. And then he asks if they want to come aboard, so they do, and then he invites them to go sailing with him. And, um, that's as far as we got."

"Well, hurry up and finish it. I want to read it, too."

"You're going to read a book?" Hetty teased.

"He has to," said Hayley. "It's a rainy day and there's no TV. Or video games."

"I read books," Nicholas said indignantly.

"About baseball," the girls said together.

"I *like* baseball. Now get out of here and go read your book or I won't let you watch *The Seaweed Strangler* tonight."

"You have to let us!" cried Hayley, but she started back down the stairs anyway.

The mention of baseball took him back to the strange experience earlier in the day. *Struck out by a girl.* That was definitely a first for Nicholas, but, oddly enough, it wasn't that sweeping curveball that was stuck in his mind; it was that *smile*. What *was* it about her that was so . . . interesting? Or was it irritating? He couldn't decide which. And why had she smiled like that at him, anyway? Was she making fun of him? *Or did she think I was . . . Oh, stop.* He shook his head sharply, trying to shake the memory of her face from his mind, and got up to look out the window at *Goblin*. The wind had shifted direction, and she pointed across the lake, bobbing gently. He took the letter out of his pocket and sat down on the edge of his bed to read it.

Dear Will,

    I still can't believe you're going back to New York. It's not fair that you got blamed for everything that happened. I know it wasn't your fault, but nobody believes me, either. My parents don't even want me to see you, so I'm going to sneak this into Nick's house when you guys go to church Sunday morning.

    Will, I know a lot has happened in the past few days, and I don't know how you feel about everything, but I have to let you know how I feel before you leave. Even though it's being cut short, and I have to wear this stupid cast for the next six weeks, this was the best summer of my life. I'll never forget a single moment we spent together, especially those times we snuck off to our "secret place." No matter what else happens in my life, you will always be special, because _every_ girl remembers her first kiss. I hope you'll remember, too.

    I cried all night when I heard your parents were coming to pick you up on Sunday (I know, not like me at all, right?) and thought about being stuck here in Deming without seeing you for a whole year. Please, please, PLEASE write to me when you get this. It's driving me crazy not being able to talk to you and know what you're thinking. I don't know what I'll do if I don't hear from you, but I guess that will mean it's over. Everyone keeps saying I'm too young to know what's best for me, but I don't care.

I love you, Will Mettleson. There, I said it.

Franny

PS I'm really sorry you didn't get to finish the movie after all the work you put into it. Maybe by next summer everybody will stop acting so crazy and you can prove to them what I already know: you're a genius!

PPS Remember, you promised me the first sail in the Heron, so you have to come back.

Nicholas's mind ran wild with questions. Who was this Franny person who was so in love with his dad? What was he being blamed for? He *kissed* her? The Heron?

He read the letter a second time, but that only led to more questions and the only possible conclusion he could imagine: *Maybe there are two Will Mettlesons in the world.*

CHAPTER THREE

For Nicholas, Hayley, and Hetty, New Yorkers who were used to the sun setting a little earlier, it seemed as if it would never be dark enough to show the movie.

"Why don't you two entertain us?" Nick asked. "Your mom tells me that you're always putting on little shows for her. Show me what you've got."

"You'll be sorry," said Nicholas. "Once they get started, it's practically impossible to get them to stop."

Hayley stuck her tongue out at him. "You're just jealous, Nicholas, because me and Hetty have *talent*."

"Let's do that song from *Junior High Musical!*" said Hetty. "That's our best one."

"Compared to what?" Nicholas scoffed.

"Give them a chance," said Nick.

The twins, who spent most Saturday mornings during the winter in a song-and-dance program for aspiring Broadway stars, belted out the pop ballad "He Passed Me a Note in the Hall!" like a couple of old pros, bringing Nick to his feet, where he demonstrated his earsplitting whistling ability.

"Bravo! Wow! I had no idea I was host to two *stars*."

"We *are* both named after actresses, you know," said a beaming Hayley. "Mom's favorite when she was a little girl was Hayley Mills—she's the one in that movie *The Parent Trap*. The *old* one, that is."

"And Dad has a great-aunt Hetty, who was on Broadway a long time ago," added Hetty. "I've never met her, but he showed us pictures of her. There's even a drawing of her in this restaurant over by Times Square. She was kind of famous in the fifties and sixties, I think."

"Well, I never met dear old Aunt Hetty, but I have to say I'm very impressed, and I think both she and Miss Mills would be proud. How about one more song, and then we'll watch the movie?"

Nicholas groaned, burying his head under the couch pillows. "No-oooo!"

But it was too late; when it came to performing, the twins didn't need to be asked twice.

* * *

As the sky to the west turned magenta, and then violet, they watched the last few die-hard fishermen pull-start their tired Evinrude outboards and head back down the lake toward the marina.

"Is it dark enough yet?" Nicholas asked.

Nick nodded and threaded the film into the projector. "Now, you have to remember, not only is the movie unfinished, it's eight-millimeter film, so there's no sound."

"What do you mean, there's no sound?" Hetty demanded. "How can you make a movie without sound?"

"You'll see. That's how everybody used to do it. Ever hear of Charlie Chaplin?"

"N-no. Who's he?"

"I'll explain later," Nick answered with a laugh. "Lights!"

The projector whirred into action and the screen flickered to life. In the first grainy images, the camera peered over the shoulder of someone sitting in a chair reading the front page of an obviously hand-printed newspaper. The headline, in enormous letters, read: *The Seaweed Strangler!* The person then turned to page two, which read: *Written, Produced, and Directed by Will Mettleson.*

"Daddy!" cried Hetty as the credits faded to black. "I can't believe we're watching a movie he made."

The first real scene unfolded exactly like the one Nicholas had read, except that the person in the boat almost fell overboard as he stood up to aim the rifle at the Seaweed Strangler. They all laughed at that, and at the frame reading *Bang!* that appeared as the person shot the poor creature, and again when the Seaweed Strangler stumbled and fell face-first in the water as he chased after his attacker.

"Who are those boys?" Hayley asked.

"Just kids from the neighborhood," Uncle Nick answered. "Summer people, some of them. Not sure about all of them, but the Seaweed Strangler is definitely Jimmy Brennan—used to live down the road. Kind of a pain in the neck. Always a little too good-looking for his own good."

Nicholas's ears perked up.

Brennan! That's the second time today I've heard that name.

After that first scene, the movie was hard for them to follow because it was unfinished; some scenes were edited, but others were not. Some were in order; some appeared not to be. And there were definitely gaps in the story, which consisted for the most part of a series of revenge killings by the Seaweed Strangler, who—not surprisingly—strangled his victims with a length of seaweed. Then, with no warning, the camera tilted down to the sand, where the words *The End?* appeared letter by letter, as if written by an invisible hand.

As the tail end of the film slipped through the projector and onto the take-up reel, the twins stood up, clapping and cheering.

"That was so good!" said Hetty. "Let's watch it again."

"Did Daddy really do all that himself?" Hayley asked. "He actually wrote that story?"

"He did," said Uncle Nick, rewinding the film. "Of course, there's the legend."

Nicholas's ears perked up again. "Legend?"

"Well, maybe 'legend' is too strong a word. But there were stories." He paused, looking at the girls. "You two sure you want to hear this? Wouldn't want you to have nightmares. Or be afraid to go out on the water tomorrow."

Hayley's eyes were wide with anticipation. "Tell us!" she shouted.

"No, wait!" said Hetty. "I'm not sure. Maybe I don't want to know. Remember that time I watched that show about those bugs that crawled into that guy's brain and started to eat it?"

"She slept with her head under the covers for a year," said Nicholas. "But that was a long time ago. You've watched all kinds of scary stuff on TV since then and I haven't heard you complaining."

Hetty squeezed her eyes shut, thinking hard. "Okay," she said, opening them again. "But if I have nightmares, I'm telling Mom it's your fault."

With the film fully rewound, Uncle Nick turned the projector off and sat back on the couch. "The story got started about the time your dad started spending summers here. It was early spring—middle of March, just after the ice broke up—and a couple of fools decided to go for a sail

44

in their brand-new boat. Just couldn't wait another month or two like normal folk, I suppose. Didn't know how to sail, but that didn't seem to bother them. They were up there at the north end of the lake, by Onion Island, and I'm sure everything was fine until the wind kicked up a bit. Now, no one saw it happen, so this is just speculation on my part, but they probably capsized—and since it was an open boat with a heavy keel, it sank like a stone, and the two knuckleheads drowned."

"That's horrible!" Hetty exclaimed.

"What's so scary about that?" asked Hayley.

Uncle Nick held up his index finger. "Wait. I'm not done. You see, they only found one of them. The other never turned up. Same thing with the boat. Not to this day. The stories really got started after our numskull sheriff talked to some reporter from Cleveland. Told him that when they found the one fellow, he was wrapped from head to toe in seaweed."

"Cool," said Hayley.

"Ewww," said Hetty. "I hate seaweed."

"Before you knew it," Uncle Nick continued, "people were talking about some mysterious Seaweed Strangler and blaming him for the whole shebang. Which was bad enough, but then old Mrs. Lindeman swore up and down that she was sitting on her porch one night and saw the boat—the one that disappeared—sail right past her house. Said she recognized it from the pictures. When she went down to the shore to get another look, it was gone.

Perfectly clear night, she said. And she was just the first. After hers, there were lots more sightings—including one by your aunt Lillie. They all happened just before three o'clock in the morning—2:53, to be exact—or so people said. Problem was, the stories just got crazier and crazier, and whenever anybody sat up late *trying* to see it, they never saw anything."

"I guess that explains that painting of Aunt Lillie's up in my room," Nicholas said. "The one called *2:53 A.M.*"

"I'd forgotten about that," Uncle Nick said, smiling at the memory it evoked. "Lillie was going to give that one to your dad, but I think she ended up liking it too much to give it away. It was one of her favorites."

"Did she believe in the Seaweed Strangler?" Hetty asked.

"She believed that she saw a boat one night, and that's about it. Nobody with half a brain believes in some creature running around the lake strangling folks with seaweed. The boat sank. Those two dingbats drowned. End of story."

* * *

At seven-thirty the next morning, the four of them—plus Nick's usual sailing partner, a life-jacket-wearing Pistol—sat in the cramped cockpit of *Goblin*, eating ham and eggs cooked by Nick on the tiny stove in the cabin below. He served it to them on translucent red plates ("Just like the ones in the book!" Hetty exclaimed) and started the day's sailing lesson by pointing out, and then quizzing them on, the different sailing terms and parts of the boat: port and starboard, mast, boom, tiller, rudder, mainsail, mainsheet, winches, cleats, halyards, and so on, until Hayley declared that her memory was full.

"Sorry, Uncle Nick, but I just can't remember another single thing. Can we please just go sailing?"

And off they went.

It was a perfect day to learn to sail. With the twins tucked safely out of the way in the cockpit, Nick showed Nicholas how to raise the mainsail with the boat pointing straight into the gentle wind, coiling the halyards neatly when he finished. Then, on the "go" signal, Nicholas unhooked the mooring line from the bow, Nick hauled in the slack in the mainsheet and pushed the tiller to starboard, and they were sailing.

No one said a word for several minutes as *Goblin* silently sliced through the ripples known to sailors as "cat's paws." Hayley was the first to break the spell, whispering to Hetty, "It's so *quiet*."

"It's not always this quiet," Nick said. "When you get a stiff north wind and some whitecaps, she'll make some noise. Okay, Het, one more question for you: Are we on port or starboard tack?"

Hetty screwed up her face, looking left and then right. "Starboard?"

"That's right! The wind is coming over the starboard

side of the boat. And I think we're ready for the jib. Nicholas! You think you can handle that? I'll head into the wind a little bit to make it easier for you. Just get it up there and snug it up good and tight."

Nicholas was a fast learner; he stood at the mast and pulled the halyard, raising the jib. When it was all the way up, he wrapped the line around the cleat just the way Nick had shown him.

"Good boy! Okay, Hayley, now, you see that line right there? That's the jib sheet, and I want you to pull it in until that sail stops luffing, er, flapping. Good, good . . . perfect!"

With both sails drawing, *Goblin* picked up speed, her blue topsides digging in a bit deeper.

"How fast are we going?" Hetty asked, leaning over the rail to watch the water slip by.

"Twenty-five miles per hour," Hayley guessed.

Nick had a good laugh at that. "Maybe four knots. Sailors use nautical miles, and one knot—or one nautical mile per hour—is a little more than a regular mile per hour."

"No way, Uncle Nick," said an incredulous Hayley. "We're going faster than four miles per hour!"

"I'm afraid not," he said. "*Goblin* is many things, but fast is not one of them. How are you girls coming with *We Didn't Mean to Go to Sea*?"

"They just lost the anchor, and now they're out at sea," said Hayley. "It's kind of scary."

"Ah, but they're in a sturdy little boat—just like this one."

"Is this *Goblin* exactly like the one in the book?" Nicholas asked.

"Not *exactly*, but she's pretty darn close—the closest thing I could find when I was looking for a design to build. They're the same size, same basic hull shape, same sail plan. I always liked the look of the cutter rig. We'll put up the stays'l later. Remember, that's the sail on the little boom in front of the mast. Then maybe we can get her all the way up to *five* knots. All right, Nicholas, come back here so I can teach you how to steer."

With a huge grin on his face, Nicholas sat on the cockpit seat opposite his uncle and took the tiller in his hand.

Nick showed him how to find a spot on the land to aim for, always watching the angle that the forestay made to the horizon, and how to make gentle corrections when he got off course. The twins watched his wake carefully, pointing out every little wiggle with a *tsk-tsk*.

"You're a natural," said Nick. "I can tell already that you're going to be a good sailor—people either have a feel for it or they don't. Now, you see that dark spot on the water ahead? That's what we call a 'puff,' a place where the wind is stronger and, lots of times, where the direction of the wind changes a little, too. A good helmsman is always scanning the water ahead, looking for puffs, so he can prepare. This time, I want you to just do what you've been doing; pretend you didn't see it, so you'll feel it in the tiller."

Nicholas bit his lip in anticipation, not sure what was going to happen when *Goblin* hit the darker water. He was on a steady course, aimed at a flagpole on the shore, when suddenly the boat heeled over several more degrees and started to turn to the right on its own. He pulled harder against the tiller, finding it difficult to stay on course for the flagpole, and glanced nervously at his uncle.

"You're doing fine—doing fine. Now feel the difference when I do this." As he let the mainsheet out a few inches, *Goblin* stood up noticeably. "Feel that in the tiller? Less pressure, right? Mainsheet's kind of like the gas pedal. When you start to heel too much, take your foot off the gas a little."

Nicholas nodded, getting back on his original course with no trouble.

"Let's do it again," said Hayley.

"Let's not," a more nervous Hetty replied.

"I'm sure we'll have more opportunities," said Nick. "But there's lots more to do. Time to put you two to work."

For the next three hours, *Goblin* made her way up and down the lake, never straying too far from home, and by lunchtime, the three Mettleson children, Nick declared, were no longer landlubbers. They were officially sailors. At noon, they anchored in the cove where their father had filmed the first scene in *The Seaweed Strangler* and

As the afternoon temperature rose to nearly ninety degrees, the wind died, until Goblin *was barely ghosting along with Hetty at the tiller for the last mile or so.*

feasted on peanut butter and jelly sandwiches, carrot sticks, and warmish cans of soda.

The twins, eager to try out the minuscule sink, volunteered to clean the dishes while Nicholas and Nick scrubbed the decks. When the girls finished, they lay down on the cushions in the cozy little cabin and began to formulate a plan of their own.

"Can we sleep here tonight?" Hayley shouted up at her uncle. "It would be just like in the book!"

"Well, I hope not *exactly*," he said. "I'd rather not have *Goblin* drifting out to sea in a heavy fog. But I don't see why not, as long as I can have one of the long berths. I'm too tall—and too old—to sleep in the forepeak."

"Jim Brading slept on the *floor*," Hetty reminded him.

"I'm definitely too old for that," said Nick with a laugh. "It should be a nice night, and you kids can use your sleeping bags, I suppose."

"Yay!" shouted the twins.

"Everybody ready for lesson number two?" Nick asked. "Come on, Nicholas. I'll pull up the anchor, and you take us out of this cove."

"Aye, aye, Captain," said Nicholas, saluting.

"We're going to head for a buoy about three miles south of here; should take us an hour or so to get there. It's going to be upwind, so we'll have to tack back and forth a few times, and then we'll have a nice reach back to the mooring."

* * *

As the afternoon temperature rose to nearly ninety degrees, the wind died, until *Goblin* was barely ghosting along with Hetty at the tiller for the last mile or so. Nick was stretched out in the cockpit with his hat pulled down over his eyes while Nicholas and Hayley sat on the foredeck with their feet dangling over the side, daydreaming.

As they approached the mooring, Nick sat up. Hetty immediately tried to hand the tiller off to him, but they were moving so slowly that he waved her off. "You brought her this far. Just point it right at the mooring and Nicholas will do the rest."

"Are you sure? Nicholas has never done this, either," said Hetty from her seat in the cockpit.

"Positive," said Nick. "Steady as she goes, Hetty. Hey, I think that's going to be your new name: Steady Hetty."

Hetty beamed as she gripped the tiller with both hands, guiding *Goblin* past a fishing boat and toward the mooring.

Nicholas reached over the bow to grab the stern of the waiting dinghy, which he then tied to *Goblin*'s stern. After double-checking that the mooring line was properly attached to the bow, he and Nick furled sails and tidied things up on deck while the twins prepared the cabin and chattered about the sleeping-aboard plan. Finally, they were ready to board the dinghy for the shore.

At the last moment, however, Nicholas decided to swim rather than ride. He stripped off his shirt and threw it and his shoes to Hetty in the dinghy. Then he dived off *Goblin*'s stern, splashing both twins in the process.

"Nicholas!" they squealed.

"It's just water," he said. "You should come in. It feels good."

Nick, who already had one foot in the dinghy, suddenly changed his mind, too. He climbed back aboard *Goblin* and, to everyone's complete surprise, leaped into the air and did a cannonball just *inches* from the dinghy, soaking the twins and sending them into a tizzy.

"Uncle Nick!"

"Nice cannonball!" shouted Nicholas, high-fiving his uncle, who then untied the dinghy, setting the twins adrift.

"Hey, you can't do that," Hayley cried.

Hetty stood with hands on hips. "What are we supposed to do now?"

"The first thing you should do is sit down," Nicholas scolded. "And then, if I were you, I'd start rowing. You'll make it to shore eventually. Unless the Seaweed Strangler gets you . . . or *I capsize you!*" He grabbed the gunwale of the dinghy and rocked it violently.

While Hetty screamed, Hayley chose a more practical solution. She picked up an oar and went right for Nicholas's knuckles. Her second swing was too close for comfort, so he let go, laughing.

"Come on, Nicholas," said Uncle Nick. "Race you to the dock!" He put his head down, his one arm and legs churning up the green-algae-tinted water. Even though his uncle had a five-yard head start, Nicholas took up the challenge. He dug in with each stroke and kicked with everything he had. The seventy-five yards between the mooring and the end of the dock was just enough for him to catch and, in his final strokes, pass his uncle. He reached up for the steel frame that supported the dock and hung from it, breathing hard.

"That was . . . farther . . . than I . . . thought," Nicholas gasped.

Nick, only slightly winded, nodded. "How are the girls doing out there?"

"Not so good," Nicholas answered, his breathing returning to normal. "They dropped one of the oars in the water and now they're going in circles trying to get it back."

"Think we should rescue them?"

"Nah. Let 'em figure it out. Hayley almost broke my fingers with that oar. She's crazy." With that, Nicholas hauled himself out of the water and up onto the dock. As he stood up, he was surprised to see someone walking down the dock toward him. He shook the water out of his hair and then blinked away the blurriness caused by the lake until he finally got a clear look at who it was. He almost fell off the dock when he realized that it was the girl from town—Charlie, the pitcher who struck him out

55

on four pitches. Correction: the really *cute* pitcher who struck him out.

What is she doing here?

For a second—maybe two—confusion was the overwhelming emotion racing through his preteen brain. And then the real horror hit him.

Where is my shirt?

For Nicholas Mettleson, a little shy, a little short for his age, and a *lot* scrawny, standing shirtless in front of a girl—especially a pretty girl like Charlie Brennan—was a thousand times worse than being struck out by one. Ten thousand times, maybe.

His shirt, of course, was in the dinghy with Hayley and Hetty, who were still trying to retrieve the second oar.

"Hey, I know you," Charlie said, smiling broadly. "You're the kid I struck out yesterday. What are you doing here?"

Nicholas looked around in vain for a towel that he could throw over his shoulders at least. "Umm, my, uh, uh, my uncle lives here."

Just then, Uncle Nick's head popped up from underwater. "Hey, Charlie! Meet my nephew, Nicholas. He and his sisters—that's them out in the dinghy—are spending the summer with me. Nicholas, Charlie here is just about the best pitcher you'll ever see. Has a curve that can go around corners."

Oh God. Here it comes, thought Nicholas.

But Charlie threw Nicholas a life ring. "Maybe I can

show you sometime," she said, winking right at him. "Nick taught me how to throw it."

"Uh-huh," mumbled Nicholas, not at all sure how to proceed with this strange ponytailed creature.

"Mom sent over a big tray of lasagna for you, Nick," Charlie said. "It's in the kitchen. I had it on the back of my bike and almost dropped it."

"Well, I'm glad you didn't—would have been a crime. Nicholas, Charlie's mom makes the best lasagna in town— maybe the whole state—and she's not even Italian. Hey, I've got an idea, Charlie. Why don't you stay for dinner? Get to know these three—tell 'em that life out here in the country isn't so bad. I've been trying my best, but they're more likely to believe it coming from someone their own age."

Charlie grinned. "I'll have to call Mom, but I'm sure she'll be okay with it."

"Tell her to come, too," Nick said. "If I know her, she made enough for a small army." He looked out at the twins, who were making slow progress toward the dock. "We're not quite that many—more of a platoon, I suppose."

Charlie's attention turned to the twins. "Are they okay out there? I mean, they don't seem to know what they're doing. Maybe I'd better help them." She pulled her T-shirt over her head and stepped out of her shorts, revealing a peach-colored bathing suit underneath. With no hesitation, she dived off the dock and aimed for the dinghy. She stayed underwater for several long seconds, finally surfacing halfway to her objective. When she reached the girls, she held on to the transom and pushed them toward the dock, kicking noisily all the way.

Once they were safely at the dock, Hayley stuck her tongue out at Nicholas as she ceremoniously dropped his shirt in the lake, and then she and Hetty walked back to the house with their new best friend Charlie, one on each side and peppering her with questions.

* * *

Dear Dad,
    First sail on <u>Goblin</u> today—a BLAST. Wondering why you never talked about sailing. Uncle Nick says you loved it when you were a kid—??
    The twins are homesick, especially Hetty. She called Mom and told her she wanted to go home RIGHT NOW. Mom told her it was either here or Aunt Betty's house on Long Island. Suddenly she wasn't homesick anymore.

                Love,
                Nicholas

CHAPTER FOUR

A few hours later, Charlie's mom pulled in the driveway at Nick's, and Nick sent Nicholas out to help carry in the huge bowls of Caesar salad and green beans and the two loaves of homemade garlic bread that Charlie and her mom had made to complete the Italian feast that was taking shape.

"Um, can I help?" said Nicholas, approaching the car. "I'm Nicholas."

As Charlie's mom was handing him the bowl of green beans, she got her first close look at him and stopped suddenly.

"Oh my," she said, continuing to stare at Nicholas, who didn't know what to make of the situation.

Luckily, Charlie rescued him. "Come on, Mom, let's go inside. You have to meet the twins. They're hilarious. And besides, I'm starving."

Nicholas held the screen door open for them, but even when the twins came running down the stairs and into the kitchen, followed by Pistol in all his tail-wagging glory, Charlie's mom still didn't seem able to look away from Nicholas.

"Hi, Fran," said Uncle Nick, kissing her on the cheek. "And hello again, Charlie. Thank you both for the feast—and the company. And I see you've met my boarders. These are Will's kids—Nicholas, Hayley, and Hetty."

Nicholas's ears had perked up at Charlie's mom's name.

Fran? As in Franny? As in Dad's old girlfriend?

Nicholas was so busy making connections to the letter he'd found that he hardly noticed her reaction to learning who *he* was.

One of her hands flew to her mouth as she whispered, "Will," and she almost dropped the salad bowl, juggling it for a few seconds before getting it back under control. "Omigosh, I'm so sorry. It's just—for a second there, I thought I had stepped into a time machine."

Nicholas, Charlie, and the twins wore confused looks, but Uncle Nick nodded in agreement. "He is the spitting image of his father, isn't he? Janet at the library had the same reaction."

"It's remarkable." She quickly regained her composure

and, after setting the salad on the counter, held her hand out for Nicholas to shake. "I apologize, Nicholas. I'm Charlie's mom, Franny Brennan. You must think I'm crazy, the way I'm staring at you. I was . . . Well, I knew your dad when he was about your age—I was Franny Sherbrooke back then. I'll bet you're probably sick to death of people telling you how much you look like him."

Nicholas shrugged. "It's okay. Doesn't really happen that often." Even so, he knew it was true; he'd seen pictures of his dad as a kid, and the two of them looked more alike than Hetty and Hayley.

"You knew Daddy when he was a boy?" Hetty asked. "Did you know he's a *doctor*? He's in Africa, helping people with mengeeitis."

"Meningitis," said Nicholas.

"I did know that he's a doctor. It's nice that he's helping people," said Franny.

"Were you in his movie?" Hayley asked. "We just saw it last night."

Franny turned to look at Nick, her eyes wide with surprise.

"Nicholas found Will's movie," said Uncle Nick.

"In a secret compartment up in the tower room," said Hayley. "That *I* discovered."

"You know, I don't think I was. Maybe one little scene. Mostly, I was the cameraman, er, person. Your dad and I were the only ones who knew how to use the camera, so we took turns—"

"Okay, kids," Uncle Nick interrupted. "Why don't you all go out on the porch for a while and let Fran and me get dinner ready."

Franny looked relieved, and immediately started tossing the salad with the dressing and croutons she had brought.

On the porch, Hetty and Hayley insisted that Charlie sit between them on the swing while they continued their interrogation about school, what she did for fun, her favorite musicians—anything they could think of.

Nicholas, meanwhile, picked up a magazine about wooden sailboats and pretended not to listen. Part of him was dying to show Charlie the letter from her mom to his dad.

Not yet. Maybe if I get to know her better. She might think I'm weird, or get mad because I read somebody else's letter. You just can't tell with girls.

So he sat there pretending to read until Uncle Nick called them all into the dining room. The twins immediately started their assault on Franny, hitting her with questions about *The Seaweed Strangler*, but Uncle Nick held up his hand for them to stop.

"Girls, what do you say? Let's let our guest enjoy this beautiful dinner—which she prepared—in peace. No more questions."

Hayley and Hetty put on their poutiest faces.

"That's not going to work on Uncle Nick the way it does on Dad," Nicholas said, laughing.

"Tell you what, girls," said Franny. "Because you're so nice, and because I just love your names, I'll tell you a little secret. I *married* the Seaweed Strangler."

"You WHAT?" the twins shouted.

"But that means," Hayley said, turning to Charlie, "that you're . . ."

"The Seaweed Strangler's *daughter!*" Charlie exclaimed.

"Absolutely true," said Uncle Nick. "Remember, I told you that the monster was a kid named Jimmy Brennan. That's Charlie's dad."

"Too bad you weren't Daddy's girlfriend," said Hetty.

Nicholas and Franny both choked momentarily on bites of salad.

"Yeah. You would have been our sister, Charlie," Hayley said wistfully.

"Um, I don't think it works like that," Charlie said. "Besides, you have Nicholas; isn't he better than another sister? I *always* wanted a big brother. I have an older sister, Natalie, but she's already away at college."

"No!" Hayley shouted. "You saw what he did to us today. He tried to kill us! If you hadn't rescued us, we would have drifted out to sea."

"It's not really fair to lay all the blame on Nicholas," said Nick. "As I recall, *I'm* the one who untied you."

"But Nicholas tried to capsize us," said Hayley. "That was way worser."

"Oh, you're right. That is definitely much worser,"

Charlie agreed, grinning at Nicholas. She then turned to Uncle Nick and said, "Why don't you and Mom go relax on the porch. Nicholas and I will do the dishes."

We will? She's even crazier than I thought.

"And then afterward, I want to see this movie you're all talking about," she continued. "Apparently, I'm the only one here who hasn't seen it."

"But what about our adventure?" Hetty asked. "Remember? We were going to sleep on *Goblin* tonight."

The distant rumble of thunder seemed to answer her question.

"Oh," she said.

"Not afraid of a little lightning, are you?" teased Nicholas.

"We'll do it another time, honey," Uncle Nick promised. "Come sit on the porch with us and watch the storm."

Nicholas wished he were going to join them, but instead found himself standing next to the sink drying dishes as Charlie handed them to him.

"You don't say much, do you?" Charlie asked after a few minutes of silent washing and drying.

Nicholas shrugged, smiling just a little. "Yeah. I mean, no, not really."

"Always, or just with new people? When you were at the ball field, I didn't think you were so shy. Actually, I thought it took a lot of guts to do what you did."

"But you still struck me out."

"Yeah, I guess I did. I couldn't help it. It just sort

of . . . happens. It's your uncle's fault. He's a great coach, isn't he?"

"To be honest, until a few days ago, I barely knew him. My dad never talked about him, or about staying here when he was a kid, or anything like that. I had no idea he even played baseball. I just figured, you know, with his arm and everything . . ."

"What about the movie? Or my mom? Did your dad ever talk about them?"

"Nope. Before we left New York, the only thing he said was something like 'You never know what you'll find.'"

"And you guys are going to be here all summer? Are both your parents in Africa?"

Nicholas hesitated a second before answering. "No, they're, um . . . divorced. My dad spends most of his summers in Africa. Have you ever heard of Doctors Without Borders? He's an immunologist, and he's been working with them for a long time on this program to get kids in Africa vaccinations for things like measles. But right now he's in Cameroon because there are a bunch of people with meningitis and they're trying to stop it from spreading. I can't wait until I can go someday."

"So you're going to be a doctor, too?"

"Yeah . . . well, I'd *like* to. It's really hard, though. And it takes a long time."

"That's cool, though, knowing what you want to do," said Charlie.

"What about you? Aren't you going to be the first girl

in the major leagues, pitching for the Yankees or something?"

"The *Yankees*! Ha! I hate them. Oh no. Don't tell me you're a Yankees fan. I don't know if I can be friends with you if you are."

"Who do you like?"

"The Indians, of course."

"The *Cleveland* Indians? Are you serious? When's the last time they won the World Series—like, 1800?"

"It was 1948, for your information. But *this* year is going to be different. So, what about your mom? What's she do?"

"She's, like, a vice president at this big public-relations company, and she works all the time. Like, twenty-three hours a day. And on top of that, they're rebuilding our whole apartment, so they decided the best thing would be to ship the kids off to Ohio for the summer."

Charlie grinned at him, her eyes twinkling. "And I can tell you're just *thrilled* about that. Do you ever get to talk to your dad when he's in Africa?"

"Not much. Usually they have to use a satellite phone, which is pretty expensive. Sometimes he has email, sometimes he doesn't. Mostly, we use regular old mail. It's slow, but it works. He talked me into sending him at least one postcard a week."

"Wow. That must be hard—not being able to see him or talk to him for that long."

Nicholas shrugged. "I guess I'm used to it. Did your mom ever talk about my dad?"

"Well, I knew that she used to have a friend who was a 'summer boy' named Will, and he was related to Nick, but that's about it." She looked out the kitchen window at the backyard, where the trees swayed wildly with the approaching storm. "Isn't it funny—strange funny, not like ha-ha—that we met—well, almost met—in town before I came over here with this big ol' tray of lasagna? I mean, if you believe in fate and all that, we were going to meet today anyway, so why did the gods have you show up at my team's practice?"

For someone who had never seriously considered the role of fate in his life—or anyone else's, for that matter—that was too much for Nicholas to digest all at once. He stared at her, unsure how to answer.

"You probably think I'm crazy," Charlie said. "I just met you and I'm yakking about fate already. It's just—well, you seem like a cool kid, and in a few weeks, baseball season will be over, and in case you hadn't noticed, there's not a lot of other kids around here, especially during the week. On weekends, there are a few summer people around, kids from Cleveland and Youngstown. We usually have a softball game on Saturday afternoons—just for fun. I only live, like, half a mile from here, and you know, I was hoping we could hang out, at least sometimes. And I would *love* to learn to sail, too. Nick could teach all of us, and he could teach *you* how to hit a curve." She couldn't help smiling as she said that.

Nicholas smiled right back. Having someone his own age to hang out with would be good—he could only take the twins for so long. And then there was that idea that had started brewing in his head the moment he had found *The Seaweed Strangler* in the tower room.

"So, do you know anything about making movies?" he asked.

CHAPTER FIVE

July 1
Dear Dad,

   You were right about the country. We don't even miss the TV, AND I'm almost done with my summer reading list for school. I give <u>The Hobbit</u> an 8, but <u>To Kill a Mockingbird</u> gets a 10. Maybe I'll be a lawyer instead of a doctor. Kidding! Been playing baseball with some locals, this kid Charlie has a WICKED curveball. Uncle Nick says he can teach me how to hit it, but so far it's pretty hopeless.

Love,
Nicholas

PS You were right about the tower room. It <u>is</u> full of secrets.

* * *

By the end of that first week of July, Nicholas and Charlie were best friends, nearly constant companions, and, quick learners that they were, well on their way to becoming expert sailors. They sailed every day with Nick, who had less and less to say and do with each mini voyage. He spent most of the time sitting in the cockpit with his hat pulled down over his eyes, peeking out occasionally to make sure they weren't headed for a sandbar or hoisting a jib upside down (that happened only once, much to the delight of Hayley and Hetty).

On one particularly fine morning—so clear that they watched a fisherman on the other side of the lake land a walleye that would have fed them all—the five intrepid adventurers rowed out to *Goblin*, intending to spend the day aboard. As usual, Pistol was the first one out of the dinghy and onto *Goblin*'s deck, followed by Nicholas and Charlie, who wasted no time, immediately uncovering the mainsail and rigging the jib sheets. When Nicholas turned to ask Uncle Nick a question about their destination, he was surprised to see the dinghy, with Uncle Nick rowing and the twins perched in the bow seat, headed back to the dock.

"Uncle Nick! What did you forget?"

Without breaking his rhythm, Uncle Nick answered, "Not a thing. The girls and I decided we don't really feel like sailing today. We're going to just stay ashore with the other landlubbers."

"What about us?" Charlie asked. "You're just going to leave us here?"

"I figured you two wanted to go for a sail. So go," Uncle Nick said. "It's a beautiful day. Pistol's ready, so what are you waiting for?"

"You're serious—we can take her out without you?" said Nicholas.

"What do you need me for? I've been nothin' but ballast the last few days."

Nicholas and Charlie looked at each other, grinning.

"Thanks, Nick! We'll see ya in a few years," said Charlie with a wave.

Together they decided that she would take the tiller as they left the mooring, with Nicholas running back to trim the sails after dropping the mooring line. They pulled it off like a couple of seasoned veterans. A gentle wind was blowing parallel to the shore, and as the sails filled, Charlie bore off perfectly onto a beam reach, with *Goblin*'s bow aimed at the public beach on the other side of the lake. They were off.

"Well done!" Nick shouted. "Have fun, and keep her off the sandbars!"

Nicholas and Charlie didn't hear that last part. Of course, who knows if it would have even made a difference;

it's not like they were *trying* to find the one sandbar Nick hadn't told them about.

If you're sailing on the ocean or the Great Lakes, you have nautical charts that show the water's depth at every location, and most shallow spots, or shoals, are marked with buoys to warn you of the dangers. Unfortunately, there's no such thing as an official chart for Forsaken Lake, or most other inland lakes, for that matter. In *Goblin*'s cabin, Uncle Nick had a laminated chart—drawn by his wife, Lillie—that showed approximate depths at most locations around the lake. He had taught Nicholas and Charlie how to identify shallow spots by watching the action of the waves and the changing color of the water.

During their sailing lessons, Uncle Nick had pointed out all the big sandbars in his end of the lake, but there was one more—a small one, a few hundred yards off the very beach where *Goblin* was aimed.

They were cruising gracefully at a comfortable clip, sails trimmed perfectly and *Goblin* heeled over just a few degrees, when it happened. Nicholas had the tiller in his hand and had just told Charlie to prepare to come about when *Goblin*'s bow suddenly dipped and she came to a lurching stop in the soft sand. Their "landing" was so soft that it took a few seconds for the two sailors to grasp what had happened. The sails were still full and drawing, but they were most definitely stopped.

"Uh-oh," Nicholas said.

Pistol seemed to agree, whining as he assessed the situation.

"What is going on?" asked Charlie. "Why aren't we moving?"

"We're on a sandbar."

"What do we do?"

"I dunno. I've never been on a sandbar before."

"Can't we just back up? Should we start the motor?"

"Not yet." He pulled the tiller toward him. The bow started to turn, and for a moment, they thought they were free. Their relief was short-lived, however, as the hull ground into the sand again.

"Maybe if we heel over a little more," Charlie suggested. "Let's both lean over the side and see if that helps." Nicholas let go of the tiller and joined her at the shrouds, where they hung out over the water as far as they could. *Goblin* heeled over a bit more, but together they just didn't weigh enough to make enough of a difference.

"Okay, I have another idea," Nicholas said. "If we're on the bottom, the water must only be about three feet deep, right? I'll go over the side and push us off."

Charlie looked skeptical. "You really think you can budge this big ol' boat?"

"Only one way to find out." He sat on the gunwale and slid down into the water, which came up to his chest. "At least it's nice soft sand. I don't think it did any damage."

With Charlie looking on, he leaned down and pushed against the sturdy wooden hull. There was some movement, and it looked as if Nicholas would be successful. The bow turned a few more degrees, slid forward two or three feet, and then came to an abrupt stop. *Goblin* remained solidly aground.

"I think all we're doing is getting more stuck," Nicholas said.

"I'm coming in to help you," Charlie announced. And before Nicholas could protest, she was at his side in the water, pushing with him.

"One, two, three, push!" they said. Still *Goblin* did not budge.

Behind them, a hundred yards away, a fishing boat was going by at full throttle, and Nicholas recognized an opportunity. "When that guy's wake hits us, it's going to rock the boat, and that's when we have to push like mad. If that doesn't work, we'll try the engine."

They got into position, watching the approaching waves over their shoulders and digging their toes into the sand in preparation. When the first one hit, *Goblin* floated up off the bottom while Nicholas and Charlie heaved with all their collective might, and as the second wave struck, *Goblin*, finally free of the sandbar, slid sideways— and started to sail away from a very surprised Nicholas and Charlie!

"H-hey!" they both yelled, swimming after the runaway boat. "Wait for us!"

Pistol, who had fallen fast asleep on his seat in the cockpit, raised his head, bewildered for a moment by all the commotion. Satisfied that *he* was in no danger, he put his head back down and closed his eyes.

Goblin wouldn't go far; eventually, an unmanned sailboat will always head directly into the wind, coming to a stop. After that, she will drift slowly in the direction of the wind. And since the wind on this day was not strong, they would have been able to catch up to her.

But Nicholas and Charlie didn't know that, so they swam frantically after her, certain that she would sail herself right up onto the beach. Just as *Goblin* started her slow turn into the wind, they managed to get hold of the starboard jib sheet, which was dangling over the side, and while both sails flapped in the breeze, Nicholas pulled himself onto the warm deck and then helped Charlie aboard.

For a full minute, they just lay on their backs, recovering from those few seconds of terror and breathing hard from the burst of activity and the rush of adrenaline. And then they busted out laughing.

"You should have seen the look on your face!" Charlie said. "You looked *exactly* like you did when I threw that curveball at you."

"I was trying to figure out how we were going to explain it," Nicholas said. "I had this image of us standing out there in the middle of the lake—no boat in sight."

"Maybe we don't tell your uncle about this." Charlie

looked in the direction of Uncle Nick's house, but it was too far away to make out any details. "I don't think anybody saw us—except maybe the guys in that fishing boat. And Pistol," she added, patting his head. "Thanks for all your help, boy."

Nicholas, agreeing that this was no time for full disclosure, took the tiller in his hands and pointed *Goblin* back out to the center of the lake.

* * *

But someone *had* seen them. Despite his apparent nonchalance as they left the mooring, Uncle Nick watched their progress across the lake through binoculars. As they approached the sandbar, he cringed, remembering that he hadn't pointed it out. He crossed his fingers, hoping they would just miss it, and groaned when he saw that they had stopped.

"Here, take a look at this," he said, handing the binoculars to Hayley.

She stared through them at *Goblin* for some time. "Why aren't they moving?"

"Remember *We Didn't Mean to Go to Sea?* After they lost the anchor and started sailing away, what were the kids most worried about?"

"The promise they made to their mom not to go to sea?"

76

"And what else?"

"The shoals?"

"That's right. Well, Nicholas and Charlie found a little shoal all their own."

Hayley's eyes grew wide. "Are they gonna sink?"

"No—the only damage will be to their pride," Uncle Nick said. "If they start the engine, they should be able to back her right off. Here, let me see." He looked through the binoculars again, shaking his head and smiling. "No, no, Nicholas. Stay aboard the boat."

"What's happening?" asked Hetty.

Uncle Nick narrated the rest of the action across the lake, roaring with laughter at the climactic moment when *Goblin* slid herself off the sandbar, leaving Nicholas and Charlie standing helplessly while Pistol and *Goblin* sailed away. He was never really concerned for their safety, because they could just stand there on the sandbar until he came to rescue them, and with the wind blowing down the lake as it was, he knew *Goblin* could drift slowly along for a long time before running into anything.

He handed the binoculars to Hetty. "Everyone's back aboard, and they're sailing. They're both looking this way—probably want to see if we're watching."

"It's a good thing we were," said Hayley.

"Are they in trouble?" Hetty asked. "I think they should be. Specially Nicholas."

"Why him especially?" Uncle Nick asked. "I'd have to say they're both equally involved. Nobody's in trouble—accidents happen, and this one was my fault as much as anyone's. Ladies, we're not going to say a word about this—right?"

Hayley pouted for a few seconds, disappointed at losing a good opportunity to make her big brother a little bit miserable. "What if *they* say something first?"

"Well, now—that's a whole different pail o' worms," answered Uncle Nick.

* * *

Two hours later, after an uneventful sail to the far south end of the lake, *Goblin* approached her mooring with Charlie at the tiller and Nicholas standing on the bow with the boat hook, ready to pick up the float at the end of the mooring line. The wind had freshened a bit, but Charlie did her job perfectly, releasing the jib sheet and turning directly into the wind at the last moment, slowing the boat dramatically and giving Nicholas the opportunity to snag the line and snap it onto the bow. Charlie met him on the foredeck and high-fived him. They had done it: they had lived to tell the tale of their first adventure (without Uncle Nick) on the high seas. When they finished folding and stowing and tidying, Nicholas stood for a moment in the cockpit, imagining that *Goblin* was his own and he had just returned from a long ocean voyage from some exotic port.

Someday.

* * *

July 9
Dear Dad,
   Best summer E-VER.
   Me and Charlie sailing <u>Goblin,</u> *Nick onshore.*
   No big deal—we rocked it.
               Your son (the expert sailor),
               Nicholas

* * *

Set well back from Nick's house was an old barn, its red paint now faded to a soft patina, the slate roof missing a tile here and there, but still standing as straight and tall as it had for more than a hundred and fifty years. Once upon a time, it held a herd of registered Holsteins, but it had been many years since any livestock called it home. Now it was a workshop. Where once there had been box stalls, Uncle Nick built *Goblin;* the braces that held the hull in place during construction still leaned against the walls. Earlier in the summer, just a few days after arriving, Nicholas had noticed a neatly painted white rectangle on one outside wall, and asked Nick about it.

"Strike zone," he answered. "For your average Little Leaguer. This is where I taught Charlie how to pitch. Do you want me to teach you?"

"Actually, I'm more interested in learning how to *hit* a curveball. Can you show me *that*?"

"Happy to. The only problem is, with my shoulder acting up the way it is, I can't put any mustard on the ball anymore. Best thing would be to have Charlie pitch to you."

"Oh, great."

Nick chuckled. "Don't sweat it, Nicholas. You're not the first boy to be struck out by a girl. And you won't be the last—especially if Charlie Brennan has anything to do with it. At one of her games this year, she struck out nine in a row. But if I can teach her to throw it, I can teach you to hit it."

* * *

But it was the hayloft inside the barn that held the real surprise for Nicholas and Charlie, who climbed the ladder one hot, windless afternoon a few days after that first sail without Nick. Back in the farthest corner, a heavy canvas tarp with several years' accumulation of dust and pigeon droppings covered an object about twelve feet long and five feet wide.

Despite the kids' fear of disturbing whatever critters might be lurking beneath it, curiosity got the best of them, and they slowly pulled a few feet of the tarp back.

"It's a sailboat," said Nicholas, running his hand over the unfinished wood deck.

"Wonder what it's doing up here," said Charlie. "Let's uncover it all the way."

Still wary of the dust—and things that creep, crawl, or slither—they slowly removed the tarp and began their full investigation of the mysterious, not-quite-completed vessel that clearly had been hidden away for a long, long time. They were immediately awed by its graceful curves and the expanses of wood on the deck and in the cockpit.

"Omigosh. It's beautiful," said Charlie. "What's it doing up here?"

"It looks like somebody was building it, and they just gave up. It's, like, ninety-five percent done, I think."

"I think you're right," Charlie said. "Looks to me like it just needs some paint and varnish. And some of the rigging stuff—the cleats and the rest of the hardware."

"And a mast. And a boom. And sails," added Nicholas, continuing to poke his head into every corner of the hull. "All right, so maybe it's ninety percent done."

"Do you think Nick built it?" asked Charlie. "Maybe he started building *Goblin* and just never got back to this one."

Nicholas pointed to a small brass plaque screwed into

the wood on the side of the centerboard trunk. "Well, *that* answers a few questions."

Heron Class Dinghy

Designed by Jack Holt

Built by
Nick and Will Mettleson

Charlie squeezed in next to Nicholas so she could read it, too. "So, your dad and Nick built it? That is *cool.*"

"Yeah, well, I think there might be more to this story."

"What do you mean?"

"Let's go inside," Nicholas said. "There's something you need to see."

* * *

The creases in Charlie's forehead grew deeper and deeper as she read the letter from her mom to Nicholas's dad. When she got to the end, she went right back to the beginning and read it again.

Finally, she looked up at Nicholas. "When you found it, was it still folded?"

"Uh-huh. Like one of those paper footballs. It was kind of in a corner; I missed it the first time, when I found the movie."

"I can't believe my *mom* wrote this. It's so . . . romantic.

82

They must have been, what, fourteen or fifteen? But what does she mean in this part where she talks about your dad getting blamed for everything? What happened?"

Nicholas shrugged. "No idea. Dad never told me anything. Neither did my mom, and she usually *likes* to tell me about all the bad stuff he did, especially since they got divorced. Maybe he never told her, either."

Charlie took one more look at the letter before refolding it and handing it back to Nicholas. "You know, I'll bet your dad never saw this. Think about it. Mom sneaks in here on Sunday morning while everybody's at church and puts the letter in their secret hiding place. In the letter, she says your dad's parents were coming to get him Sunday afternoon, but what if they showed up a little early and he never had the chance to look? You said yourself it was still folded up. Why would he read it, refold it, and put it back? It just doesn't make sense."

"I guess it's possible," said Nicholas. He wasn't sure why it mattered one way or the other.

"Nicholas! This letter is . . . an important piece of history. If your dad never read it, he may not have known how my mom felt about him, and maybe he never wrote to her because he was expecting a letter from her that *never* came. Omigosh, it's so *tragic*."

"Hold on," said Nicholas. "Don't you think that's a little dramatic? It was a *long* time ago. And what are we supposed to do about it now? Your mom got married. So did my dad."

"And divorced."

"So?" A pause. "Oh no. You're not thinking what I think you're thinking. Are you?"

Charlie smiled at him—the very same smile she'd flashed at him after striking him out—and started down the spiral staircase. "Come on, let's go look at that little boat again. I have an idea."

* * *

"It can't hurt to ask," Charlie said, caressing the smooth deck of the Heron.

"It does seem like kind of a waste, just sitting up here collecting dust," Nicholas agreed.

"And pigeon poop," added Charlie.

Hayley, standing on the top step of the ladder, stuck her head up into the hayloft. "Cool. What are you guys doing up here?"

"Hayley! Get down from there before you get hurt," Nicholas scolded. "Where's Hetty?"

"Right behind me," said Hayley. "We're not babies, you know, Nicholas. We know how to climb a ladder. Come on up, Hetty. Nicholas is just mad because we're interrupting him and Chaaarlieeee. *Aren't* you, Nicholas?"

"No," said Nicholas, glad that the hayloft was dark enough that they wouldn't see him blush. "For your information, we were just looking at this boat."

Hayley clambered through the opening in the floor, followed by the slightly more cautious Hetty, and soon both were oohing and aahing over the striking little day sailer perched in the unlikeliest of settings.

Before long, Nick began to wonder where everyone had disappeared to, and stuck his head into the barn. "Nicholas? Girls? You in here?"

Nicholas leaned over the edge of the loft. "Yep, we're all up here."

Nick grunted.

"We found a *beautiful* little boat!" Hetty exclaimed.

"I think he probably knows about it," said Nicholas.

Nick knew this day was inevitable, but he still wasn't quite prepared for it as he climbed the ladder to the hayloft.

"So you found her," he said gruffly, pulling himself to his feet with a helping hand from Nicholas.

"You and Dad built this? It's amazing," Nicholas said.

"Your dad was being nice, putting my name on that plaque," Nick said. "He did all the work. I just gave him a little advice now and then. And maybe a little lumber." He rubbed his hand down the length of the starboard gunwale, reminiscing. "She's a beaut, no?"

"Is it fast?" Charlie asked.

"Oh, I'm sure she'd scoot right along in a little breeze. These little boats are very popular in England, partly because they're so stable. Hard to capsize. Thousands of them, most homebuilt like this one. Your dad saw a picture of one in a magazine and sent away for the plans. Spent most of two summers working on it. Shame he didn't—"

"Can you take us out on it?" Hayley interrupted. "It's so cute."

"*Adorable*, really," added Hetty.

Nick scrunched up his face, scratching his chin and squinting at Nicholas and the twins. "Well, it may not be my place to say, but after all these years, I don't think your dad would object to somebody finally finishing her up. It's kind of a shame, her sittin' up here like this. But I have to warn you, she still needs a good bit of work before she'll be ready to sail. Think you'd be up for that?"

Charlie and Nicholas nodded enthusiastically.

Nick sighed. "Well, I suppose she's been imprisoned long enough."

"Why is it up here, anyway?" Hayley asked. "Why didn't Daddy finish it?"

"Long story," Nick answered, not offering to tell it.

"Does it have a motor?" Hetty asked.

Nick found an oar leaning against the wall and showed it to her. "Yep. Finest kind. Look, I think this one even has your name carved into the handle. H-E-T-T-Y," he teased. "There's a suit of sails somewhere in the house. Will bought them used from a fellow from Cleveland. If I had to guess, I'd say they're probably in the back of that hall closet."

"Is there anything you *don't* have in that closet?" Nicholas asked.

Nick laughed. "You sound just like Lillie."

Hayley cleared her throat to interrupt. "Um, don't we have a little problem here, people? The boat is in a *hayloft*."

"Oh, don't let that bother you," Nick said. "I got her up here; I can get her down. There's a block and tackle around here somewhere we can use to lower her over the edge."

Hetty walked all the way around the boat, then stood with her arms crossed. "She doesn't have a name."

"Hetty, the boat isn't even painted yet," said Nicholas. "The name won't go on until last."

"*IMP!*" shouted Hayley and Hetty together. *Imp* was the name of the dinghy used by *Goblin*'s owner in the book to go between his mooring and shore.

"Please, pretty please, Great-uncle Nick—allow us to name her *Imp*," said Hetty in the fake British accent she'd started using after reading *We Didn't Mean to Go to Sea*. "It's *ever* so perfect."

Nicholas and Charlie laughed at Hetty's over-the-top plea.

"I thought you didn't like books, Hetty," said Nicholas.

"*Most* books," she replied, doing her best to sound like a sophisticated English child. "That one is *quite* special."

* * *

Nicholas was in his room reading over the faded construction plans for the Heron and suddenly feeling a little intimidated by the childhood version of his own dad. A movie. A boat. A girl, even. Who said she *loved* him.

Yikes. Not sure I'm ready for that.

And all at the age of fourteen.

I have a couple of years to catch up.

Nick knocked on the staircase and then slowly spiraled his way into the tower room. "Now I remember why I don't come up here that often," he joked as he sat on the edge of Nicholas's bed and took a few deep breaths. "This room is meant for young people. Ah, I see you're looking at the plans. Nifty little boat."

"Did you have plans like these for *Goblin*?"

"Very similar. Building big boats is a lot like building little ones."

"I wonder why Dad never told me about this," said Nicholas.

Nick nodded. "Yes, about that. Tell me, Nicholas, did your dad ever say anything . . . well, about what happened the last summer he stayed here with me and Lillie?"

Nicholas shook his head. "It was something bad, right?"

"What makes you think that?"

Nicholas thought about the letter and all that it revealed about his dad, but decided that this wasn't the time to bring it up. "I don't know. I just have a feeling. You know, the movie—he didn't finish that, and now this boat. So close to being done. Something bad must have happened."

"Not much gets past you, does it?" Nick said. "For tonight, let's just leave it at that. It was all a long time ago. For now, I think your dad will be pleased that you're going to finish up the Heron."

"I'm going to keep it a secret from him," Nicholas said. "I want it to be a surprise when . . . *if* he ever comes out here."

CHAPTER SIX

Nicholas woke with a start at 2:53 a.m. He had fallen asleep while reading an old *National Geographic* about Robin Lee Graham, the sixteen-year-old boy who sailed his boat, *Dove*, around the world, and wondering if he would be ready for a journey like that in four years' time. He reached up and turned off his reading light, and was surprised that the moonlight pouring into the tower room was still bright enough to read by. Out on the lake, the lunar spotlight fell directly on *Goblin*, tap-dancing on the rippled surface of the cove.

He was about to turn away and try to go back to sleep when something far out on the lake caught his eye. He blinked his eyes a couple of times to make sure he wasn't seeing things, but there was no doubt about it: someone was out sailing! By the time he saw it, the boat was nearly at the edge of his line of vision, and within seconds was out of sight. If Nicholas hadn't at that moment looked at Aunt Lillie's painting, mysteriously titled *2:53 A.M.*, which seemed to capture a moment exactly like the one he had just witnessed, he probably would have crawled back into his bed without another thought. But he did see it, and it was all just too much of a coincidence for him.

Nicholas grabbed his sneakers, pulled them on quickly, and spun down the spiral staircase. He almost stepped on Pistol, who was stretched across the hall at the bottom of the stairs. The dog lifted his head long enough to watch Nicholas disappear out the front door, and then returned to chasing the slow-moving rabbits of his dreams.

Knowing that he wouldn't be able to see anything from the dock, Nicholas sprinted around the edge of the little cove to the sandy point of land that the twins had named Beach End, which came from *We Didn't Mean to Go to Sea*, naturally.

The breeze was steady but light, and Nicholas had sailed enough to have a pretty fair idea of where the boat *should* be when he reached Beach End and looked down the lake.

There was, however, not a boat in sight.

The moon had ducked behind a cloud, and for a few seconds he thought the blanket of darkness that had been thrown over the lake was the explanation. When the clouds parted, though, no boat appeared.

What the . . . ? Was I dreaming?

He stayed there for a few minutes, letting his eyes get used to the darkness, but it made no difference. He tried to picture in his mind the shoreline north of where he stood—was there someplace a boat could hide? There were no docks or moorings for a good half mile, much farther than a small sailboat could have traveled in the short time it took him to get from his room to Beach End. It seemed to have just . . . vanished.

* * *

July 14
Hi, Dad.
    3:15 a.m.—the moon's shining on <u>Goblin</u> and I'm wondering if you can see the moon where you are. Crazy, right? I know I should be in bed, but my brain is going, like, a million miles an hour. This place makes New York seem boring.

                                        Nicholas

* * *

When Nicholas went down for breakfast in the morning, he found Nick already out on the porch, drinking coffee and reading the paper.

"Mornin', champ," said Nick. "Did you get some breakfast?"

"In a minute. I, um, wanted to ask you about something."

Nick lowered the newspaper. "You saw it, didn't you? The 2:53—that's what I call it."

Nicholas's eyes widened. "How did you know?"

"Heard the screen door bang against the frame and looked over at the clock in my room. When I saw the time, I knew."

"So you *do* believe in it?"

"Well, I believe that you saw a sailboat out your window. However, I believe that there's a perfectly logical explanation for it. What happened when you got down to the lake?"

Nicholas shrugged. "It was gone. I thought maybe I dreamt the whole thing."

"Do you remember anything about the boat?"

"It was a little smaller than *Goblin,* I think, but it did have a cabin. Normal-looking, I guess. I only saw it for a few seconds. Then the moon went behind some clouds and that was it."

"Sounds about right," said Nick. "I wouldn't worry about it. Lillie never saw it again; you probably won't, either."

* * *

An hour later, as a delightful offshore breeze ruffled the water, *Goblin* paced impatiently at her mooring, like a dog on a leash waiting for its morning walk. But Nicholas and Charlie had turned their attention to *Imp*, which they had carefully lowered from the hayloft with a little help from Charlie's teammates Zack Cooper and Ryan Crenshaw and the ancient block and tackle that Uncle Nick set up and operated. They were determined to finish the job that Nicholas's father had started so long ago, even though it meant sacrificing precious sailing time aboard *Goblin*.

They set the boat upside down on some boards inside the barn and wedged a block of wood under each side to keep it from tipping every time they leaned on it. Uncle Nick supplied them with a shopping bag full of sandpaper and showed them how to sand with the grain of the wood, starting with coarse sandpaper and gradually using finer and finer grit. The wood seemed to come to life with just a few strokes, and the dull gray-brown surface quickly began to show signs of its original color and grain.

Zack and Ryan were supposed to stick around to help out with the sanding, but bolted when they realized that sanding was actual work.

"Sorry, Charlie, but I don't do physical labor," said Zack. "Helping you move the boat is one thing, but

The wood seemed to come to life with just a few strokes, and the dull gray-brown surface quickly began to show signs of its original color and grain.

standing there with sandpaper in my hand and breathing in all that sawdust, which is probably toxic? No way."

Nicholas scoffed under his breath, "And you called *me* a city boy."

"Uh, have fun, guys," said Ryan. "See you Saturday, Charlie. Softball game over at the field by my house."

"You should come, too, Nicholas," said Zack. "Don't worry, you can be on Charlie's team—that way you don't have to worry about her striking you out again."

"Hilarious," muttered Nicholas as they hopped on their bikes and rode off.

"Don't let Zack get to you. He's like that to everybody. And if it's any consolation, he can't hit my curve, either."

* * *

For the next hour, they sanded and sweated, and sweated and sanded, in the dim light of the barn. Hearing a noise in the back of the barn, Nicholas moved closer to Charlie and whispered, "Don't turn around. We're being watched."

She grinned at him from across the hull. "I *thought* those little monkeys were being awfully quiet. Where are they?"

"Behind the tractor. They must have snuck in the side door."

"I should, like, kiss you or something. Really give them their money's worth."

Nicholas laughed nervously. "Yeah, that would be . . . I have a better idea, though. You just stay here; keep sanding." Then he added, loudly, "I'll be right back. I need to get something from Uncle Nick," and walked out of the barn toward the house. Instead of going inside, though, he ran around the barn to the side door, next to Charlie's painted strike zone. He slipped inside without a sound and ducked behind a pile of old farm equipment about ten feet from the twins' hiding spot, where he waited for the perfect opportunity.

"Do you think Nicholas likes her?" Hayley whispered.

"Of course he does," said Hetty. "He's just too dumb to know it yet. Remember—Mom used to say that about Dad."

Nicholas slid a few feet closer, smiling to himself at how clueless they were. Then he pounced on them, shouting "ARRGGHH!" and throwing a filthy blanket over their heads.

They screamed, trying to escape the trap, but Nicholas managed to keep them in custody long enough to tell them, "You know what else Mom used to say? *Mind your own business!*"

"Nicholas! Stop it!" Hetty cried as she poked her head out from under the blanket.

"You are going to be in *so* much trouble," Hayley added, jumping to her feet with hands firmly planted on her hips.

"I'm going to tell Mummy," said Hetty, returning to her British accent.

Nicholas laughed. *"Mummy?"* He added, in his own bad accent, "Well, when you ring Mummy, just make *bloody* sure you tell her about how you were spying on me."

"We weren't spying," said Hetty. "We were just listening."

"Oh, that's different," Nicholas said.

"C'mon, Hayley. Let's get out of here and leave them . . . *alone*." The twins stormed out of the barn.

"What was *that* all about?" Charlie asked when Nicholas returned.

"Oh, nothing. They were just snooping, like usual. Mom calls them the Snoop Sisters."

"Are you going to get in trouble?"

"No. They won't tell her, because they know they're not supposed to be spying."

"You hungry at all?"

The change of subject caught Nicholas off guard. "What? Uh, yeah, I guess. Let's just try to finish this section, and then we'll go in."

They went back to their sanding, and were soon so caught up in what they were doing that they didn't notice when Nick came in twenty minutes later. The twins, a few feet behind, stopped at the threshold, refusing to step inside the barn.

Nick ran his hand over the hull, took a deep breath, and smiled.

"Ah, nothing like the smell of freshly sanded wood. *Almost* makes me want to build another boat."

"I'm just happy she's only twelve feet long," said Nicholas. "I can't imagine doing this to *Goblin*."

"And with only one arm," Uncle Nick reminded him. "You can switch hands when you get tired. You two have done a great job. Let's flip her over, and then you can tackle the deck and the inside."

They rolled the boat up on one edge and then all the way over so she was sitting deck-side up. Charlie and Nicholas both sighed when they saw the expanse of unsanded wood that lay before them.

"Maybe you two are ready for a break," said Uncle Nick. "She'll still be here tomorrow. Nice breeze blowin' out there. Good day for a sail." He raised his eyebrows questioningly.

Nicholas and Charlie looked at each other. They were both tired and a little sore from all the sanding, and a relaxing sail around the lake with a few stops for swimming thrown in would certainly be more fun than an afternoon of back and forth, back and forth, back and forth.

Charlie spoke first. "I know it's a beautiful day, but we still have a lot of work . . ."

Nicholas nodded. "Even if we finished sanding today, we need to buy paint and varnish and brushes, and then you have to show us how to do all that, and we have to put on *how* many coats?"

"Four or five, at least," admitted Uncle Nick. "If everything goes according to schedule, you could be sailing her in a couple of weeks. Today's probably the worst day.

Lots of sitting around and waiting for paint to dry from here on."

"Two weeks?" Nicholas said, sounding surprised and a little disappointed.

Uncle Nick put his hand on Nicholas's shoulder. "No shortcuts, I'm afraid. Better to be patient and do it right the first time. So go ahead, you can stay and work. There's fixin's for sandwiches and iced tea in the fridge when you're ready for lunch. The twins and I are going for a sail."

"Yay!" cried Hayley and Hetty, who turned and ran toward the lake, with Pistol trotting along beside them.

* * *

As Nicholas and Charlie sanded (and sanded, and sanded) on opposite sides of the Heron's deck, they returned to the topic of the letter.

"What should we do about it?" she asked.

"Do? What do you mean? What *can* we do?"

"Maybe I should tell my mom."

"I'm not sure that's a good idea. At all," Nicholas said.

"Why not? Don't you think she deserves to know the truth—that your dad never found her letter?"

"We don't *know* that. And what good will it do now? It'll probably just make your mom mad at us for reading it. It's kind of personal, you know. And it's ancient history. It's not like they're going to get back together or something like people do in the movies."

"Maybe you're right, but old people—like our parents—are always talking about 'closure.'"

"What's that?"

"I think it just means that they finally know the truth, and then they can stop worrying about whatever it was that happened."

"You seriously think your mom has been worrying about why my dad didn't write to her for thirty-some years?"

"That's just it! I don't know! Maybe she has. Maybe the only reason she married my dad is because she got tired of waiting for *your* dad."

Nicholas was too exasperated to respond, which made Charlie smile.

"You're starting to see it my way, aren't you?" she asked. "What about your dad? Do you think we should tell him, too?"

"No!"

"Why not?"

"Because."

"That's not an answer. You know, I think I know what this is about. Your parents have only been divorced for a year, right? You've seen too many movies where these adorable, clever kids do something to get the parents back together. Look, I know this isn't what you want to hear, but trust me, Nicholas: it's not gonna happen. Life isn't like the movies. When my parents got divorced, I used to spend hours planning crazy schemes to get them together.

I'd get my hopes up and then I'd be disappointed when nothing happened."

"That's *not* what I think is going to happen," Nicholas said. "I'm not some little kid, like Hayley or Hetty, you know. You don't know anything about it, so just . . . drop it, okay? Jeez, like you're an expert on my life or something."

He put his head down and concentrated extra hard on the section of deck he was sanding so he wouldn't have to look at Charlie, who was trying to make eye contact with him. What really annoyed him about the whole thing was that she was right, of course. He *did* still hope that his parents would get back together, even though he knew, deep down, that it would never happen.

"Nicholas."

He pretended not to hear.

Why do you have to be such an annoying girl sometimes?

"I'm sorry, okay? I just don't want you to have to go through what I did."

Nicholas grunted, but still didn't look up.

"And . . . for *now*, I agree that we won't say anything to your dad. Unless my mom wants to. That would be different, right? Nicholas? C'mon! Are you ever going to talk to me again?"

He shrugged, still annoyed by her know-it-all ways, and still refusing to look at her. But Nicholas Mettleson had met his match in stubbornness. Charlie moved over to his side of the boat and started to sand the same spot he was working on. When he moved over a few inches, she followed him, smiling to herself all the while. After a few more attempts, he was frustrated enough to slam his hand down on the boat and look up at her.

To his credit, he *tried* to maintain his composure and stay mad at her, but it was no use. She looked back at him with the "strikeout smile" smeared across her face, and he couldn't help himself—his own mouth betrayed him and broke into a smile. He shook his head in frustration.

Charlie put her arm around his shoulders as they went inside for lunch. "You're a nice kid, Nicholas. Just don't mess with me."

* * *

Charlie invited Nicholas to dinner at her house that evening, and after they filled up on meat loaf, baked potatoes, and the first sweet corn of the season, Charlie led her mom into the living room and sat down next to her on the couch.

"What's *this* all about, Charlie?" Franny asked, forcing a smile. "Oh no, you're going to ask for a raise in your allowance, aren't you?"

"No-ooo. Nothing like that. We . . . well, Nicholas, actually . . . found something that belongs to you. In the tower room over at Nick's."

"Oh?" Her face brightened instantly. "My ID bracelet? I got it for my twelfth birthday, and I lost it a couple of years later, the summer that . . . the last summer your dad spent here."

Charlie shook her head. "Nope, not a bracelet. It's a letter. That you wrote."

"That *I* wrote? Why would there be a letter that . . . Oh my. The letter I wrote to Will."

Nicholas then produced the letter from the right front pocket of his shorts.

"I'm sorry I read it," he said, handing it to her. "I know I shouldn't have. But when I found it, I didn't know you; I didn't know anything *about* you. It was just an old letter."

Franny held the letter in the open palm of her hand and ran her index finger over the name "Will" that she had so neatly printed twenty-five years earlier. The corners of her mouth softened into a semblance of a smile, and her eyes glistened as memories came flooding back to her.

"Aren't you going to read it?" Charlie asked.

Nicholas stirred uncomfortably in his chair. Clearly, Charlie and her mom had a very different relationship from the one he had with his parents. He couldn't imagine confronting either of them on something so personal. It just wasn't done in the Mettleson family. Private meant private, which is one reason Nicholas felt guilty for having read somebody else's letter.

"I'm getting there," said Franny. "Still mustering up my courage. I'm a little afraid of what I might have said. I was a lot like you, Charlie, when I was your age—*very* emotional. Not at all like the rock I am today," she added with a laugh.

"Uh-huh. A rock. That's just what I was thinking," said Charlie. "C'mon, read it!"

Franny unfolded the letter as if she were handling a priceless document from a museum, and Nicholas noticed that her hands were shaking as she finally held it before her and began to read.

Just as he and Charlie had both done, when she got to the bottom, she went right back and read it a second time. Her eyes were shiny with tears, and Nicholas turned away, embarrassed to be caught in the middle of this very private moment.

"I should probably get going," he said cheerfully. "Thanks for dinner, Mrs. Brennan. That corn was amazing. I have to admit, Charlie's right about that—the corn in Ohio is better than in New York. See you tomorrow, Charlie." He stood up to go.

"No, don't go," said Franny, wiping a tear away and reaching for a box of tissues. "Stay, Nicholas. I'm sorry. I guess there's still a little of the old emotional me in here."

"So here's what we think, Mom: Will never got the letter." Charlie explained her theory about Will's parents arriving early and whisking him back to the city before he had a chance to check the secret hiding place one last time. "It makes perfect sense," she continued. "Why else would he leave it behind? And the movie."

"What you say is certainly possible," Franny said, then

gave a sad sigh. "His parents *did* come earlier than expected that day. In fact, I barely got out of Nick's house in time. But I think there's another explanation. Maybe he just wanted to forget about me. And the movie. That's what got him into all the—"

"All the *what*, Mom? What *happened?*" Charlie pleaded.

Franny sighed deeply and then smiled at Charlie and Nicholas. "Let's invite Nick and your sisters over for some ice cream and then I'm going to tell you two a little story."

CHAPTER SEVEN

When the ice cream bowls had been emptied and the spoons licked clean, the twins went into Franny's room to enjoy a special treat.

"You have a *television?*" Hetty asked as Franny led them away. "That is just *brilliant*. I do so miss the telly."

Nicholas shook his head. "Oh brother. Uncle Nick, please, no more books about England for those two. Hetty is driving me crazy with that stupid accent."

When Franny came back, they took seats out on the porch, where they watched the sunset and listened to the familiar, relaxing sound of outboard motors putt-putting up the lake. Although it felt a bit like snooping to him, Nick read the letter that had remained undiscovered for so long in his house, sighing sadly as he folded it and handed it back to Franny.

"I wanted Nick to be here, too," started Franny, "because he'll remember some things I've forgotten, and on top of that, he probably knew more about it than I did. It's funny—it was a long time ago, but as I read this letter, my stomach did flip-flops when I got to the part about Will leaving. For a second, I felt like I was fourteen again."

"Nicholas tells me that his dad never told him anything about that summer," said Nick. "And he hasn't set foot in my house since that day. Even when Lillie died, he came to the funeral, but he never came back here to the lake with everybody else."

"Jeez, you guys!" cried Charlie. "You're killing me here. Will you *please* just tell us what happened!"

Franny leaned back in her chair and told her story:

"It was the perfect summer. I'm sure there were days when it was too hot, and days when it rained, but I don't remember them. They just wouldn't have mattered. Will had spent the previous two summers with Nick, so we were already good friends, but that summer was . . . different. We were older, more, um, sophisticated, I suppose. Nicholas, your dad really was amazing—he wasn't like any of the other boys I knew. He knew so much, about *everything*, and was convinced that he could do anything if he put his mind to it. He saw some Disney movie about kids making their own horror movie, and decided that he could do that. Nick had a sailing magazine with a story about a kid who built his own boat, and the next thing I know, Will's building a boat."

Nicholas glanced over at Charlie, who winked at him. She still hadn't told her mom that they were working on the boat in Nick's barn.

"He bought an old movie camera at a garage sale, and then he made all the neighborhood kids pitch in their lawn-mowing money to pay for film and developing while he wrote the script. Your dad was a real wheeler-dealer, Nicholas; he told them if they wanted to be in the movie, they had to cough up some cash. He said, 'I'm gonna make you all famous!' and most of us believed him. Well, you've seen the parts of the movie that he finished—it's pretty good, considering the equipment we had."

"Why didn't he finish it?" Charlie asked.

"I'm getting there," Franny answered. "*Patience*, Charlie. We shot scenes out of order, just like in Hollywood, because some days Jimmy—that's Charlie's dad—had baseball practice, or somebody else had to go fishing with his dad, or mow somebody's lawn, and besides, we just couldn't wait to film this exciting finale that Will had dreamt up. It's near the end, when the Seaweed Strangler gets his revenge on the rich hunter who has been harassing him. Just as the guy is about to set sail in his big sailboat, which we had borrowed from Jimmy's cousin, Teddy Bradford, the Seaweed Strangler climbs aboard. He ties the owner of the boat to the mast, facing forward, and then he takes the wheel. It's a really windy day, and he aims the boat right for the pier over by the causeway, where there are all those sharp rocks and old iron things sticking up out of the water. When the boat hits all that, it explodes in a big ball of fire."

"What! My dad blew up a boat?" Nicholas asked.

"Well, no, not really," Franny explained. "It was all going to be done with special effects. Here's how it was *supposed* to work: I was running the camera that day because Will was playing the part of the rich guy tied to the mast. Everything was going perfectly. The boat was anchored, and Will pulled up the mainsail, and then went up on the bow to pull up the anchor. When he turned around, the Seaweed Strangler, who had climbed up the ladder on the stern, was standing there waiting for him. They struggled for a few seconds, and Will ended up tied to the mast with a bunch of seaweed, facing forward and watching in horror as the Seaweed Strangler turned the boat so it was heading right for me and the rocks. According to Will's plan, when the boat was still about a hundred feet away from shore, Jimmy was supposed to dive off the back of the boat, and then I could stop filming, because the rest of the scene—the boat crashing onto the rocks, the explosion, and the fire—was going to be done with a model boat that Will made to look just like the real one.

"The second Jimmy jumped off, Will got loose from the seaweed and ran back to the steering wheel. The wind had picked up and the boat was moving faster than he expected, I think, but there was still plenty of time for him to turn the boat safely away from the rocks. Except . . . something happened. Will couldn't turn the boat. I still remember seeing him at the wheel, and the boat getting closer and closer. For some reason, I kept the camera running. And that's all I remember."

"What do you mean?" demanded Charlie. "What happened next?"

"Your mom got a bump on her noggin the size of a grapefruit is what happened next," said Uncle Nick.

Nicholas and Charlie looked at one another, confused.

"But . . . I thought you were on the shore," Nicholas said.

"Yep. Standing there with the camera up to her eye, according to the people who witnessed it. That boat had its mainsail up and was moving pretty good when it hit the rocks. Well, when the boat stopped suddenly like that, the backstay broke and the mast and sail just kept right on going, right over the bow. The mast came down on Franny before she could move. Got a good concussion and a broken arm out of it, and I'd have to say she got off easy. Might have killed her."

"Ahh, that explains the *cast*," Charlie said. "In the letter, you talked about having a cast on for a long time."

"I don't get it," said Nicholas. "Why didn't Dad turn the boat?"

Uncle Nick and Fran looked at each other with uncertain expressions.

"Nobody knows," said Uncle Nick. "Will swore that

he had the wheel all the way over, but the boat didn't respond. Boat crashed so hard that Will had two broken ribs from where he hit the steering wheel."

"Maybe it was in a dream while I was in the hospital, but I always swore that I remembered him turning the wheel and screaming something about the rudder. But in the end, it just didn't matter. My parents went crazy. They threatened to sue Will's family, saying he'd done it all on purpose for the movie. He had left some sketches at my house of how he wanted the scene to look on film, and when my dad found them, he said they were proof. They showed the boat crashing on the rocks with the mast broken—and the drawings looked *just* like the photos of the wreck that ended up in the paper. They printed them side by side, and after that, everybody just assumed he was guilty."

"What about the model boat? Didn't he tell everybody about that?" Nicholas asked.

"He tried, but it didn't seem to matter," Uncle Nick said. "Like Fran says, it all looked bad for him, right from the start. I remember him sitting on the porch swing after it happened. He looked terrible—he felt just awful about Franny—but he swore to me that it was an accident. And I believed him. He never would have lied to me. The worst part was, they wouldn't even let him visit you in the hospital."

"I know," Franny said. "He tried calling, but my dad answered the phone. Told him never to call me again, and then he hung up. That's when I decided to write the letter."

"And this letter—you say it never made it into Will's hands?" Uncle Nick asked.

"That's the way it looks," Franny said.

"Lot of water under the bridge since then," said Uncle Nick with a sad shake of his head. "For both of you."

"So that was it?" Charlie said. "He left and you never heard from him again? Mom, you said yourself that you believed in him—didn't you even *try* to prove his innocence?"

"Charlie, I think you've been watching too much TV," Franny said. "What was I supposed to do? I was fourteen and in love with a boy from New York—who my parents hated. It was hard for me to imagine a happy ending to the story."

Nicholas looked at Charlie and in an instant knew how he'd be spending the rest of his summer.

* * *

With the sanding completed and inspected by Nick, it was finally time to start the painting and varnishing of *Imp*. Hayley and Hetty had their hearts set on pink, but Charlie and Nicholas—and Uncle Nick, who cast the deciding vote—chose a glossy fire-engine red for the hull.

"Sorry, girls," Nick told the twins, "but these two are

doing all the work. I think they should get to choose the color. Tell you what, though. If I build another boat, you can paint it any color you want." He winked at Nicholas.

That seemed to satisfy the twins for the moment, and they ran off to sit on the dock, dangling their toes in the water. Nick, with Pistol riding shotgun in Betty, rumbled off to the hardware store in Deming to pick up the paint and brushes while Nicholas and Charlie wiped the dust off *Imp* one last time.

"I've been thinking," said Charlie.

"Uh-oh. About what?"

"Mom's story. Your dad. That whole thing with the boat."

"And?"

"There's something missing. There's about a million holes in that story. Think about it."

"I've *been* thinking about it," Nicholas admitted. "And you're right. I couldn't sleep last night because I was thinking about it. I even wrote down a bunch of questions that I want to ask your mom."

"Me too!" said Charlie, unfolding a sheet of paper that she'd taken from the front pocket of her shorts. "And then she left for work this morning before I had a chance to ask any of them. Get your list; I want to see what you said."

Nicholas ran up the stairs to get his journal and then they began to compare notes.

"What was your first question?" Nicholas asked, his hand covering a page in his journal.

"Okay," Charlie said. "Here goes: Did anybody ever check out the boat to see if your dad was telling the truth?"

Nicholas smiled and then slid his hand down the page a few inches and showed Charlie the two words he had written: *Boat investigation?*

Charlie's mouth dropped open. "Omigosh. That is so obvious, right? I mean, somebody must have looked at it, right?"

"Maybe not," said Nicholas. "But that's not my number one question. I want to know what happened to the film that your mom shot that day."

Charlie held up her list with a smile. "Yep. Here it is on mine, too. Because the scene that she described is definitely not in the movie that you found."

"It couldn't be. Even if Dad had taken the camera that day, he would have had to send the film away to get developed and then add it to the parts he'd already edited. He just didn't have time to do it; his parents came and took him back to the city."

"Maybe he still has the film."

"It's possible, but why wouldn't he have just stashed it where he put everything else? It was a good hiding place."

"Good point. Well, somebody must know what happened to it."

A few minutes later, as Nick pulled Betty into the driveway, Pistol barked and then jumped from the passenger-side window of the still-moving pickup truck, tearing across the yard after a very surprised rabbit.

"Go, Pistol, go!" Charlie cheered.

"When we're talking to Uncle Nick, let's focus on the boat for now," Nicholas said. "I'm going to do a little more snooping in the tower room. Maybe Dad stashed the film in another hiding place that only he knew about."

For the next hour, Nick taught them how to paint, slowly dipping into the can and brushing on the white primer ("You're not Tom Sawyer, whitewashing a fence here; think of this as a piece of fine furniture"), while the interrogation began.

Charlie started gently. "So, Nick, um, we were wondering if there was, you know, any kind of investigation after that whole boat-crash thing. Like with the police or something."

Nick scratched his head, getting some of the primer in his hair in the process. "Oh well, at least it's white. Nobody'll notice. An investigation, you say. What's gotten into you two? Why do you want to dig up things that have been buried away for twenty-five years?"

"It's kind of like this boat," Charlie answered. "*It* was buried, too, but now we've sanded away the old wood and we're going to make it perfect and show the world just how beautiful it is. That story of Mom's needs a little sanding, too, if you ask me. The truth is there—it's just hiding under the surface. I'm sure of it."

Nick looked up at her, smiling. "Here, you take the brush for a while. Just keep it moving, and spread this primer out nice and thin. When it dries, we'll give it a quick sanding, and then we'll be able to lay down the first coat of red before lunch."

"And then what?" Charlie asked.

"And then we wait," answered Nick. "We'll let that dry overnight and hit it with the second coat tomorrow morning."

"So, about the investigation," said Nicholas. "Does this mean you don't know—"

"Or you *do* know but don't want to talk about it?" Charlie interrupted. "Is there something we're not *supposed* to know?"

"Slow down, Charlie," said Nick. "There's no conspiracy, I promise you that—at least as far as I'm concerned. If you two want to go digging around in the past, by all means dig away. I don't know about any kind of police report or anything like that, but it wouldn't surprise me if there was one. Must have been an insurance company involved somewhere. As I recall, Teddy Bradford got a brand-new boat a few weeks after the wreck. Money must've come from somewhere. He sure didn't get it from working hard, if you know what I mean. But why don't you go take a look at the old boat for yourself."

"What? It's still around? Where is it?" Charlie cried. "Why didn't you tell us that in the first place?"

"Well, sure it's still around," Nick answered calmly. "Fiberglass boats sure aren't as pretty as wood, but the dog-gone things last forever. It's over at Tressler's—the other side of the lake. They've got a big old barn they use for storing the summer people's boats and campers during the winter. It's been a few years, but I saw it out behind the barn when I was over there looking at an old Lyman runabout. Can't imagine it's gone anywhere."

*　*　*

"What do you mean, you can't ride a bike?" Charlie looked at Nicholas with a mixture of horror and disbelief as she pulled open the garage door at her house.

Nicholas shook his head. "I live in Manhattan. I just never learned. You make it sound like I'm the only one who doesn't know how."

"Well, *yeah*. Everybody knows how."

"Everybody who *learned* how. My dad is always away during the summers, and I guess Mom never got around to it. I'm not even sure she knows how herself. Some of my friends don't know how, either. Plus, we live in an apartment. It's not like we have a garage, you know. Where am I supposed to keep a bike?"

"Unbelievable. Why would *anyone* want to live in a place like that?"

"Because it's *New York*. It's cool," Nicholas said.

"Uh, yeah. Sounds *fantastic*. Well, you're just going to have to learn. How are we even supposed to go look at the boat if we can't ride bikes?"

"Walk?"

"It's, like, ten miles! Okay, maybe not ten, but it's

more than five. We're not walking when we have two perfectly good bikes just sitting here doing nothing. You can ride my mom's."

"A *girl's* bike?"

"Boy, you have a lot of attitude for somebody who doesn't even know how to ride one," Charlie said, pushing a navy blue bike toward him. "Here. It's a mountain bike—it doesn't have daisies painted on it or anything like that."

"Have you ever taught anyone before?" He glanced nervously at the array of brake and gear levers on the handlebars.

"No, but I think I can handle it."

"Yeah, it's not your face that's going to be hitting the gravel."

"That's what this is for," said Charlie, smiling broadly and setting a helmet on Nicholas's head. "C'mon, follow me. We'll start on the grass, like I did. That way, when you fall, it won't hurt so much."

"*When* I fall? I thought you said you could teach me." He placed his hands on the handlebars, both feet still firmly rooted to the ground.

"I never said you weren't going to fall, though. Falling is part of the deal. *Everybody* falls at first. Are you ready? I'm going to hold the bike steady for you, and you're going to put your feet on the pedals, okay?"

Nicholas lifted his right foot and set it on the pedal, and then s-l-o-w-l-y picked up his left and moved it into place. He took a deep breath. "Okay. So far. Now, what about all this stuff?" he asked, pointing at all the levers on the handlebars.

"Don't worry about shifting gears yet. I put it into a nice easy gear for starting out. You just need to know about the brakes. The one on the right is the back; the left is for the front. For now, just use the back brake. Later on, I'll teach you when you'll need to use both. Got it?"

Nicholas nodded. "Right, back. Got it."

"Okay, here we go then." Charlie, with one hand on the handlebars and one on the back of the seat, began pushing Nicholas across the yard. "Start pedaling!"

Together, they did a lap of the yard like that, and then, without warning, she let go.

"Hey! What are you—" He never finished his question. The bike tilted one way, and when he tried to straighten it, he overcompensated. For a few terrifying (for Nicholas, that is) seconds, the bike wobbled and wiggled along before the front wheel finally turned a little too sharply, and Nicholas and bicycle went flying in opposite directions.

To her credit, Charlie *tried* not to laugh, but she just didn't have the willpower to resist the urge that overcame her as Nicholas lay sprawled across the lawn. "Are you okay?" she managed to ask between giggling fits. "I'm sorry—it was just, the look on your face . . ." More giggling. Much more.

Nicholas stood up, rubbing his shoulder, which had taken the brunt of the impact with the ground. Without a word, he turned and started walking toward the road, and home.

At first, Charlie thought he was kidding around, but when she realized he was serious, she ran after him, stopping right in his path. "Come on, Nicholas. I'm sorry. I didn't mean to laugh. I won't do it again, I promise."

He stepped around her without a sound and kept right on walking as she stood there dumbfounded.

"What about the boat?" she asked. "*Both* boats. The movie? Nicholas! Come back. I swear I'll never laugh at you again."

But Nicholas just kept walking.

CHAPTER EIGHT

Nicholas spent the rest of the afternoon alone in the tower room. He told himself that he was there to search for another of his father's secret hiding places (which he didn't find), but deep down, he knew that he was the one doing the hiding this time. Charlie had injured his pride, and that hurt a lot more than his banged-up shoulder. At dinner, he barely spoke, and when he finished picking at his food, he went right back upstairs.

He was staring out the window at *Goblin* when he heard a knock at the spiral staircase. "What?" he growled.

"Nothing," said Nick. "I'll leave you alone."

Nicholas leaped out of bed, feeling guilty. "No, come

on up. I'm sorry, I thought it was Hayley and Hetty bugging me again."

Nick chuckled. "Not this time. They're on the phone with your mother. You know, these stairs are getting easier. Maybe I'll move in here after you go back to New York."

"Really?"

"I don't think so. For one thing, Pistol won't come up here, and in the winter he likes to sleep at the foot of my bed. Keeps my feet warm." He sat on the edge of the bed and motioned for Nicholas to sit, too. "Awful quiet today. You seem like a young man with something on his mind. Everything okay?"

Nicholas shrugged. "Yeah, I guess."

"You know, all this talk about your dad—is it making you miss him? Because that would be a pretty natural thing to happen, I think."

"No, it's not that. I mean, I do miss him, but that's not why I'm . . ." His voice trailed off into silence.

"Okay—I don't want to pry. Just wanted to make sure you're okay. When Charlie gets here in the morning, we'll give that first coat of paint a light sanding, and then lay on the second. If it's a nice dry day, we might even get another coat on later in the day."

From the look on Nicholas's face when he mentioned Charlie, Nick knew something had happened.

"Um, yeah, I don't know if she'll be coming over tomorrow," Nicholas mumbled, mostly to himself.

"Oh?"

"Uncle Nick, do you know how to ride a bike?"

Nick was caught off guard by the question. "A bicycle? Sure. Boy, I didn't see that one coming. Right out of left field. Can I ask why?"

"I can't. Ride a bike. Nobody ever taught me. So today, Charlie was going to, but then I busted, and . . ." He stopped to compose himself. "Why do girls have to be like that?"

"I'm afraid you've stumbled onto one of the great mysteries of the universe, son. Ask me about bikes and boats, or what kind of oil to use in your car, or even how to stuff a turkey, and I'm fine. Women, though, that's another story. But I think I can help you out with your bicycle problem. Come with me out to the barn."

From a spot behind some ancient, rusted farm machinery, Nick wheeled out an old single-speed bicycle—the kind with fat tires, a sturdy frame, and heavy metal fenders. With the sleeve of a long-retired flannel shirt, he wiped away a thick layer of dust and grime, revealing the gleaming red paint with SPEEDSTER emblazoned in gold letters across the top bar of the curvy frame.

"Wow. Is this an antique?" Nicholas asked.

"Hmm. Never thought about it, but I suppose it qualifies. Picked it up for ten dollars at a yard sale a few years ago, when my knees were in a little better shape. Put new tires on it, and it was ready to go." He found an air pump and filled the tires, squeezing them between his finger and thumb until he was satisfied. "There you go. It's a little late now, but tomorrow morning, we'll get—" He stopped when he saw the disappointed look on Nicholas's face. "Oh, right. Well, I suppose we have enough light to get started right now."

Nicholas smiled for the first time since leaving Charlie's yard as Nick wheeled the bike outside and leaned it against the long side of the barn, just a few feet from the painted-on strike zone. Pistol tagged along behind them, his tail wagging in anticipation of excitement and adventure.

"All right. Here's what you do. Climb aboard, and let's get you situated so you're the right distance from the wall of the barn. When you reach out to your side, you should be able to *just* touch it."

Nicholas lifted his leg over the frame and then stood with the bike between his legs, moving it a few inches farther from the barn. Then, with one hand on the wall and the other on the handlebars, he pushed himself up and onto the seat.

"Good, good. Now just sit there for a while—as long as you want—getting a feel for the balance."

After a few rather shaky moments, Nicholas started to feel more confident. "Okay, now what?"

"Keep that one hand on the wall like you've been doing," said Nick. "Be careful of splinters, but just start pedaling—nice and easy!—using that hand to help keep your balance. If you feel yourself starting to fall, just stop

125

For a few terrifying (for Nicholas, that is) seconds, the bike wobbled and wiggled along before the front wheel finally turned a little too sharply.

pedaling. That's perfect. . . . Oops!" Nick caught bike and rider before they toppled over onto the grass.

I can do this. Think of all the seven-year-olds out there who can do it.

Nicholas took a deep breath and steadied himself for a second attempt. This time, he was determined to make it to the end of the barn. What would he do when he got there?

I'll cross that bridge when I get to it.

He pedaled away from Nick and Pistol, slowly "riding" down the length of the barn, occasionally reaching out to steady himself with his hand.

When he got near the end, Nick shouted at him, "Keep going! You're doing great!"

Pistol joined in, running after Nicholas and barking his encouragement.

That was just what Nicholas needed. He grabbed the handlebars with both hands and kept right on pedaling across the front yard—aimed directly at a hundred-year-old oak tree!

"Turn! Turn!" shouted Nick.

"I'm trying!" said Nicholas. He jerked to the right, then left, then right again, finally flopping over onto his side just inches from the immense tree trunk.

Nick hurried over to him and was relieved to see Nicholas smiling. Laughing, even. "That was *cool!*" he said. "I want to do it again!" He jumped to his feet and pushed the bike back to the barn.

"This time, when you turn, take it nice and easy," Nick advised.

"Got it."

And he was off. He touched the wall only once after starting, sailing past the end of the barn and sweeping around the oak tree in a semi-controlled turn. "How do I stop?" he said, laughing.

"Stop pedaling and then push backward—gently!—on the pedals."

Nicholas stopped pedaling and promptly fell over onto a rosebush with only a handful of pink roses, but countless prickly thorns.

"Or you can just fall over," Nick teased. "You all right?"

But Nicholas was already on his feet, grinning as he wiped away the blood from a series of scratches on his arms and legs. "Fine. It's just a couple of scratches."

On his next attempt, he wobbled and wavered, but each time, he caught himself before falling, and then swept past the barn, the oak tree, and the rosebushes in a sweeping arc that was as wide as his smile.

"Bravo. My work here is done," Nick said, applauding. "I'm going inside."

"Is it okay if I stay out here for a while?" a beaming Nicholas asked. "Oh, and Uncle Nick—uh, thanks."

"You're welcome. Just don't stay out too late. Don't go out on the main road. Oh, and Nicholas?"

"Yeah?"

"Watch out for trees."

Nicholas stayed outside for almost two hours, and when he raced up the stairs to the tower room that night, he felt as if a weight had been lifted from his shoulders. He dug through the collection of postcards from the drugstore until he found one that pictured a boy riding a bicycle across Deming's town square. With a fine-point marker, he drew an arrow pointing right at the rider and wrote across the front of the card:

THAT'S ME!

After addressing the postcard to his father, he stared at the back for a few minutes before finally deciding not to add another word. As he set it on the bedside table and switched the light off, he wondered if his dad even knew that he couldn't ride a bike.

Until now, that is.

* * *

Nick made himself a breakfast of soft-boiled eggs, toast, and coffee and sat at the kitchen table, enjoying a few minutes of quiet before the three children would clamber down the stairs in search of orange juice and cereal. He had just turned to the sports section of the newspaper when, out of the corner of his eye, he saw a flash of red fly past the kitchen window. A cardinal? A low-flying airplane? Superman? He stood up to get a better look.

"Son of a gun," he said. It was Nicholas, already circling the yard and drive on the red Speedster, which he had polished to a glossy sheen that Nick wouldn't have believed possible.

"Hey, Uncle Nick," he said nonchalantly as he came to a smooth stop just outside the window. "What's for breakfast?"

"How do you like your eggs?"

Nicholas pondered the question for a second or two. "Scrambled. Do you have any bacon? That sounds *really* good to me."

"Scrambled eggs and bacon, coming right up," said Nick. "Why don't you get the twins up, too. We can all start the day with a good breakfast. That old bike looks good, by the way."

"I used some of your car wax. Hope that was okay."

"Sure. Maybe I'll give ol' Betty a little of the old spit and polish later on. She looks like she could use it. Say, why don't you ride over to Charlie's and see if she wants to join us for breakfast. I've got an extra dozen eggs."

Forgetting momentarily that he was mad at Charlie, Nicholas took off down the road. When he reached her driveway, it all came back to him, and he considered turning his bike around and hightailing it back to Nick's.

What if she's already seen me? If I turn back now, I will look like such a loser.

He parked the bike in the yard, turning around to admire it one last time before knocking on the screen door.

Franny bounded down the steps, dressed for work and in a hurry. "Oh, hi, Nicholas. Come on in, make yourself at home. Charlie's awake, but she hasn't made it downstairs yet. Sorry, I have to run—late for work!" And she was gone.

He sat at the kitchen table, poured himself a glass of orange juice, and waited for Charlie, who padded down the stairs a few seconds later. She gasped and stopped suddenly when she saw him, her hand flying to her chest.

"Oh my God! Nicholas! You scared me to death! What are you doing here? I come downstairs and there's somebody sitting there." She sat down to collect herself.

"Your mom let me in. I just kind of figured that you heard her talking to me. Sorry."

"What if I'd come down here, you know, naked or something?"

"Do you do that often?" He felt himself blushing.

"No! But that's not the point." She waved her hands around wildly, embarrassed by the direction the conversation had taken. "Besides, I thought you were mad at me—not that I blame you."

"Yeah, w-well, I—I, uh," he stammered. "Uncle Nick kind of helped me out last night. And I realized that I, um, you know . . ."

Charlie went to the front door and looked out at the lawn.

"No *way*! You rode that here? That is the coolest bike *ever*! Where did you get it? Can I ride it? When did you learn how to ride?"

"It's Uncle Nick's old bike. He taught me how last night. Had a few minor crashes along the way." He pointed out the scrapes and scratches from his run-in with the rosebush.

"Ouch. Look, Nicholas, about yesterday. I'm really— I mean, I didn't mean to hurt . . ."

Nicholas felt himself blushing; he was embarrassed by the way he'd acted. He waved off the rest of her apology. "Let's just forget it ever happened, okay?"

"Deal."

* * *

After breakfast at Nick's, Charlie led the way across the two-mile-long causeway that spanned the lake. Nicholas, determined to keep up with her despite his lack of experience, pedaled as hard as he was able. He was breathing hard and his heart was pounding as they swung their bikes into the parking lot of Tressler's Marine and RV Center, which was completely empty of cars. They rode right up to the entrance of the showroom, where a hand-printed sign had been taped to the glass door: FAMALY AMERGANCY

CLOZED TIL NEXT WENSDAY. CALL KEN IF YOU NEDE TO GET YER
BOTE OUT. HE GOT THE KEY.

"Nice spelling," Nicholas said. "And I guess we're just supposed to know Ken's phone number."

Charlie scoffed at the sign. "Well, we're not waiting until next Wednesday, that's for sure. Come on, let's check it out. Bring your bike over here."

They wheeled their bikes around the side of the building and hid them behind an old shed. A six-foot-high chain-link fence separated the building from the back of the property, which consisted of a weed-covered gravel lot filled with a motley collection of rundown boats and even sadder-looking rust-stained campers.

"The boat must be behind *that*," said Charlie, pointing at a large unpainted barn. "Nick said it was behind the barn."

"So, what are we supposed to do now?" Nicholas asked.

Charlie grabbed the fence and stuck a toe between the links. "We go in and take a look." When she reached the top, she swung her feet over and jumped down to the ground.

"Um, isn't that trespassing?"

"Only if we get caught. Don't worry—nobody's going to see us."

That's what they always say right before the FBI swoops in and arrests them.

Nicholas looked around, half expecting to see police

helicopters hovering overhead and a SWAT team racing toward him with guns drawn. But this was Deming, Ohio, on a quiet Tuesday morning; in all likelihood, there wasn't a helicopter within fifty miles as he mimicked Charlie's climbing technique and dropped onto the gravel on the other side of the fence.

They were in.

Just in case someone was watching, they ran to the back of the barn. There were three old sailboats sitting in wooden cradles, but it didn't take a detective to determine which was the one they were looking for: it was the one with the *big* hole in the bottom.

Charlie whistled. "Boy, when your dad wrecks a boat, he does it *right*."

"Man. No kidding," Nicholas added, reaching up inside the boat with his hand.

The hole was big enough for them to crawl through, and even more of the fiberglass around the keel was crushed and broken where it had landed on the sharp rocks outside the marina. The rudder, which should have been perfectly vertical, was heavily damaged and bent at a crazy angle; it looked like it belonged on a submarine. Above the waterline, one side of the hull had escaped unscathed, but the other had obviously pounded on the rocks and the marina seawall for some time.

"Let's take a peek inside," Charlie said, looking around for a way up onto the deck.

They found a ladder on the ground behind one of the

other sailboats, and soon they were on the deck, peering into the cabin through one of the portholes.

"Looks pretty nasty in there," Nicholas said. "But it's dry, at least. I guess the one good thing about having a two-foot hole in your boat is that water drains right out."

"Hadn't thought of that," Charlie admitted with a smile. "I wonder if there's anything living in there. Guess we'll find out." She gave the main hatch a good push forward with her foot and braced for a frontal attack by an angry raccoon.

"You're crazy," Nicholas said, marveling at this strange creature who seemed to fear nothing.

But Charlie was already on her way into the cramped, empty cabin, so Nicholas followed once more. The cushions had all been removed, as had the lines, sails, and every other piece of sailing equipment.

"What are we looking for?" Nicholas asked.

"First, I want to see how the steering wheel works— I mean, what connects it to the rudder? On Nick's boat, and on the Heron, it's simple: the tiller just connects directly to the rudder." She lay where one of the berths had been, and began to crawl toward the stern of the boat along the wood box that enclosed the inboard engine. Behind that was a small compartment—too small, in fact, to fit her head inside. After a little experimenting, though, she found that if she turned her head *just so*, she could see inside. And what she saw definitely got her attention.

"Nicholas! You have to see this. Come back here. On the other side."

He wiggled his way back, finally arriving at the point directly opposite Charlie. Their heads were separated by only eighteen inches or so.

"Where am I supposed to be looking?" Nicholas asked.

"Turn your head so you can look behind this . . . thingie. Can you see the pulleys?"

"Pulleys? No. No, wait, I see them."

"Those are part of the steering system," Charlie explained. "There are wire cables that run from the steering wheel up on the deck, then down here, where they change direction and connect to this thingie that's attached to the top of the rudder."

"Ohhhh. Yeah. That's pretty cool. Hey, how do you know so much about stuff like this?"

"Helping my dad fix old tractors, I guess," said Charlie. "You know, this probably worked pretty well . . . until somebody cut this cable."

"What?"

Charlie managed to reach one hand into the compartment, where she took the two ends of the cable and held them up for Nicholas to see. "This cable was cut. On purpose. If it had broken, it would be frayed at the ends."

Nicholas brought one end closer to get a better look.

"You're right. But . . . why? Who?"

"Good questions," said Charlie, reaching farther into the compartment. "I can't answer those, but I can tell you *how*. With *these*." She handed him a pair of wire cutters—the kind electricians use—rusted but still lethal-looking.

Back up on the deck, Nicholas stood behind the steering wheel, trying to imagine what must have been going through his father's head as he helplessly saw the boat headed for the rocks. Nicholas ran his hand around the stainless-steel wheel, bent forward where the young Will Mettleson had slammed into it.

"One more thing before we leave," Charlie said. "Let's see if the mast is here someplace. I want to check something out."

They found it on a rack with several other aluminum masts and booms. It, too, was not hard to spot. Unlike all the others, which were all arrow-straight, this one had a definite kink about two-thirds along its length, where it suddenly veered off at a quite noticeable angle.

Nicholas tried to lift one end; it was heavier than he thought. "Man. I can't believe your mom got hit in the head with this thing. And survived. No wonder her parents were freaked out."

Charlie was more interested in the four wire stays that had supported the mast than in the mast itself. She followed each down from the top, paying especially close attention to the backstay, which ended abruptly in a tangle of sharp strands of wire.

She turned to Nicholas. "Can you do me a favor? Go back up on the boat and see if the rest of the backstay is still attached. I forgot to look."

He climbed up the ladder and went to the stern of the boat. "Yep. It's here. It looks just like that end." Using the wire cutters that Charlie found in the cabin, he cut through the rusty cotter pin that secured the backstay turnbuckle to the hull and lifted it free.

Back on the ground, he and Charlie held the two broken ends of the wire together like two pieces of a puzzle.

"You seein' what I'm seein'?" Nicholas asked.

"Yep. This was no accident." She pointed to a group of strands on both halves, all severed at exactly the same place. "It's pretty obvious that somebody used a saw to cut at least halfway through the backstay."

"Yeah, there's no way they would break like that," Nicholas agreed. "Especially when you see how the rest of the strands look—all jagged and twisted."

"So, somebody cut the steering cable *and* sawed most of the way through the backstay to make sure the mast would come down."

"Which brings us back to the same two questions: Who? And why?"

Charlie adjusted her baseball cap. "Let's find out. Race you back to Nick's."

CHAPTER NINE

It wasn't exactly a fair race. Charlie rode a modern lightweight twenty-seven-speed mountain bike, while Nicholas chugged away on his old-fashioned heavyweight cruiser. Once she made the turn onto Lake Road, Charlie slowed down and let Nicholas catch up. They switched bikes for the homestretch to Nick's house, racing neck and neck the whole way. Nicholas turned into the driveway a few feet ahead and swung around the house, heading for the front-porch screen door. He leaned Charlie's bike against the house while she skidded to a stop, set the kickstand, and ran into the house ahead of him.

"I win! Again!" she shouted.

Pistol, sharing the porch swing with Nick, barked his approval and jumped to the floor. He pressed his nose against Charlie, insisting on some behind-the-ears scratching in return for his enthusiastic support.

"Totally. Not. Fair," said Nicholas, between gulps of air.

Hetty and Hayley, squeezed into a chair and reading *Black Beauty* together, clapped loudly. "Yay, Charlie!"

Nicholas shook his head at them. "Thanks a lot. My own sisters are against me. Family support—ha!"

"What have you two been up to all morning?" Nick asked. "Hope you don't mind—I gave the Heron a light sanding while you were out. She's ready for another coat of paint whenever you are."

Charlie poked Nicholas in his side. "Show him what we found."

Nicholas held out the remains of the backstay he had removed from the wrecked boat.

Nick took it from him and put on his reading glasses to get a better look. "What do we have here?"

"It's from the boat my dad wrecked," said Nicholas. "The backstay."

"Uh-hmmmmm. What'd you do, climb over the fence?"

Charlie and Nicholas stared at him, openmouthed. "How did you . . ."

Nick winked in the twins' direction. "The twins and I

know *everything* that goes on here at Forsaken Lake. Don't we, girls?"

Hetty and Hayley nodded enthusiastically.

"That's right, Uncle Nick," said Hayley.

"Even that time you and Charlie got stuck in *Goblin*," added Hetty. As soon as she said it, her hand flew up to her mouth. "Oops. I wasn't supposed to say anything about *that*."

Nicholas felt his face reddening as he turned to look at Nick again. "Wait—you *knew* about that? Why didn't you say anything?"

"One, because it wasn't your fault, and two, no harm done."

"Okay, that one I can understand," said Charlie. "You must have been watching us with binoculars. But this morning . . ."

"I ran into Ken Dulman the other day at the filling station. He said something about Joe Tressler's kid getting arrested down in West Virginia, and that Joe was heading down there to try to get him out of jail. And then when I drove by, I didn't see any cars in the lot, so I figured the place must be closed up for a few days. Was I right?"

Nicholas and Charlie nodded.

"You should be a detective, Uncle Nick," said Hayley.

Nick returned to his examination of the backstay. "I don't know about that, Hale. I think these two are doing just fine without me. Looks like somebody took a hacksaw to this, don't you think?"

"Uh-huh," said Charlie. "That's exactly what we said. And that's not all we found. You know how that boat has a steering wheel? Well, we went down in the cabin and figured out how it all worked—when you turn the wheel, it pulls on cables that move the rudder—but guess what? Somebody cut the cable!"

"With these," said Nicholas, handing Nick the wire cutters.

Nick whistled. "Well, I'll be dogged."

"It couldn't have been Daddy," said Hayley. "He was going to use a model boat, remember? And besides, he loved Franny. He felt terrible when she got hurt."

Nick, Charlie, and Nicholas all turned to face Hayley; it would be hard to say which of the three was most surprised by what she'd said.

"Hey, I thought you were watching TV in the other room when we were talking about all that stuff," Nicholas said.

The twins shared a conspiratorial smile and shrug.

"We don't always do what we say we're going to, Nicholas," said Hayley. "Even *you* should be smart enough to know that by now."

"You little sneaks," Charlie said. "I'm impressed."

Nicholas scoffed. "Don't encourage them. They know they're not supposed to do that."

"Well, it's just not cricket—keeping secrets from us," sniffed Hetty.

"Not *cricket*? Do you even know what that means?" asked Nicholas.

Nick held up his hand, signaling a truce. "What's done is done; there's no going back. Now, back to this boat. You're certain about the steering cable, are you?"

"Positive," said Charlie.

"I have to hand it to you two," Nick said. "Somebody should have caught this. And a broken—or cut—steering cable. Doggone it, *I* should have caught it."

"So, what do we do now?" Nicholas asked. "I mean— does all this really prove anything?"

"No, I don't suppose it does," said Nick. "Even if somebody had noticed this way back when, folks still would have blamed your dad. They'd have said he had plenty of time alone on the boat, and then they'd have pointed at those pictures he drew."

"Motive and opportunity," said Hayley, which made everyone turn and stare at her. "*What?* Can I help it if I've been reading a lot of detective stories?"

"If only we knew what happened to Dad's camera," said Nicholas. "And the film they shot that day. It must show *something*."

Charlie nodded in agreement. "Maybe that's why we haven't found it. Maybe somebody was afraid of what was on it."

"So, where do you want us to start?" Hayley asked.

Nicholas knew that the only way to keep the twins out of his hair was to give them a job. Besides, they *had* proven themselves to be plenty sneaky; who knew what they might find if they put their minds to the task.

"I've checked every inch of the tower room, so stay out of there. I want you two to start with your room," he said. "You need to check every crack, every gap, every board in the floor, every piece of molding, behind pictures, under furniture—everywhere. Pretend you have a search warrant to look anyplace you want—*except* my room, and Uncle Nick's room. Those are out-of-bounds. Got it?"

"Got it," they said, running up the stairs together.

"Do you think they'll find anything?" Charlie asked.

"Who knows? But at least they won't bug us for a while."

They went out to the barn, and while Nicholas wiped the dust from the Heron, Charlie stirred the paint and used a rag to squeeze the excess paint thinner from the brushes.

"Only two more coats," she said. "Then we flip her over and start on the varnish. I can't wait."

"I can't wait to take her sailing," said Nicholas as he dipped his brush into the paint for the first time. He looked out at the lake, which was as smooth as glass for the third day in a row. "*If* the wind ever blows again, that is."

"It always looks like that when it gets hot. Mom says it's going to be cooler next week, so it'll be better for sailing."

Nicholas considered for a few seconds what he was about to say, and then proceeded carefully. "About your mom. I was thinking."

Charlie looked up from her painting. "Oh?"

"Yeah. Do you think she'd be willing to, um, go back in time?"

With eyebrows raised, Charlie said, "Nicholas Mettleson, did you invent a time machine? That is so cool! It'll be just like in all those books." She set her brush down and stood up straight, hands on hips. "What are you talking about?"

"I don't mean *literally*," he said. "Okay, I know you know that. I'm talking about re-creating the scene of the crime, sort of. Just to see if she remembers anything else."

Charlie dropped her hands from her hips. "I see what you mean. It always works on TV."

"You think she'd do it?"

"I'll ask her tonight. I think she'll go along with it. All we have to do is remind her about that letter she wrote to your dad. She kind of owes it to herself—and him—to find out the truth."

* * *

July 17
Dear Dad,
    My first drive-in movie! REALLY dumb movie, but I think the whole town was there. Nick drove

in his pickup and we brought lawn chairs. Met a bunch of Charlie's friends from school—they can't believe I really live in New York. They keep asking me if I ever saw anyone get murdered. Or if I know anybody famous.

Nicholas

PS Do you ever wish you could go back in time, to when you were a kid? Uncle Nick said he wouldn't do it even if he could. He said that someday I would understand why.

* * *

Later in the afternoon, Nicholas was earning some extra money from his uncle by mowing the lawn. As he pushed the mower back and forth across the front yard, he thought about what his dad had told him before he got into the taxi for the airport and the long flight to Africa.

"Nick—and Lillie—and the summers I spent in Deming helped make me the person I am today. New York is amazing, and I love it, make no mistake, but I don't want you to grow up thinking that it's the only place, the only way to live. You need to get a taste of another way of life, and I can't think of a better place to start. Give it a chance. It'll be good for you to get your hands a little dirty."

Nicholas looked at his hands—callused, grease-stained, and tan—and smiled. It *did* feel good. And even though he wasn't crazy about lawn mowing, the money he *earned* seemed very different from the spending money his parents had given him for the summer. A moment later, he stopped in his tracks, startled to hear the twins screaming his name over the sound of the noisy engine. He hit the kill switch and wiped the sweat from his forehead with the bottom of his T-shirt.

"Did you bring me something to drink?" he asked.

Hetty shook her head vehemently. "No. Something *much* better."

"Pictures," said Hayley. "Of Daddy. And Charlie's mom, we think. At least it looks like her."

Nicholas took a plain white envelope with no writing on the outside from Hayley. Inside were five pictures, all of their father and Franny, taken from far enough away that it seemed likely to Nicholas that they didn't know someone was taking their picture.

"Where did you find these?" he asked.

Hetty looked worriedly at Hayley, who backed up a step from her older brother. "I know you said not to go in your room—"

"Hetty!" Nicholas shook his fist at her. "I can't believe you found them in there. I looked everyplace."

"Not behind the pictures," Hayley said. "They were inside the paper that's stuck on the back of one of Aunt Lillie's paintings. Not the Seaweed Strangler one. The other one, with the house in it."

"We heard something when we shook it," said Hetty.

"Why were you *shaking* paintings?"

Hayley rolled her eyes at him. "You said to look *everywhere*."

"Well, anyway, I don't know what good they are," said Nicholas. "You can barely see their faces, let alone anything else that might be helpful. You can't even tell where they were taken."

"Then why did Daddy hide them like that?" Hayley asked.

That's a really good question. Maybe there is something to all those detective stories she's reading.

Nicholas shrugged, not giving away how impressed he was with Hayley's thought process. "Maybe he, uh . . . Actually, I have no idea. But hold on to these—I might need them later. Now be good little sisters and bring me something to drink."

He pulled the starter cord, and the engine roared to life, almost, but not quite, drowning out the twins' laughter as they ran away—with absolutely no intention of returning with a cold drink for their brother.

* * *

Franny expertly speared another green bean with her fork and looked across the table at her daughter. "Explain it to me again. *Why* do you want me to take this little stroll down memory lane? Because, I have to tell you, I usually reserve those trips for *good* memories."

"I know, but this could be important," Charlie replied.

"You're always talking to me about standing up and doing something when I see injustice, and this is one of those times."

"Just to be clear, O little one, I was referring to *real* injustices in the world. Racism. Discrimination of any kind. Poverty. Not two teenagers who had a bad breakup."

"It wasn't a bad breakup, Mom. I'm not saying you would have married Nicholas's dad, but at least you would have had a *chance*."

"And you think by doing this I'm going to get that chance? Sweetie, it just doesn't work like that in real life. I love that you think it does—I don't want you to stop being so . . . hopeful, I suppose, but in this case, I'm afraid you're going to be disappointed."

Charlie wasn't ready to give up yet, though. Without a word, she pulled out the pictures of her mom and Will that the twins had found earlier in the day and set them on the table.

"What's this?" Franny picked up the first of the pictures, a puzzled look on her face. "Where on earth did you get these?"

"Over at Nick's."

"But these were taken at . . . Nobody knew about that place. Who took these?"

"So you've never seen these before?"

"No, absolutely no."

Charlie looked closely at one of the photos. "Where did you say this is? It looks nice."

Franny smiled secretively. "I *didn't* say."

"Ohhhh, I get it. This is the secret place you wrote about in the letter. You're really not going to tell me?"

Franny shook her head. "Maybe someday. But my guess is, when you're in need of a special place, you'll find it."

"What's *that* supposed to mean? Mom, you're being very mysterious all of a sudden."

"A mother's prerogative," said Franny with a sly smile.

"So you won't do it? Go over to the marina with us to re-create the scene on the day of the wreck?"

"Oh, I'll do that. I just wanted you to explain it better. And now I want you to tell me more about Nicholas."

Charlie smiled at the mention of his name. "What about him?"

"Well, you two are spending a lot of time together this summer."

"Are you asking if history is repeating itself, Mom? If Nicholas and I are, you know . . ."

"Something like that, yeah."

It was Charlie's turn to be secretive. "I guess we'll just have to wait and see."

* * *

The Saturday morning sky seemed to *dare* boaters to venture out onto the lake; slate-gray clouds raced from the northeast, bringing fierce breezes and waves with them.

"Blowin' the oysters off the rocks out there," said Nick, sipping his second cup of coffee.

"There's no oysters in Forsaken Lake, Uncle Nick," Hayley said. "They're only in the ocean."

"Just an expression, kiddo. You three ready to go? Franny just pulled in the drive."

They all piled into Franny's car and drove the three miles to the marina, where the plan was for Franny to walk them through the events of that fateful day so many years before. Nicholas brought a notebook with him so he could make notes about who was where, and when they were there.

"It's kind of ironic, actually," Franny said as she put the car in park and turned off the engine. "It looks *exactly* like it did that day. Waves were crashing into the break-wall and spraying everything just like they are now."

They walked right to the edge of the breakwall and stopped. A few of the gusts were so strong that Nicholas had to hold on to Hayley and Hetty to keep them from blowing away.

"I guess it's a good thing the wind is blowing at us," he said. "You two would get blown out to sea."

"Just like the oysters, right, Uncle Nick?" said Hayley.

Nick grinned. "Blowin' the twins off the dock. That's got a nice ring to it."

"Okay, let's get this show on the road," Franny announced. "Before the rain hits. I have my limits."

151

"We'll start with you," said Charlie. "Where were you? And the camera?"

Franny backed up a few steps, getting her bearings by looking to her right and then her left. "I was standing right about here." She made an X in the gravel with the toe of her shoe. "The camera was on a tripod right in front of me."

"Where was the boat when the scene started?" Nicholas asked, pencil and notebook at the ready.

Franny pointed to her left, to the protected side of the marina seawall. In contrast to the rough, white-capped lake, the water behind the wall was barely rippled. "It was anchored right over there. That way, all I had to do was swivel the camera on the tripod to follow the boat. Nice and smooth. Will *hated* it when the camera jerked around. He was kind of a perfectionist."

"So Dad was already on the boat," Nicholas noted.

"What about *my* dad?" Charlie asked. "Where was he?"

"In the water, hanging off the back of the boat, out of sight," Franny said. "He was supposed to climb up the ladder as soon as Will went up to raise the anchor."

Nicholas made a quick sketch in his notebook. "Okay, what about other kids, even if they weren't in the scene? Some of them must have been with you guys, right?"

Biting her lower lip, Franny closed her eyes and went back in time. She stayed that way for almost a minute, gesturing occasionally with her hands. Finally, she opened her eyes to find everyone staring at her.

"That was scary," said Hetty. "I thought you were, you know, being zombiefied or something."

"Just concentrating," Franny said. "There were two kids—Kevin Willard and Petey Truman. There used to be another dock over *there*, and they were sitting on a pontoon boat—I think it may have belonged to Petey's dad. They had a good view of everything without being in the way. Kevin was Jimmy's best friend growing up. He was best man at our wedding. Lives outside of town, on Melvin Road. I think he just got divorced for the third time. Maybe the fourth."

"What about the other kid? Petey?" Charlie asked.

"He was kind of an odd kid. Had every allergy known to man, I think. Wouldn't go in the lake, and he couldn't touch seaweed, so he could only take a small part in the movie. He was the gun salesman—remember? I ran into him a few weeks ago."

"Wait a minute—his last name is Truman? Is he Kacey Truman's dad? She was in my class last year. She's nice. Super quiet. Misses a ton of school. I mean, she's absent twice a week at least. I remember one time she was just sitting next to somebody who was eating a peanut butter sandwich and her whole face broke out in this rash and she had a hard time breathing."

"Yep, that's him," said Franny. "Petey Truman. Sounds like his daughter inherited his allergies."

"And those were the only two there?" Nicholas asked, scribbling some notes.

"Kids, yes. There may have been some other people on the docks watching what we were doing, but I don't remember anyone in particular. I'm afraid I'm not being very helpful."

"Tell us what happened next," Charlie said. "After you started filming."

Franny narrated as she pretended to operate the camera. Her story didn't differ from the account she'd given them earlier, until she got to the part where she was regaining consciousness after getting hit on the head by the mast.

"When I got knocked down, I ended up in this position," she said, lying on the ground. "This was grass then, not gravel. I remember hearing voices talking about somebody being hurt, and I wanted so much to open my eyes to see who they were talking about, but I just couldn't do it. Not yet, anyway. I remember hearing Will's voice. And then an adult—that would have been Mr. Parker, who owned the marina. He must have seen the mast fall. I heard tires—that crunching sound they make on gravel—getting closer and closer, and then somebody I didn't know was talking. He sounded angry, and he asked a lot of questions—how it happened, that kind of thing. Frankly, he seemed more concerned with the boat than me—he left me lying on the ground without a blanket, or something under my head. Someone told me later it was the sheriff."

"Humph. I'm not surprised *he* was worried about the boat," Nick said. "The sheriff back then would have been Ned Randleman. Moron. And a good friend of Jimmy's cousin Teddy, who *owned* the boat."

Franny continued: "A little while later, I opened my eyes, and there was Will, looking really relieved, alongside Mr. Parker. And some other people I didn't know—they must have been people who had boats in the marina. I remember they all laughed because I kept apologizing to Will for dropping the camera."

Nicholas's eyes brightened. "Did he—did *anyone*—say anything about the camera to you?"

Franny shook her head. "Just that I shouldn't be worried about it. And then the ambulance came and they took me to the hospital."

Suddenly, Franny's eyes filled with tears and she turned away.

Charlie moved to her instantly, hugging her. "Mom, I'm sorry," said Charlie. "This was a stupid idea. It's my fault. Let's go home."

Franny quickly pulled herself together, wiping the tears away with her fingertips. "No, no, I'm fine, really. I just didn't expect to see it all so . . . *clearly*. Especially those few seconds right before they closed the door at the back of the ambulance. Will held on to my hand until the last possible moment, squeezing it, telling me I was going to be okay. But it was the look in his eyes. . . . Honestly, I don't think anyone has *ever* looked at me like that since then. And how I felt—it was . . . well, indescribable. And that was the last time I ever saw him."

For the next few seconds, the waves crashing against the seawall and the screeching of seagulls—the only sounds she could hear—seemed very distant, as if she were listening to them through a long tunnel. Finally, she shook herself with a little laugh, trying to lighten the mood.

"Well, that was all a long time ago. And I don't know about anybody else, but I'm getting hungry. Sorry I wasn't more help." She walked slowly toward the car.

Charlie was frozen in place by her mom's words. Only her hair moved as she stared at the trees bending and swaying on the far shore, two miles away.

Nicholas stood by her side, his fingers twitching as he fought off an almost irresistible impulse to reach for her hand.

CHAPTER TEN

Franny treated everyone to an early lunch at Cole's Diner, on the square in Deming, where the twins entertained everyone with a performance of their new favorite song while they all waited for their hamburgers and fries.

"Wow—you girls really *are* good," said Franny after they took their bows. "When you're both big Broadway stars, I'm going to tell all my friends that I knew you when."

Hayley and Hetty made faces at their brother. "See, Nicholas," said Hetty. "You don't know what you're talking about. Franny thinks we're going to be stars."

"Yeah, you should definitely put us in your movie," Hayley said.

Franny raised an eyebrow. "Movie?"

"I'm still just *thinking* about it," Nicholas said. "Nothing is for sure, you guys."

"He's thinking about finishing Daddy's movie," said Hetty. "He's writing a script. We saw it when . . . um . . ."

"When you were *snooping* around my room," said Nicholas.

"It's going to have a different ending, of course," Charlie was quick to add. "We have some ideas about that. We want to make the creature more . . . human. When I watched the movie, I felt sorry for him. He's not a monster, actually—he's just misunderstood."

"I see," said Franny, laughing. "I had no idea. To me, it was just Jimmy Brennan running around in torn jeans and some dime-store fangs, carrying a big bunch of seaweed. Which he used to *strangle* people. I'm trying to imagine what's so sympathetic about him."

"Well, for one thing, all these people are trying to kill him—like, for sport!" said Charlie. "We're going to show his childhood. You know, what happened that made him become the Seaweed Strangler."

"The way we see it is, he didn't become the Strangler *until* people started shooting at him," Nicholas explained. "He's not just some random serial killer. He was just a guy—okay, a creature—trying to mind his own business, to live his own life."

"He might even have a wife," Charlie said. "And a bunch of little Seaweed Stranglers."

"Is he going to die in the end?" Hetty asked. "Please don't let him!"

"I—we haven't decided that yet," said Nicholas. "Like I said, we were just thinking about it."

"Well, it sounds like you've both put a *lot* of thought into this," Franny said.

Charlie looked across the table at Nicholas and smiled.

"They're *always* out in the barn working on the boat together," Hetty said. "That's when they talk."

Charlie choked on her soda and looked to Nick for help. He wasn't quite sure why, but he knew that Charlie was hoping to keep the Heron a secret from her mom.

Franny tilted her head questioningly at Charlie. "You're building a boat, too? My, you have been a busy girl."

"Looks like the cat's out of the bag," said Nick after a secretive wink at Charlie. "Sorry, kids. You see, Franny, in addition to finding that old movie, these two also dragged out that old cedar-strip canoe that's been up in the barn for ages. Remember, you and Will used to talk about fixing it up."

Franny smiled at the memory. "Oh, right. I do remember. It was hanging from the ceiling next to the door to the milk house, right?"

"Yep, that's the one. I've been helping them get it ready to go in the water. I'm supplying the materials, and they're providing all the labor. It's shaping up real nice. You'll be canoeing before long."

"Wait a minute," said a very bewildered Hetty. "What canoe? I thought that was—"

Nicholas put his arm around Hetty's shoulders. "We've been teasing you, Het. It's not really a submarine."

Hetty looked even more puzzled until Hayley, who understood what was happening, whispered something in her ear.

"Ohhh," said Hetty. "*That* canoe."

"Boy, you all are just full of secrets, aren't you?" Franny said. "I can't believe that old thing was still in one piece. I seem to remember that it was in pretty rough shape."

"It's been up in the barn for thirty or forty years. Nothing really wrong with it—at least nothing that a little paint and caulking can't fix. I should have checked with you first, to make sure it was okay with you to have her over working on it, but they wanted to surprise you. They've been working like crazy on it."

She waved off his concerns. "I think it's great. In fact, I can't wait to see it. And your movie, you little sneaks. But I think you'd better work fast. It'll be August in a few days. Summer'll be over before you know it."

As the horror of that statement began to sink in with everyone at the table, the front door of the diner jangled and a well-dressed woman entered. Nicholas almost fell off his chair when she took off her sunglasses.

"*Mom?* What are you doing here?"

"Mommy!" screamed the twins, who then raced to hug her, almost knocking her down in the process.

"I've been on the road since five o'clock this morning, so I stopped in here for a cup of coffee and to ask for directions," she said when Hayley and Hetty finally let her up for air. "As soon as I saw this place, I remembered that Nick used to come here for— Hey, Nick, it's nice to see you. It's been a long time."

Nick stood and kissed her on the cheek. "Good to see you, too, kid. These are some friends—Franny Brennan, and her daughter, Charlie."

"Hi—I'm Jo Mettleson," she said, waving at them. "You know, from the looks on all your faces, I get the feeling that *somebody* forgot to tell you that I was driving out this weekend."

"Oops," said Hayley.

Nicholas shook his head. "Wait—you knew she was coming?"

"Welllll, ummmm . . . yes," said Hetty.

"I told them the other night. They were *supposed* to tell Nick so it wouldn't be a big surprise when I showed up on your doorstep. Sorry, Nick—I should have talked to you about it."

"Not a problem," said Nick. "Plenty of room at the inn."

* * *

161

After three hours of softball at Ryan Crenshaw's house, followed by a long swim in the lake, Charlie and Nicholas were relieved to have a few minutes to relax on Nick's porch swing.

"Your mom seems nice," said Charlie. "She's not how I pictured her at all."

"What were you expecting?"

"I don't know—kind of uptight. Like really intense."

Nicholas laughed. "Oh, she's plenty intense. Trust me."

"*Who's* so intense, Nicholas?" asked his mother, joining them on the porch.

"That would be you, Mom," he said. "It's okay—I'm used to it."

"So, do you live close by, Charlie?" asked Jo. "How did you find Nicholas and the girls?"

"Actually, Nicholas found me," said Charlie. "I live about a half mile down Lake Road, but we met in Deming. He stopped to watch my baseball team practice. And then, the next day, I was bringing Nick some lasagna that my mom made, and there he was again."

"Well, I'm glad Nicholas has someone his own age to . . . do things with. Nick tells me that you have become quite the sailors, that he lets you take his boat out without him on board. I'm . . . not sure how I feel about that, but I'm going to trust Nick. And you. All I ask is that you be *careful*. Promise?"

"Promise," said Nicholas.

"And really keep an eye on the twins, although they

162

seem to be doing fine now. After Hetty's little meltdown on the phone, I was a little worried. Now I get the feeling that if I tried to take them back to New York with me, they'd mutiny. I imagine that has something to do with you, Charlie. I'm sure they like having a 'big sister.'"

"They're great," said Charlie. "It's been fun for me, too. And I guess Nicholas isn't too bad, either."

* * *

Kevin Willard's head was buried far beneath the hood of a maroon 1967 Ford Galaxie 500 when Charlie and Nicholas turned their bikes into his yard the next day. He looked up when he heard their tires hit the gravel and adjusted the trucker-style cap (GIT 'ER DONE! it implored) that covered his greasy shoulder-length hair. He set a wrench on the car's fender and nodded approvingly at Nicholas's classic ride.

"Cool bike, kid."

"Thanks."

"Y'wanna sell it?"

"I, uh, no . . . It's not really mine. I'm just borrowing it."

Kevin took his first good look at Nicholas. "Do I know you? Y'look familiar."

"You knew my dad. A long time ago."

Kevin squinted at him, trying to make the connection.

"Will Mettleson," Charlie said.

"Yep, I see it now," Kevin said. "Y'do look a lot like

yer old man, now that I think about it. What's he doin' these days?"

"He's a doctor," said Nicholas. "Right now he's in Africa with Doctors Without Borders—you know, helping people."

"Huh. Y'don't say. Guess he done all right for himself." He turned his gaze to Charlie. "You one o' Will's kids, too?"

Charlie grinned. "No, but you know my mom and dad. You were in their wedding."

"No way. You're Jimmy and Franny's kid? Look at ya, all grown up. Last time I seen you, you wuz still a baby. How're yer folks? I heard they split up a while back. Hear from yer dad much?"

"Not too much, no. He's still trying to get rich raising ostriches."

Kevin chuckled. "That sounds like Jimmy. He's a good egg, though, yer dad. We had some good times together."

"Um, yeah, that's why we came out here," Charlie said. "We were kind of wondering about something from back when you were kids. Remember when you guys were making that movie?"

"*The Seaweed* . . . somethin' or other?"

"*Strangler*," Nicholas said. "*The Seaweed Strangler.*"

"We're really just interested in one day—the last day," Charlie said. "When the boat crashed and my mom got hit in the head with the mast."

Kevin winced, remembering the moment. "Not likely

to forget that day as long as I live. Felt like I was watchin' it in slow motion. Yer mom dropped like a stone."

"But *after*, when everybody was around her, and the sheriff and the ambulance came—do you remember what happened to the movie camera? It was on a tripod, and it went down with Mom."

Kevin shook his head and offered an apathetic shrug. "No idea. Can't even picture it in my head. Just yer mom, and that pretty little boat poundin' on the rocks. So, what's yer mom up to these days? She seein' anybody?"

"Wh-what? Mom?" Charlie tried hard not to gag at the thought of her mom dating a creep like him. "Um, yeah. She has a boyfriend," she lied.

Nicholas got him back on track. "And you never heard anything about it—the movie camera—later on, like from Petey Truman, or the sheriff, or anybody?"

Another shake and shrug. "Why're you kids lookin' for that old camera, anyway? Ain't worth nuthin' now. Probably can't even buy film for it no more."

It was Charlie's turn to shrug. "It's kind of like a piece of family history."

"Yeah? Well, good luck with that, kid." Kevin grunted and picked up his wrench. "Oh, and be sure to tell yer mom I said hi."

"Yeah, I'll get right on that," said Charlie as she and Nicholas spun their bikes around and rode away.

* * *

Petey Truman, whose house was spotless inside and out, was not much help, either.

"Come in, come in! Get out of the sun for a minute. I sure hope you kids have UV protection on. The sun is a killer, you know. Do you mind taking your shoes off outside? Dust sets off my allergies something fierce. Now, let's see. You were asking about Will's movie camera." He paused, his brow furrowed in thought. "Huh. I just assumed the sheriff confiscated it for evidence. But that's just a guess. I have to be honest, I don't remember paying any attention to the camera once that mast fell. Have you asked the sheriff? He's not sheriff anymore, of course, but he lives just down the road. It's worth a shot—he might remember what happened to it. And what about Teddy Bradford? There's another one you could ask."

Charlie and Nicholas turned to look at one another; Franny had mentioned that it was Teddy's boat that was wrecked, but his name didn't come up when she was standing in the marina reliving the experience of the big event.

"You mean my dad's cousin Teddy—the guy who owned the boat? He was there that day?" Charlie asked.

"Sure—at least at the end. I'm not sure about him being there earlier, but I definitely remember seeing him after the ambulance pulled away. Wasn't saying much. A bit odd, now that I think of it. He'd just watched his boat get wrecked, the mast toppling over and almost killing a kid, but instead of yelling and screaming, or trying to do something about the boat, he was just kind of wandering around in a daze."

"Hmmm," said Nicholas and Charlie, agreeing that it did seem like strange behavior.

"But I'd start with the sheriff if I were you," said Petey, and he gave them Ned Randleman's address. They thanked him for his help and rode down the bumpy gravel road, stopping in front of a run-down mobile home where a life-sized plastic Santa stood guard in the yard.

"I guess this is it," said Charlie. "Kinda creepy. I'm glad I'm not alone."

They parked their bikes and knocked firmly on the door.

"Who is it?" a man's voice shouted from somewhere behind the screen door.

Nicholas put his face close to the screen and tried to peer inside. "Nicholas Mettleson and Charlie Brennan."

"Who?"

"We just want to ask you a question," Charlie said. Under her breath, she added, "So get off your butt and answer the door."

"Are you sellin' something?" the voice demanded.

Charlie sighed loudly. "No. Sir. We want to talk to you about something that happened a long time ago, back when you were sheriff."

Suddenly, they were staring up at a giant in a stained tank top and boxer shorts that were decorated with big red hearts—exactly like the ones cartoon characters wear. No one had bothered to tell them that Ned Randleman was six feet ten inches tall.

"What *about* when I was sheriff?" he growled through the screen.

Charlie and Nicholas each said a little prayer that he wouldn't invite them in or join them outside. It was just a screen door, but they felt better with *something* between them and Underwear Guy.

They explained the purpose of their visit while he listened, occasionally slurping noisily from a can of beer and scratching his belly where it hung out below a shirt that was clearly meant for someone several inches shorter and many, many pounds lighter.

"Don't know what you're talking about. Nobody ever told me about a camera. Let me get this straight. You say your dad was making a *movie*? That's a good one. Haw-haw-haw! And he was *how* old? Haw-haw-haw!" He was laughing at Nicholas for believing such a dubious story. "All's I can tell you, kid, is that your old man shoulda been sent up to juvie hall for what he done. I think he wrecked that boat 'cause he thought it would be fun."

"Look, just forget it," said Nicholas, turning to walk back to his bike. But then something growing inside him made him stop in his tracks and spin around. "I don't care if you believe it or not, but he was making a movie, and if you knew *anything* about being a cop, you would have asked a few questions and found out there was a camera with potential *evidence* on the film. Evidence that would have *proved* that my dad didn't do it on purpose."

"Hey, you can't come around here bad-mouthin' me, you little—"

Nicholas wasn't done, though. "And if you had taken five minutes to look at the boat, you would have found some other very interesting evidence. Somebody *cut* the steering cable and sawed halfway through the backstay. But I guess you were too busy worrying about whose boat you were going to go drinking on, now that your buddy's boat was trashed. Come on, Charlie, let's get out of here."

"Gladly."

Nicholas threw his leg over his bike and turned to face the trailer. "Oh, and one more thing, mister. Put some *pants* on. And buy a shirt that fits. *Nobody* wants to see that."

* * *

When they got back to Nick's house, they found him standing on the dock with the twins and Jo, about to row out to *Goblin* for an afternoon sail. The morning's strong winds and rain were long gone, replaced by deep blue skies and a pleasant breeze, and the twins admonished their older brother to hurry so they could take advantage of the perfect conditions.

Nick smiled while Jo watched in wonder as Nicholas and Charlie took charge after climbing aboard *Goblin*. Without a moment's hesitation, they removed the cover from the mainsail, hanked on the jib and staysail, and rigged the sheets. Then they raised the main, tying off the halyard and coiling it neatly. Nicholas then casually walked to the bow and reached down and unclipped from the mooring after Nick gave him the "okay" sign. Charlie trimmed in the mainsail while Nick, at the tiller, slowly bore away onto a beam reach. Not a single word had been spoken.

Hayley and Hetty noticed, too.

"Why is everyone so quiet?" whispered Hetty.

"Shhh," said Hayley. "Just listen. It's like a ghost ship."

And so they went, up and down the lake, silent except for the sound of the bow creaming through the water and the occasional creak of the wooden mast, until Hetty could take it no longer.

"I'm sorry, but I just *have* to talk."

Everyone burst out laughing at her admission.

"Why don't you come back here and take the tiller awhile, Het?" Nick asked. "It's a good day for you and your sister to get some time at the helm."

"R-really?" Hetty said, looking nervously at the sails and water. "I've never steered when there was wind—when we were actually *moving*."

"No time like the present," said Nick. "Come on. You too, Hayley. I'll be right here next to you. Show your mom what you've learned."

As the twins joined him and their mother in the aft part of the cockpit, Nicholas and Charlie moved up to the foredeck, where they sat side by side, dangling their feet over the edge.

"That was pretty cool, what you did today," said Charlie. "Sticking up for your dad like that. God, what a *creep* that guy was. I can't believe they ever let him be sheriff."

"Can I tell you something? Just between us? I was shaking like mad after I said all that stuff. I thought he was going to *shoot* me or something. I've never done anything like that before. He just ticked me off—it's like he was making fun of my dad, *and* of me, all at the same time."

"That reminds me—I need to call my dad tonight. Maybe he'll remember something different. Or explain why his cousin was acting the way he was."

"So . . . um, you've never really talked about your dad. He raises ostriches?"

"Yep, that's my dad. The Ostrich King of Trumbull County, Ohio. He got remarried last year to this woman named Linda. She's all right, I guess—she has two kids. My dad is . . . well, the way Mom puts it, he's kind of a dreamer. To tell the truth, though, I think she's being . . . I mean, he's my dad, and I love him and all, but calling him a dreamer is sugarcoating the truth. He's always looking for some crazy way to get rich without really having to work."

"And you can do that raising *ostriches*?"

Charlie laughed. "I know, right? But he swears that

ostrich meat is the next big thing. I've had it—it's not bad, actually. But Mom never says anything negative about him around me, even when he forgets to show up on the weekends I'm supposed to stay with him, or just completely misses my birthday."

"Youch. Your birthday?"

"That's only happened a couple of times."

"You're only twelve! Two birthdays is a lot. You know, I don't understand grown-ups at all. There's all these movies and shows and books about people meeting and falling in love, but it's all so phony because, like, five years later, they're all divorced. They don't show you that part."

"Not everyone gets divorced."

"All my friends' parents are."

"All?"

Nicholas hedged a little. "Okay, not *all*. But most."

"Ah, so there's still hope for true love, you see. It may be on life support, but it's not dead yet."

* * *

July 22
Dear Dad,
    <u>Weird</u> week. Mom's here for a few days, worried that I'll drown or get run over on the bike. But another first! I cooked the whole dinner last night—hamburgers, baked potatoes, and corn.

And watermelon for dessert. (I made the twins clean up—LOL.)

Uncle Nick gave me this old <u>National Geographic</u> about a kid who sailed around the world when he was only sixteen. Get ready—that's me in four years!

Nicholas

* * *

It had been a long, busy day, and after a late dinner of hot dogs and baked beans, the Mettleson kids said their good-nights and good-byes to their mom, who planned to be on the road for New York by five o'clock in the morning. As the twins tramped upstairs to their rooms with their books in hand, Jo marveled at Hetty, the twin who, just a few short weeks earlier, had claimed not to like reading.

"This is my *seventh* book so far," said Hetty. "The librarian has a list of kids who read the most books over the summer, and I'm in eleventh place."

"I'm in second," bragged Hayley. She held up *Misty of Chincoteague*. "This is my *thirteenth* book. It's my last one, Uncle Nick. Can we go to the library tomorrow?"

Jo laughed. "Who *are* you kids? And what have you done with my Hayley and Hetty?"

Meanwhile, Nicholas, who had already finished the books he'd borrowed from the library, scrounged around the bookcase in the living room, finding Lillie's collection of Agatha Christie mysteries. He chose *Murder on the Orient Express*. He had heard of the book and its eminent detective, Hercule Poirot, and smiled at the memory of the day's detective work. He and Charlie hadn't really discovered answers—just more questions, really—but he couldn't remember a time in his life when he felt more energized.

A half mile down the road, it had been essentially the same story with Franny and Charlie. Charlie fell asleep reading a romantic book about young time travelers that Janet, the librarian, had insisted she would just love, while Franny struggled to concentrate on the thriller a friend at work had lent her. Her mind kept taking her back to the marina with Will and all of her old friends, and she couldn't help thinking about how her life—*all* their lives—had turned out. Would everything have turned out differently, she wondered, if Will had chosen a simpler, less spectacular ending to his movie? Or if she had been standing six inches away, in either direction, and the mast had missed her completely? She knew it was a pointless exercise, but she couldn't resist imagining a version of her life that might have been—*if* Will had found her letter, *if* he had written back, *if* he had returned to Nick's the following summer. Instead, she had started hanging out with Jimmy as a freshman in high school, a few months after Will's departure, brokenhearted but blessed with the resilience of youth.

She wandered into Charlie's room, where she found her daughter sleeping soundly—still dressed, her book resting on her chest. She covered her with a quilt and turned off the light, but didn't move toward her own room. Instead, she stood silently at the threshold for a long time. The moon shone through the upper window onto Charlie's peaceful face, and the curtains billowed gently as a cool north breeze filled the room. The scene gave Franny goose bumps, and in the perfect beauty of that moment, any misgivings, or questions, or doubts about her own life were put to rest.

She stayed for a few minutes longer, wrapping her cotton cardigan tightly around her and soaking up the loveliness of the picture before her. As she was about to turn and leave, she heard a crinkling sound coming from her sweater pocket. She reached in and felt something— the pictures that the twins had found of her and Will in their secret spot. When she saw them this time, however, Franny pounded her palm against her forehead. "I *know* who must have taken these pictures. Mikey."

CHAPTER ELEVEN

Although she must have known it when they were kids, Franny couldn't remember his last name. He had always been just Mikey to her. A long time ago, her mother had explained that he was "slow," which was why he went to a different school, with other kids like him. That summer, he had latched onto Will for the simple reason that Will was always nice to him. The other kids would get tired of Mikey hanging around and either ditch him or flat out tell him to get lost, but Will never did. And so, on the rare days when Mikey's mom would let him out of the house, Will had himself a shadow. He let Mikey follow wherever he went—with one exception: the secret place. When he and Franny were on their way there, they made sure Mikey wasn't around. Or so they thought.

Franny smiled. "So Mikey spied on us."

While she stood there looking at the pictures by moonlight, she suddenly remembered something else about Mikey: he had been at the marina on the day of the accident. She was certain of it.

"He was there!"

"Mom?" A groggy Charlie lifted her head. "What are you doing?"

"Oh, honey, I'm sorry. I didn't mean to wake you. Go back to sleep."

"Who were you talking to?"

"Nobody. Myself. I couldn't sleep, and I was thinking about . . . and then I came in here to turn your light off, and you were just so beautiful that I couldn't stop looking at you."

"Mo-ommm. What is the matter with you?"

"There's been a break in the case, as they say. I *know* who took the camera," Franny said.

Charlie sat up suddenly in her bed. "You do?"

Franny nodded.

Charlie waited a few seconds, staring at her mother, until she couldn't take it anymore. "Well? Are you going to tell me?"

"Wouldn't you rather wait till morning? Then I can tell you and Nicholas together. He's been working so hard on this; he ought to hear it from me."

"Okay, fine. What time is it?"

"Little after eleven. Why?"

Charlie jumped out of bed and pulled on her sneakers. "Well, let's go tell him."

"Now?"

"Why not? He'll be awake. If the light's off in his room, we'll come home."

Franny laughed. "I can't believe I'm saying yes to this plan, but why not? You two have got me thinking about and doing all kinds of crazy things. Suddenly, I'm fourteen again."

Charlie was right; Nicholas was still awake. The rest of the house was dark, but the tower room seemed to be glowing, with warm golden light spilling out of the windows and onto the roof. Nicholas stood facing the lake, his hands resting on the windowsill.

"Oww!" Something hit him squarely on the head and bounced across the room. He spotted a fluorescent green tennis ball on the bed. "What the . . ." He didn't finish the question because he already knew the answer.

There's only one person in the world who could throw a ball through an open window three floors up and hit me in the head.

"Charlie?" he said, looking out the window toward the backyard while keeping a hand in front of his face in case there were more tennis balls on the way. "You out there?"

She waved up at him. "Did I hit you?"

"Right in the head," Nicholas answered. "You scared the—" He paused when he realized Franny was standing next to Charlie. "The *heck* out of me. What's going on?"

"Come down and we'll tell you," Charlie said.

* * *

Down on the dock, they sat and drank hot cocoa from a thermos while Franny told them all about Mikey.

"He was kind of obsessed with cameras and taking pictures; he must have cost his family a fortune in developing expenses. This was before the days of digital cameras, remember. I think that he took those pictures of me and Will, and then gave them to Will, who probably didn't want anyone else to see them."

"Why not?" Nicholas asked.

"Because he was afraid people would figure out where our hiding place was. That's my best guess, anyway."

"Okay, but what makes you so sure he has the movie camera?" Charlie asked.

"Because the second I remembered his name, his face flashed in front of me—and it was at the marina. It was after I came to, and I was lying on the ground looking up at Will. And Mikey was right behind him—like he always was—and he was holding the camera. It was all so clear in my mind that I'm sure it's real, not something I'm imagining. He was there."

Down on the dock, they sat and drank hot cocoa from a thermos while Franny told them all about Mikey.

Charlie frowned. "What makes you think he still has the camera?"

"I never said that. I think he *took* it. Whether he still has it—that's for you two to find out. I need to talk to your father tomorrow anyway, Charlie. He'll remember Mikey's last name and where he lived." She gazed out at the lake and took a long, deep breath of the cool air. "This was fun. We should do this more often. The lake is so beautiful at night."

"Mom, what has gotten into you?" Charlie asked. "I wake up to find you in my room, talking to yourself, and then when I make a crazy suggestion to come over here to tell Nicholas about this Mikey guy, you go along with it, and now you're all . . . like, weird about the lake. Have you flipped or something?"

Franny turned to her and smiled. "Maybe."

* * *

Mikey Bishop still lived with his mother in a cottage at the northernmost corner of the lake, a good ten- or twelve-mile bike ride for Charlie and Nicholas. The Bishops' cottage was one of five, all constructed of cement blocks and clustered around an overgrown flagstone patio and a crumbling brick barbecue. Mrs. Bishop, who owned the cottages, barely made a living renting them to fishermen by the week during the summer and to the occasional group of hunters the rest of the year. If word spread that the ice fishing was good, she might have a few busy weekends in January and February, but most years it was pretty quiet until the ice broke up and the walleye started biting.

Mrs. Bishop answered the door and smiled warmly. They introduced themselves and she pushed open the screen door to invite them in.

"Mommy!" cried a man's voice from behind her. "Who is it?"

"Why don't you come out and see for yourself," she answered, winking at Charlie. "That's my son, Mikey. Now, what can I do you for? How about a drink of water? You look like you could use it."

Mrs. Bishop poured ice water from a pitcher into two glass canning jars and handed them to her visitors.

"Thanks," they said together.

Charlie gulped down her water and held her glass out for a refill. "Actually, it's Mikey we'd like to talk to."

"Mikey? Why, in heaven's name? Do you *know* him?"

"No, but a long time ago, when they were all kids, he used to hang out with my dad and her mom," said Nicholas. "We were hoping we could ask him about something that happened back then."

Mikey, wearing a crisp yellow button-down shirt tucked into perfectly pressed blue jeans, clomped into the room in pristine sneakers and stood behind his mother. He

smiled shyly and said, "*Hello!* My name is Mikey Bishop."
He moved closer to Charlie—a little too close, actually—
and asked, "What's your name?"

She leaned back a few inches and held out her hand.
"Hi, Mikey. My name is Charlie."

"Hi, Charlie," he said, shaking her hand vigorously,
and not letting go. "My name is Mikey."

"Yes, I know," Charlie said.

Nicholas reached over to shake Mikey's hand, and
when Mikey looked at him, something in his memory
seemed to click.

"I'm Nicholas. Nicholas *Mettleson*. You used to know my
dad. Do you remember him? His name is Will Mettleson."

Mikey's eyes grew wide and he *ran* out of the room
without a word.

Mrs. Bishop made the sign of the cross. "Glory be."

"What's wrong?" Charlie asked.

Before Mrs. Bishop could answer, Mikey was back,
holding a small cardboard box.

"From the time he was fifteen years old—every morning, mind you—you know what the first words out of
Mikey's mouth are? He comes out here, sits down with
his Cheerios and his glass of Tang, and asks me the same
question: 'Is Will coming today?' "

Nicholas and Charlie sat there, mouths hanging open,
for several seconds before regaining the ability to speak.

Finally, Nicholas stammered, "Y-you've been

waiting . . . for my dad? All these years?" He couldn't take his eyes off the box in Mikey's hands.

Mikey nodded vigorously. "He told me to take care of his camera. He said he would come and get it."

"That's his camera—in the box?" Charlie asked. "And you've taken care of it for all these years. That is amazing!"

"Will asked me," Mikey stated, unimpressed with his own persistence. "He's my friend."

"Well, I'd say that you're about the best friend anybody ever had," said Charlie. "Can we see it?"

Mikey set the box on the table. Nicholas stood up and lifted out the camera, handling it as if it were a relic from King Tut's tomb, turning it over and over in his hands. Charlie leaned in close to him, unable to wipe the smile from her face.

"This is unbelievable," she said. "Thank you, Mom."

"The film is still in it," Nicholas whispered.

Mikey went to the door and looked out into the yard. "Is Will coming, too? He told me not to give the camera to anybody but him."

Nicholas's eyes met Charlie's. What if, after all they'd been through, Mikey refused to give them the camera? They *had* to have it, no two ways about it, but he didn't want to lie to the poor guy, either.

"Um . . . no, my dad's not coming today," Nicholas said, returning the camera to the box. "He's very far away—in Africa—helping people. He's a doctor. But I was kind of hoping I could surprise him with this when he gets back."

Mikey was unmoved. "Will said, 'Mikey, take care of my camera. Don't let anybody have it.' A man with a beard came here looking for it, but I told him that it was Will's and I can only give it to him."

"A man with a beard? When?" Charlie asked.

"Right after Mikey brought the camera home," said Mrs. Bishop. "Just a few days later, I think."

"I wonder who that was," Nicholas said.

Mrs. Bishop shook her head. "Never seen him before or since. Now, Mikey, this is very different. You can trust these two young people. This is your friend Will's *son*. And Franny's daughter. Will would *want* you to give them the camera."

"But Will said—"

"Yes, I know what he said," Mrs. Bishop interrupted. "But, sometimes, you can do the right thing without doing *exactly* what you were asked to do."

"My dad *will* be here later in the summer," Nicholas said. "I'm sure he'll want to see you, and thank you for taking such good care of his camera."

"Do you promise?" asked Mikey.

"I promise," said Nicholas.

"I think you can trust him, Mikey," said Mrs. Bishop.

Mikey handed the box to a relieved Nicholas, who shook his hand again and mouthed a silent thank-you to Mrs. Bishop.

Back outside, as Nicholas mounted his bike, he said, "Wow, this is just great, Mikey. My dad is going to be very excited. And when he gets back, we'll come see you again."

"Or you could come over," Charlie said. "We could take you and your mom sailing. Do you like boats?"

Mikey smiled broadly. "Yes. Will used to take me sailing sometimes. With Franny."

"Maybe," said Charlie with a wink in Nicholas's direction, "you three can go sailing again."

They rode away from the cottage without speaking, but when they were out of hearing range, Charlie pulled her bike off to the side of the dirt road.

"What's wrong?" Nicholas asked.

Charlie tilted her head toward the bright blue sky and screamed while Nicholas watched, fascinated.

"I don't even know why I'm so happy," Charlie said. "I mean, after all this time, the film is probably no good. But just finding it is so . . ."

"I know. It's crazy. Boy, was your mom right, or what? And what about the other guy who came looking for it? Who was *that*?"

"A guy with a beard, he said. Can't be too hard to find out who it was. Of course, for a while there, I didn't think Mikey was going to give it to us, either. Thank God his mom believed who we are."

"I wasn't too worried," said Nicholas with a sly smile. "I had the situation under control." He reached into the front pocket of his shorts and held out a black Super 8 film cartridge.

"What? H-how did you . . . ? Wh-when?" Charlie stammered.

"I only had a few seconds. Mikey was looking out the door to see if my dad was out there, and Mrs. Bishop was filling the water pitcher. I just popped it open and slid the film out. Just in case."

"Very sneaky, Mr. Mettleson. I'm totally impressed."

"Well, I'm glad he gave us the camera, because I would have felt guilty about taking the film like that. But once I knew it was in there, there was no way I was leaving without it."

"So now what? You up for a ride into Deming? I say we take the film to the drugstore right now. Mr. Leffingwell has been there forever. He'll know where to send it to get it developed."

"And then we hope," said Nicholas.

* * *

Mr. Leffingwell whistled when he saw the Super 8 film cartridge. "Haven't seen one of these for a while," he said, and then disappeared into the back room for nearly ten minutes.

"Okay," he said upon his return. "Good news and bad news. The good news is that they still process this type of film. *But* I have to warn you. This film was exposed a long time ago and there's no guarantee that anything is going to show up. The woman on the phone said it all depends on the camera, how it was stored, and so on, and said not to get your hopes up. So, fair warning. No refunds if it's all blank. You okay with that?"

Charlie and Nicholas nodded.

"Now the bad news: it's going to be a couple of weeks. *Maybe* ten days, the woman told me—if you're lucky. I'll write *Please Rush* on the envelope. Sometimes that helps."

"Two weeks!" Charlie exclaimed on the way out of the store. "I'll never make it. I'm going to explode."

"Oh, it won't be that bad," said Nicholas. "We have a lot of work to do on *Imp*—that's going to take the next few days at least. And then maybe we should get started with the movie. Your mom has a video camera we can use, right?"

"Don't you need to finish the script first?"

"Yeah, but I just thought of a *great* idea—a way to use the scenes my dad shot, to combine them with what we're going to do."

"Are you going to share this idea with me?"

"I'll explain it later—after I work out some more of the details. But first we need to get the Heron done."

* * *

Dear Dad,

Found an old book at the library, by that kid who sailed around the world. It's called <u>Dove.</u> It has one of those old cards inside where you sign your name if you're checking the book out, and YOUR name was on it. Remember?

Uncle Nick has been teaching me how to throw a curve like Charlie's. If I can't hit it, at least I'll know how to throw it—ha-ha. I can make it curve, but I have ZERO control!

Maybe the infield is the right place for me.

Nicholas

PS The twins want to take <u>Goblin</u> out by themselves, but Uncle Nick says they can't do it until they can raise the mainsail by themselves. So now they're making poor Pistol play tug-of-war every day so they'll get stronger.

CHAPTER TWELVE

Three days later, with the fifth coat of varnish on *Imp*'s deck dry at last, it was time for the final step—attaching the hardware to the deck and mast. The day before, they had all piled into Betty for their weekly trip to the library, where Nick found a diagram and some pictures of fully rigged Herons. With those, Nicholas made a list of everything they needed from the marine hardware store in Ashtabula. The next morning was windy and rainy, so Nick and Pistol made the drive together while all the kids spent a few hours at Franny's, baking and eating chocolate chip cookies.

The skies cleared a little after lunchtime, so, with Nick and Pistol back, and hardware in hand, they set *Imp* on the grass in the front yard and got right to work. While Nicholas and Charlie were busy with screwdrivers and wrenches, the twins watched impatiently from the porch, waiting for their big moment—stenciling the name on the Heron's transom, the final step before the launch. With the help of the librarian, who knew them well enough to be able to tell them apart, Hayley and Hetty had created the stencil on a computer. They found the perfect font and printed out "Imp" on heavy paper, then the librarian cut out the letters with a razor blade.

"Is it time yet?" Hayley asked, her face pressed against the screen.

"This is the last piece of hardware," said Charlie, holding up a small bronze cleat. "Get ready!"

"Yay! *Finally*," Hetty said.

They ran out the door and handed the stencil to Nick, who taped it to the transom, to the right of the rudder. He took a few steps back to make sure it was perfectly straight, made a slight adjustment, and gave Hayley and Hetty the go-ahead. They practiced using the can of spray paint on a scrap of plywood, taking turns until Nick was sure they were ready for the real thing.

"Okay, girls, you're ready," he said. "Nice and easy, just like you were doing . . . Good . . . Not too thick now—you don't want it to run. Perfect." He peeled the stencil away and stood back. "Ladies and gentlemen, I give you . . . *Imp*!"

Everyone clapped and cheered, and even Pistol barked his approval.

"Isn't there usually some kind of ceremony when you launch a ship?" Charlie asked.

"Absolutely," said Nick. "Every boat needs a proper christening. Usually they have somebody like the Queen, or the First Lady, break a bottle of champagne on the bow right before they launch a boat for the first time."

Nicholas's eyes grew wide as his hand glided over *Imp*'s glassy varnished deck. "I don't think that's such a good idea," he said. "Even if it is tradition."

"Don't worry, we won't be breaking anything on little *Imp* here. I think that some ginger ale—*poured* over the bow—will suffice," Nick said. "And since the twins named her, I think they should have the honor of doing the pouring. Now let's get this thing in the water and see what she'll do. Perfect breeze for a maiden voyage."

They pushed the boat and trailer to the lake's edge, where the five of them lifted *Imp* and gently set her in the sand, with her stern just touching the water. As Nicholas and Charlie fitted the mainsail into the boom and attached the jib hanks to the forestay, Hayley and Hetty ran into the house to find the ginger ale.

"We got it!" Hayley yelled from the porch.

"Everything else ready?" Nick asked. "Rudder and tiller? All the safety equipment? Anchor? Life jackets?"

Nicholas responded "Check" to each item on Nick's list.

Hetty swung the bottle of ginger ale around and around. "Is it time?"

Nick whispered something in her ear, which she passed on to Hayley.

"Okay, *now* we're ready. Take it away, girls," said Nick.

Hetty held the ginger ale over the bow. "Ladies and gentlemen. By the power vested in me by, um . . ."

"By Sir Nick Mettleson, lord of the manor and captain of the good ship *Goblin*," said Hayley.

"Oh, right. By, um, what she said," added Hetty. "We hereby christen thee . . ."

"*IMP!*" they shouted in unison. Hetty unscrewed the top of the bottle, spraying *Imp*, themselves, and the three spectators with warm ginger ale.

"Speech! Speech!" cried Nick. "Nicholas, I think it's also customary for the builder to say a few words."

Nicholas felt himself flush. He hated talking in front of the class at school, and all of a sudden, this felt like one of those times. "Ummm. Thanks, Uncle Nick. For letting me and Charlie . . . and for showing us how to sand and paint and everything . . . and for buying all the stuff, you know, the paint and the hardware. So, anyway, thanks again. Now, can we *please* go sailing?"

"Bravo!" shouted Nick. "Absolutely! Take her away, you two. You earned the first sail."

With *Imp* floating alongside the dock, Charlie climbed

aboard and hoisted the sails. Nicholas joined her, attaching the rudder and tiller to the stern and then performing a quick inspection of all the lines and rigging.

"Ready, Captain?" asked Nick.

Nicholas tried to hide his excitement, but a smile broke through. "I think so. Give us a little push, will you?"

"Aye, aye," said Nick, kneeling on the dock and pushing *Imp* and her crew out into the lake. "Have fun!"

Nicholas and Charlie sheeted in the sails and they were off, accelerating quickly away from the dock as Hayley and Hetty waved and shouted, "Bon voyage!"

Sailing the twelve-foot, two-hundred-pound *Imp* was nothing like navigating the twenty-eight-foot, six-thousand-pound *Goblin*. Nicholas and Charlie were well prepared, and were exceptionally fast learners. In practically no time at all, they were tacking back and forth smoothly up the lake, looking like a well-seasoned team.

"Well, what do you think?" Charlie asked when they returned to the dock. "How does it feel?"

"Great. I'm still getting used to how tippy she is. One little movement and she heels over ten degrees. You can jump up and down on *Goblin* and nothing happens."

"Have you sent your dad a postcard about it yet?"

"You mean about *Imp*? No. How about you? Did you tell your mom?"

Charlie shook her head. "Nope. She still thinks we're working on that old canoe. Now I'm afraid she's going to be disappointed; she's mentioned a couple of times how much she's looking forward to going canoeing with me. But then I think about that letter she wrote, and the promise your dad made, and something makes me want to make it all come true. It's dumb trying to keep it secret, because she's going to find out sooner or later."

"Sooner, if the twins have anything to do with it," said Nicholas with a laugh. "Keeping secrets isn't exactly their strong point. Except when they're not supposed to, like when Mom showed up." He offered the tiller to Charlie. "Here, you take it for a while."

She took the tiller and they sailed along the causeway toward the marina, where, long ago, their parents' futures had been interrupted by a falling mast.

"You know," began Nicholas, "there still might be a way for my dad to keep that promise. I just have to figure out *how* when he gets back from Africa."

"But didn't Nick say that he hasn't been in the house in twenty-five years?"

"I know, but I think he's ready. I mean, why else did he send me and the twins out here for the summer if he didn't want to, um, reconnect with Nick? And he definitely wanted me to find the movie and *this*," he said, pointing at *Imp*. "All that stuff about secrets."

Charlie's eyes lit up. "And maybe he wants to connect with other parts of his childhood, too."

"Maybe."

"So how do you get him here?"

Nicholas smiled and shrugged. "No idea. But we'll think of something."

"True. Never underestimate the power of two smart, devious kids."

* * *

A few muggy, windless days later, as the sun dropped into the haze, Hayley and Hetty gathered Nick, Nicholas, and Charlie—and Pistol, of course—into their bedroom and insisted that everyone take a seat for a "special presentation." The guests assumed it would be another musical performance, or the two of them acting out a scene from a book they'd recently read, but they were all in for a surprise.

Hetty taped a map of Forsaken Lake to the wall while Hayley held up Nick's copy of *We Didn't Mean to Go to Sea*.

"Thank you all for coming tonight," Hetty said in a very formal voice. "We hope you're comfortable while we explain why you are here. I will now turn the presentation over to my sister, Miss Hayley Mettleson."

Polite applause greeted Hayley, which she acknowledged with a smile.

"We're going on a voyage," she announced. "We have it all planned out. Everyone here is invited to join us—and, Charlie, we want your mom to come, too. We can all fit."

"Where are we going?" Nicholas asked in a sarcastic big brother–y voice.

"Please, hold all your questions until the end of our presentation," Hetty said officiously.

"Thank you, Hetty," said Hayley as she picked up a wooden yardstick (DEMING HARDWARE: FOR ALL YOUR HARDWARE NEEDS!) to use as a pointer. "As I was saying, we are going on a voyage like the kids in this book did. We're going to spend two nights aboard *Goblin*, and we're going to circlenav— er, *circum*navigate the lake."

She traced their proposed route around the lake with the yardstick as she continued. "We start here at Uncle Nick's house, then go all the way up to *here*, and we can anchor for the night. The next day, we sail over here, around these two big islands, and then back down the other side of the lake until we get to someplace safe to anchor again. And in the morning, we go down to the dam, turn around, and come back to where we started."

"Just like Christopher Columbus," Hetty added.

"Ferdinand Magellan, actually," Hayley corrected. "He was the first to sail around the world."

"Except he didn't quite make it," said Charlie. "His ships did, but he died along the way."

Nick rubbed his chin thoughtfully. "I have to say, I'm

very impressed, girls. This is a well-thought-out plan. The distances for each day are about right, assuming we have *some* wind, and there are good spots for anchoring where you want to stop for the night. It'll probably be seventy or eighty miles of sailing, depending on how much tacking we have to do. I'm sorry I never thought of it, to tell you the truth. I love the idea."

"Well, I can't believe I'm saying this," said Nicholas, "but I totally agree with Uncle Nick. It's a great idea, *and* it fits in perfectly with my idea for finishing up Dad's movie. You'll see what I mean."

"When do we leave?" Charlie asked. "And I'm not sure my mom will be able to go—you know, with work and everything. She'll let me go, though."

"We can't go for a few days," said Nick. "I have some things to finish up around here, and we'll need to do some planning and provisioning. In the meantime, you two girls need to come up with a menu and a shopping list for me. How about Sunday, a little after noon? That'll give us plenty of time to get up to the north end of the lake. We'll be back here Tuesday morning."

Hayley and Hetty threw their arms around each other, hopping and screaming.

"We're really going to do it?" Hayley asked.

"Sure," said Nick. "We can all use a little adventure."

"A real sea voyage," Hetty said dreamily.

* * *

The next morning, Mr. Leffingwell called from the drugstore to say that the movie film had finally arrived. Nicholas couldn't wait for Nick to drive him into town in Betty; he flew his bicycle down the road to Charlie's house, and they rode together into town, where Nicholas insisted on using his hard-earned lawn-mowing money to pay for the processing. Then they raced back to Nick's, where they set up the screen and projector in the basement (because it was the darkest place in the house), threaded the film through the sprockets, and held their breath.

"Cross your fingers," said Nicholas as he flipped the switch and the projector whirred into action.

Their hearts sank as the first fifteen seconds of film flickered and fluttered by without a recognizable image. But suddenly, there she was: the teenage version of Franny, standing on the seawall at the marina, smiling and waving at the camera. The picture was grainy, and shaky, and faded—a far cry from the sharp images they were used to—but there was no doubt about what they saw.

"Yes!" cried Charlie. "That's my mom! The picture's not too bad, either."

The wind whipped the hair around Franny's face as she turned to look out at the lake, which looked angrier than either Nicholas or Charlie had ever seen it. The next thing they saw was Will, standing on the deck of a sailboat. It took Nicholas a few seconds to realize it was the same boat that was rotting away behind the storage barn—the one with the hole big enough to stick his head through.

"Wow—that's my dad," he said.

"I can see why Mom freaked out when she saw you," Charlie said. "You look just like him. You're a little darker, and your hair is a *lot* shorter."

Next came a brief shot of a hand turning pages in a notebook, stopping on the page that read *Scene 13, Take 1*.

After that, the scene unfolded just as Franny had described it to them. The action began with Will standing on the bow of the boat, about to raise the anchor. As Jimmy, playing the Seaweed Strangler, climbed aboard, he was almost knocked overboard by the boom, which swung crazily across the cockpit. He steadied himself and went after Will with his seaweed "rope."

Their struggle was cut off after a few seconds, and when the scene resumed, Will was already tied to the mast. The Strangler pulled in several feet of mainsheet and took his place behind the steering wheel. The bow of the boat dived deeply into a wave as it sailed clear of the seawall, nearly sending Will face-first onto the foredeck. The camera then cut away to a close-up shot of waves crashing on the rocks and pilings in front of the seawall before returning to the boat, which had traveled a hundred yards or more out into the lake. Jimmy spun the wheel to tack the boat, and aimed the bow directly at the rocks. For the next thirty seconds or so, the scene jumped back and forth between shots of the boat getting closer and closer to the rocks and of the rocks themselves.

Even in the film's rough, unedited state, the effect was remarkable; the Seaweed Strangler appeared to be steering the boat purposely on a path of certain destruction. Running with the wind and the high waves, the boat was hard to control, and at one point, it spun nearly sideways to the shore before returning to its original course.

Then, after one last close-up of the rocks, the camera zooms in on Jimmy, poised to dive off the side of the boat. He looks at Will, baring his fangs and beating his chest, and leaps into the waves.

"Wow!" said Nicholas. "Your dad had guts."

"Either that or he was just plain crazy." She thought about it for a second and added, "Probably just crazy."

They watched as Will threw aside the seaweed that had "tied" him to the mast and ran back to grab the wheel. On the film, he is clearly turning the wheel hard to the right, but the boat doesn't respond at all; it just barrels along—aiming right at the rocks. Even on the grainy, dark film, the panic in his face is obvious as he tries turning in the other direction, with the same result. He shouts something moments before the boat slams into the rocks, and he nearly somersaults over the wheel. An especially large wave picks up the stern and drives the boat forward again, where the bow hits the seawall—and suddenly the mast is coming toward the camera like something from a bad 3-D movie.

Amazingly, the screen doesn't go black. When the mast hit Franny, she must have knocked the tripod over, but the camera continues filming the action—sideways, and from ground level—until the film runs out, after about twenty more seconds.

"*That* was amazing," Charlie said as the projector's take-up reel spun the tail of the film round and round. "Mom described it exactly like it happened, but until you see it for yourself . . ."

Nicholas turned the projector off. "I know what you mean. I know it's a silent movie, but I swear I could *hear* everything—the wind, the waves, the crunching sound that the boat must have made, even my dad scream-ing."

"And when that mast comes down . . ."

They both cringed. "Youch."

"Let's watch it again," said Charlie. "But this time, can we stop it along the way and check out some individual frames?"

"Did you see something?"

"I don't know. Maybe. Before I say anything, you take another look."

Nicholas rewound the film and they watched a second time. When they got to the part where Jimmy was about to jump, Charlie said, "Freeze it! Okay, now back up a little bit, to the place where the boat turns sideways. Right there! Now watch carefully."

They watched it three times, and each time, they moved closer to the screen. On the fourth try, Nicholas froze the film. "Do you see what I see?"

"Is that a face in the porthole?"

"It sure looks like it. I can't get it any clearer than this. It *could* just be a shadow."

"But it stays in the same place as the boat turns," Charlie replies. "I don't think a shadow would do that."

"Why would there be somebody in the cabin?"

"To cut the steering cable. Whoever it was had to wait for the perfect moment—*after* the boat was turned around and heading for shore. Now let's watch the next part, where my dad jumps off."

Nicholas let the film run through that scene once, and then backed it up to the shot of the crashing waves that preceded Jimmy's big jump. They watched a second time, and then a third and a fourth.

"Huh," said Nicholas. "That's weird."

Charlie's eyes didn't move from the screen. "Yeah."

As Nicholas advanced the film frame by frame, they saw what they had missed when it was going by at full speed: as the camera tilted up from the rocks, Jimmy, who had been at the wheel when the camera last left him, was clearly climbing into the cockpit *from inside the cabin*.

"He wasn't supposed to be down there," Charlie said. "What was he doing?"

Nicholas chose not to say what he was thinking because this *was* Charlie's dad they were talking about.

"Maybe he just wanted to, you know, make sure he didn't, uh . . . I don't know. He must have had a reason."

"Well, I don't know what that could have been," said Charlie. "Look at the whole picture. The boat *conveniently* turns sideways away from the camera when he's at the wheel, then we see what looks like somebody's head through the porthole, and then him crawling up the stairs. And all the while, *your* dad can't see what's going on because he's facing forward."

"Huh. So, what are you saying? That your dad was the one who . . . But *why?*"

"*That* is a good question."

"Yeah, but how do you find the answer to a question like that? Without, you know, sounding like you're accusing your own dad."

Charlie considered the question for a moment. "All this was a long time ago, right? I mean, he wasn't my dad *then*—he's just a kid named Jimmy Brennan. And besides, there could be a perfectly reasonable explanation for everything."

Nicholas sighed. "Yeah. Like, *my* dad really did it."

* * *

August 5

Found your name in another library book! Did you read EVERY book about sailing they had? It's about a guy from Cleveland who sailed a thirteen-foot boat called <u>Tinkerbelle</u> across the Atlantic. When I sail across the ocean, my boat is definitely gonna have a tougher-sounding name than that.

Went back to the drive-in last night with Charlie and some other kids. No one even watches the movie, it's just a place to hang out. Confession: I told a little lie. I said I once saw a guy get shot on the subway, and everyone believed me. They think NY is, like, this crazy, out-of-control place.

Nicholas

PS Do you ever wonder what would have happened if you'd never left Deming? I do.

CHAPTER THIRTEEN

Hayley and Hetty, who had not stopped vibrating with excitement and pride since Nick had told them that he was certain they would be the youngest ever to circumnavigate Forsaken Lake, sat on the porch swing twenty-four hours before departure. There, Charlie and Nicholas imparted an even more exciting bit of news: the twins were to be the stars of the re-imagined Seaweed Strangler movie, which they would be filming during the voyage.

"Okay, here's the situation," Nicholas explained after calming the girls down. "You two are famous archaeologists—"

"What's an archaeologist?" Hetty interrupted. "Oh, they're the dinosaur guys, right?"

"That's only one kind," said Charlie. "You're the kind who goes around looking for old stuff, like tombs and bones and ancient tools and other things."

Hetty smiled. "Cool. Can I use my British accent? I think it sounds *quite* lovely."

"No British accents!" Nicholas said. "Okay, now pay attention to this part, because it's important. We're going to be using some of Dad's old film for the story, but you have to pretend that what's on that film is *real*—in other words, that the Seaweed Strangler is a real creature."

Charlie took over the explanation. "In the first scene, you two are snooping around in an old house that was owned by one of your professors, an archaeologist who recently disappeared while on a secret expedition. He was obsessed with finding this creature that everyone called the Seaweed Strangler. Most people thought he was crazy, that it was just a legend—but not you two. So, you're digging around in his house and you find a secret compartment where he has hidden a journal and some movie film that shows the creature. It doesn't take you long to realize that those things are *proof* of the existence of the Seaweed Strangler."

"And that's where *Goblin* comes in," said Nicholas. "Using the film and the notes in his journal, you figure out where he was when he found the creature, and you decide to go on an expedition in search of your old professor— and the Seaweed Strangler. Nick is going to play the ship's captain you hire to take you into the dangerous waters you need to explore, and Charlie here is going to play this woman who is going with you, filming everything you do. She's like a reporter or something, and she's making a documentary film about the expedition for an adventure channel. We'll explain the rest later; that's all you really need to know for now."

"And who are you, Nicholas?" Hayley asked.

"I'm going to be the cameraman, and I'll also play the Seaweed Strangler."

"When do we start?" asked Hetty. "I can't wait. It sounds just *super*!"

"Right now," said Charlie. "Meet you up in Nicholas's room in five minutes. We're going to shoot the scene where you discover the film in the house today, and then tomorrow we'll be filming on the boat as we leave."

Hetty turned to her twin. "We should ring Mummy, don't you think? I'd love to chat her up a bit and tell her all about our new careers."

"Brilliant!" cried Hayley, joining in the fun. "That's a jolly good idea."

As they leaped off the swing and ran past Nicholas, he couldn't help smiling. "You're going to be *stars* . . . unless you use those stupid British accents!"

Saturday night, with just hours to go before the start of the voyage round the lake, and the twins safely tucked in their beds, Nick and Nicholas sat on the porch and listened to the weather forecast on the radio.

"Temperatures slightly below normal for the next three days, possibly dipping into the fifties overnight, with a slight chance of thunderstorms Monday evening and early Tuesday morning. . . ."

"Going to be a bit chilly," said Nick. "We need to make sure everybody has enough warm, dry clothes. I borrowed some foul-weather gear to keep you dry, but the twins'll need either a nice wool sweater or a fleece. You too. No fun being cold and wet."

"I think the twins packed everything they own," said Nicholas. "But I'll make sure."

"We'll put the three girls forward in the V berth, and we'll sleep on the nice wide berths in the main cabin. How's that sound?" He scratched Pistol behind the ears. "Pistol, old boy—you're going to be on the floor. Like a dog. Tragic, really."

Pistol seemed to agree, his beagle eyes looking sadder than usual.

"I guess it's a good thing Charlie's mom couldn't come after all," Nicholas said. "I don't know where she would have slept."

"One of us would have been up in the cockpit, sleeping under the stars," said Nick. "Done it lots of times. It's not so bad—unless it rains." He turned off the light and started up the stairs to bed.

"Uncle Nick?"

Nick stopped on the stairs and turned to face Nicholas. "What's up, sport?"

"Thanks. For, you know, teaching me to sail, letting us finish up Dad's boat, everything. This summer isn't what I expected—at all. It's been . . . awesome."

"Well, you're welcome. Glad to hear that you're having some fun. I know you kids have had a rough time lately, with your parents and all. Now get some sleep—we've got a couple of big days ahead."

* * *

Charlie stared directly into the camera lens, waiting for a signal from Nicholas. "My name is Charlie Brennan, and I'm standing here on the deck of the good ship *Goblin* with twin archaeologists and adventurers Hayley and Hetty Mettleson. Standing behind me are Captain Nick and his first mate, Pistol, who will be taking us into the perilous, uncharted waters of the north end of Godforsaken Lake—which is all I have been told so far." She pointed the microphone at Hayley. "Hayley, you and your sister have been very secretive about this expedition, but now that we're under way, can you tell us something about where we're going and what you're seeking?"

"I guess so," said Hayley. "We should have told you before, but you wouldn't have come if you knew . . . that your life would be in danger."

"Cut!" cried Nicholas. "That was beautiful."

And so it went for the rest of the first day, as *Goblin* made her way toward the undeveloped and unpredictable north end of the lake. While Charlie interviewed the two young archaeologist-adventurers, Nicholas quickly grew to appreciate the advances in technology that had occurred in the years since his father started *The Seaweed Strangler*. A Super 8 film cartridge lasted only about three minutes, after which there was the one-week (or longer) wait for the film to be developed. With a digital camera, he could continue shooting for as long as he liked, and he could view the results immediately.

After a lunch of roast chicken and potato salad, he showed everyone the video they'd shot the day before— the twins in the tower room, followed by the long scene with the boys Nicholas called the Three Stooges. Zack and Ryan, from Charlie's baseball team, and a friend of theirs, a summer kid named Kirk, played a group of hunters who stumble across the Seaweed Strangler and foolishly try to get close enough to capture him. They were almost impossible to work with—constantly fooling around and ruining take after take when one of them would burst out laughing. Only when Nicholas started to fold up the tripod and put the camera away, telling them it would be easier to just rewrite the script and eliminate their scene, did they get serious.

Later in the afternoon, along with more of the "interview" scenes with Charlie and the twins, he got plenty of sailing footage—some of it while standing at the bow and stern, and some from the tiny inflatable boat they'd brought along as a dinghy. The conditions were ideal: blue sky and water, puffy white clouds, and a ten-knot breeze pushing *Goblin* along quite nicely. Down in the cabin, the explorers pored over the details of the chart, explaining to Charlie where they expected to find the missing archaeologist—and, possibly, the Seaweed Strangler himself.

They reached their Day One destination ahead of schedule and found a secluded, well-protected spot to anchor for the night. After dinner, they watched the sun set beneath a purple sky. Nick brought out a book of poems, and they took turns reading "The Cremation of Sam McGee," "The Highwayman," and others by the light of the kerosene lantern hanging from the boom. Like the ticking of a clock, waves lapped at the side of the hull, and shortly after ten, the twins, yawning loudly, crawled into the V berth, leaving little room for Charlie.

"That's okay," she said, gathering up her sleeping bag in her arms. "I think I'm going to sleep up on the deck."

"Wow. Really?" said Nicholas.

"Why not? It's beautiful, and there's no bugs. Look at the stars! I don't think I've ever seen the Milky Way look so . . . milky. Come on, get your sleeping bag."

Nick slapped him on the back. "Life is too short to pass up sleeping under the stars on a night like this. I'd join you, but if I slept on one of those hard benches, I wouldn't be able to move in the morning."

Nicholas blew out the flame in the lantern and stretched out on the bench across the cockpit from Charlie, who stared up at the sky. They lay quietly for a while as their eyes adjusted to the near-total darkness.

"Shooting star!" said Charlie. "Did you— Oh, there's another one!"

"Where are you looking? I've never seen one before."

"What? Never?"

"I live in the city—I've barely seen stars, period. I never saw the Milky Way until this summer. The sky around New York is just too bright."

"I don't think I could live someplace where I couldn't see the stars. They're so . . . *amazing*. It's like they're up there just to remind me that I'm only one little speck of dust in the universe, like the flash of light from a spark. There one second and gone the next."

"Gee, that's a cheerful thought," said Nicholas. "Hey, look—the moon's coming up, behind those clouds over there."

"Oh, so you know what the moon is, city boy," Charlie teased.

"Ha-ha. As a matter of fact, I have an amazing view of the moon from my room—some nights. In fact, my dad and I have this thing we do when he . . . No, you'll think it's stupid."

"No I won't. I *promise*. Come on, you can't leave me hanging like that."

"Well, when Dad's in Africa, sometimes he can't call for weeks because phone access is limited, but then he'll finally get through. Usually, it's pretty late, and he always makes me go to the windows and look at the moon while we're talking—the same moon he's looking at, halfway around the world from me. It always makes me feel better, like he's really not that, you know, far away. I told you, it's stupid."

"That's *not* stupid. I never use this word, but it's, like, the *sweetest* thing I've ever heard. My dad lives thirty miles away, and he doesn't do *anything* like that—when he remembers to call."

Nicholas, unsure of how to respond, said nothing.

After a few more moments of silence, Charlie asked, "So, what do you think he's doing right now?"

"My dad?" Nicholas checked his watch by the light of the moon. "They're five hours ahead of us, which makes it, like, three o'clock in the morning. So, probably sleeping. But with Dad you never know. He could be stitching somebody back together in the hospital. He kind of does whatever needs to be done."

"Well, wherever he is, whatever else he's doing—I'll

bet he's looking at the moon and thinking of you and the twins right now."

Nicholas stared at the sliver of orange moon peeking through a thick blanket of clouds just above the horizon. He blinked back a tear, grateful for the darkness that hid his face from Charlie, and then drifted off to a peaceful sleep.

* * *

The smell of bacon frying woke Charlie first. She sat up, struck by the sight of the vivid red-orange sky and a layer of mist hanging over the lake's unbroken surface.

"Brrrr! It's cold up here!" she shouted down to Nick, who was cracking eggs into a bowl.

"Nice and warm down here," he said. "Come on down. You can get the twins up and dressed and make sure they have their cabin shipshape before we weigh anchor."

Charlie saluted him stiffly. "Aye, aye, Captain."

The twins, however, informed Charlie that they were going for a swim before breakfast. "When the Walker kids slept on board *Goblin* with Jim Brading, *they* went swimming in the morning," Hayley insisted.

"I see," said Charlie. "You may change your mind when you climb out of those sleeping bags. It's kind of chilly up on deck."

"R-really?" Hetty asked, clearly having second thoughts.

Nicholas burst into their tiny cabin baring his plastic fangs. "Aaarggghhh! The Seaweed Strangler's next victims!"

Hetty screamed, but Hayley sat up with her arms crossed. "That's not even scary, Nicholas. Now get out of our room."

"*Cabin*," corrected Nicholas. "Boats don't have rooms."

Two minutes later, there were three splashes as Nicholas, Charlie, and Hayley hit the water. Hetty remained on deck, looking uncertainly at the water beneath her.

"*Come on*, Hetty," cried Hayley. "It's like a big bathtub."

Her eyes squeezed shut, Hetty counted, "One, two, *three*!" and jumped. When she surfaced, she was beaming. "Blimey! It's bloody warm! Uncle Nick! You absolutely *must* come in the water. It's simply divine."

"Oh brother. Here we go again," said Nicholas.

Nick stuck his head through the main hatch. "I'll go later. Breakfast is ready. You kids come and get something to eat while I row Pistol over to shore so he can do his business. As soon as I get back, we'll head for the bay on the far side of Onion Island. I know the perfect spot to anchor for lunch, and you kids can work on your movie there. The island itself is a little swampy, but along the edge there's some pretty scenery."

The swimmers climbed the rope ladder and then stood shivering in the cockpit while they toweled off.

"I say," Hetty continued, in her way-over-the-top accent. "I do believe I was warmer when I was in the water."

"No doubt about it," Nick said. "Lake's a good ten degrees warmer than the air temperature this morning. But it's that red sky that has me a little worried."

"Red sky at night, sailor's delight; red sky in morning, sailor's warning," chanted Hayley and Hetty.

"What do you think it means?" Nicholas asked.

"Hard to say, exactly," said Nick. "Sometimes nothing. Other times . . ."

"A storm?"

"It's possible. We'll keep an eye on things. Barometer's steady so far. Something you always have to remember about the lake: storms seem to come out of nowhere. Seen it a million times. Clear sky, beautiful day one second, and next thing you know, it looks like somebody turned off the lights and it's blowing fifty. There's a reason folks call it Godforsaken Lake. When one of those storms hits, you're on your own."

"What do you do if you're out in the middle of the lake and something like that happens?" Charlie asked.

"Best thing is probably to *stay* out in the middle—away from shore. I usually just tack back and forth until it blows over." Nick saw the concerned looks on the faces of the twins. "Don't you worry. If you have to be in a squall out on the lake, *Goblin* is the place to be. She's built to take it—and then some."

* * *

Aboard <u>Goblin,</u> anchored in Weaver's Cove.

Dear Dad,

 Forgot to tell you—we're sailing around the lake. On our way to Onion Island today for a little exploring. Thought about you last night. I've never seen a sky like that before, and I saw my first shooting star! I don't want this summer to end, but I can't wait to see you to tell you EVERYTHING that's happened. I have some big surprises for you—I hope you like them.

Nicholas

* * *

The sun burned off the mist, and they had a slow, uneventful trip to Onion Island, where they dropped anchor shortly after noon. Nicholas took Charlie to shore in the inflatable dinghy, and then returned to *Goblin* for the twins. While Nick and Pistol stretched out on the cockpit benches, Nick with a paperback and an iced tea, and Pistol with a rawhide bone, the kids spent the afternoon on the island filming new scenes for their production of *The Seaweed Strangler*.

 In the day's first scene, the two young archaeologists row ashore with Charlie's character, in search of their friend, the missing professor. Following the clues they found on the film, they discover a beat-up canvas back-pack that they immediately recognize as the professor's. Inside is his camera and another leather-bound journal (exactly like the one hidden in his house) filled with barely legible notes and sketches of the creature.

Hetty turns and speaks to the camera. "We have just found the professor's journal. Here is a random entry: *Saw the creature again this morning. I watched with amazement as he caught a two-pound fish with his bare hands and ate it raw. I fear that he knows he's being followed. Every few seconds, he lifts his nose high in the air and sniffs, as if he has caught a whiff of something strange to him. I know it is dangerous, but I must follow him, even if it takes me to places no human has ever set foot. Something tells me that he is not alone back here in these woods; I feel certain that there are others like him. If I am correct, it will rank as one of the greatest discoveries of all time. He is heading southwest. More later.*"

"Cut! That was *awesome*, you two," said Nicholas, high-fiving his sisters. "Even with that stupid accent, Hetty."

"Oh, you noticed," Hetty said. "I didn't mean to—it just kind of came out."

"It's all right," he said. "Now it's my turn." He changed into the Seaweed Strangler costume—no shirt, an old pair of jeans cut off raggedly just below the knee and held up with a piece of rope, and his plastic fangs. Except for his face, he looked exactly like Charlie's dad in the original version.

"Isn't it going to be weird having two different

Seaweed Stranglers in the same movie?" Hayley asked. "People are going to notice that you don't look just like Charlie's dad."

"Ah, but that's just it. Maybe there *are* two Seaweed Stranglers. In fact, there might be a whole bunch of them living back there in the swamp. Okay, follow me, everybody."

They trudged into the interior of Onion Island and spent the next two hours on the movie's crucial, and tricky, final scenes—for some of which the twins were *behind* the camera, much to their delight. By the time they wandered back to the shore and the waiting dinghy, they were wet, tired, mosquito-bitten, and very hungry.

"There you are," said Nick from *Goblin*'s bow. "Thought I was going to have to send Pistol in after you. It's time we got moving if we're going to make it down to Heller's Cove by dark. Still not much wind out there."

When the dinghy bumped the hull, he reached down to help the twins up the ladder. "Jolly good timing, you two. Just in time for ahhhhfternoon tea." He pretended to drink from an imaginary teacup, his pinkie properly extended.

"Oh no!" cried Nicholas, rowing back to the island to pick up Charlie. "Not you, too, Uncle Nick."

CHAPTER FOURTEEN

Ghosting along in a dying late-afternoon breeze, *Goblin* hugged the western shore of the lake as her crew, worn out from the day's activities, took turns napping on deck. When dinnertime came, they were still several miles from their destination, so Nick went into the tiny galley and heated up some canned chicken noodle soup, which he served in plastic mugs, while Hetty made ham and cheese sandwiches for everyone.

"There's nothing like hot soup when you're sailing," Nick said, tilting his mug up to get every last drop. "Especially when you've got weather on the way."

Nicholas twisted his head around to look over the trees behind him. "D'you still think we're going to get a storm today?"

Nick nodded. "Weather reports are all talking about scattered storms around the county tonight. We might get lucky. Either way, we'll be safe and sound in the cove. If the storm comes from the north or west, there's no better place to be—it's very protected."

As they edged around a point of land littered with driftwood, a serene farmhouse, surrounded by pastures filled with grazing Holsteins, came into view.

"It's like a *picture* of a farm," Hayley noted.

"*Moooo*," said Hetty. Her voice carried over the calm water to the shore, where several cows looked up at her. "Hey! They heard me! *Mooooooo!*"

"That's the Kuerners' place," Nick said. "Just the two of them now, both in their sixties, running the farm. Had a whole passel of kids, but none of them wanted to farm—they all moved away. Sad to think what'll happen—" He stopped, noticing that a woman was running toward the shore and waving her arms about wildly.

"Who's that?" asked Hayley.

"Sue Kuerner. Something's wrong. Take us in a little closer, Charlie. Nicholas, can you take the mainsheet? Good, good."

"Nick!" shouted the panicked woman. "Come quick! It's Ethan—he collapsed in the barn."

"Did you call 911?"

"They sent an ambulance—it's on the way. But . . . please, can you come up to the barn with me? I'm afraid he's . . . and they take so long to get here."

"You go back to Ethan. I'll be there in a second."

Luckily, the dinghy was still inflated, resting upside down on the foredeck. Nick took a quick look at *Goblin*'s young crew. "Charlie, you come with me. We may need an extra set of hands. Sue must have left a gate open, because she's got cows running loose; we'll need to get them back in the pasture. Nicholas, here's what I want you to do. There's a place where you can anchor, a couple of hundred yards south of here. As soon as you get around that bend, you'll see a bright yellow house. It's not perfect, but you'll be safe there until Charlie and I get back. Just wait there for us."

"Got it," said Nicholas, taking the tiller from Charlie's hands as the first rumble of thunder sounded its warning in the distance.

"Better get moving," said Nick. "Make sure you really get that anchor set. Hayley, Hetty—you girls listen to Nicholas. He's the captain until I get back."

Pistol barked as Nick climbed down the rope ladder to the waiting dinghy.

Nick pointed a finger at him. "No—you stay right there, boy. Keep an eye on him. He may try to come after me."

"I can't believe he's leaving," said Hetty, watching Nick rowing away.

"Moooo," said Hetty. Her voice carried over the calm water to the shore, where several cows looked up at her. "Hey! They heard me! Mooooooo!"

"He'll be right back," said Nicholas. "Don't worry about it."

Hayley sighed. "That's just what the kids in *We Didn't Mean to Go to Sea* said."

As he nosed *Goblin* around the bend, Nicholas was astonished by the sight that greeted him. Ominous clouds barely skimmed over the treetops, dabbing dark brush-strokes of gray onto a world that, moments before, had glowed with the bright greens and blues of summer. With the second drumroll of thunder came a gust of wind, filling the sails and heeling the boat over rather suddenly.

He barked orders at the twins. "Hayley, come here—now! Take the tiller for a minute while I get the sails down. Head right for that house. Hetty, go below and get those red sail ties. Now!"

Whether it was his no-nonsense tone or the frighten-ing sky above them, they both sprang into action. In a matter of seconds, Nicholas had wrestled the jib to the deck and secured it with the sail ties that Hetty handed him. He opened the anchor locker and lifted out the Dan-forth anchor and chain.

"Okay, Hayley, when I say '*Go!*' I want you to turn the boat directly into the wind. Then just keep the bow pointed in that direction, okay?"

Hayley nodded, her eyes wide with excitement—and maybe just a pinch of terror.

"Hetty, you take the mainsheet. The second Hayley starts turning, you uncleat that thing and let it out two or three feet. Then cleat it again, and keep your head down, because the boom's going to swing around like crazy. All right?"

Looking as if she might bite through her bottom lip, Hetty gave him a thumbs-up. "I'm ready."

Nicholas stood at the forestay, watching the fast-approaching shoreline, where the overturned maple leaves seemed to be waving him off. When they reached the spot he had chosen, he gave Hayley the signal. The twins did their jobs perfectly, and he tossed the anchor in front of the boat as far as he could and waited to see if it would "catch" in the mud while *Goblin* began to drift slowly backward.

"Come on, come on," he said, tugging on the anchor line. He was about to give up on it when he felt a jerk as the anchor snagged on some submerged object. "Yes! It's holding. Let's get that mainsail down."

* * *

While Nicholas and the twins prepared themselves and *Goblin* for the approaching storm, Charlie and Nick had their hands full. Ethan Kuerner, conscious but still doubled over in pain, sat on a hay bale inside the barn.

"Kinda like somebody's . . . driving a railroad spike into . . . my chest," he said when Nick asked him how he was feeling. Like most farmers, however, he was more concerned about the livestock than his own well-being. He looked up at Charlie. "You've got . . . to get the cows . . . in the barn. Bad . . . storm coming. Can you do that for me?"

"Yes, sir," she said, bolting out the door as the ambulance pulled in the driveway.

Charlie was no expert on cows, but she had spent enough time on friends' farms to know how to get a herd of the black-and-white behemoths moving back to the barn. She raced around the pasture, yelling and slapping rumps until they started in the right direction. Then she ran down to the lake to retrieve the "escapees" that had wandered through the open gate. As they moseyed along the path to the barn, a flash of lightning lit up the sky, followed a few seconds later by the booming of thunder. The cows picked up the pace after that, and Charlie closed the gate as the first drops of rain splashed onto the dusty barnyard. She glanced up at the sky and thought of Nicholas and the twins huddled in *Goblin*'s cabin, sorry that she was missing out on the experience.

The paramedics had removed Ethan from the barn by then, and were closing the ambulance doors, ready to leave, when Nick intercepted Charlie.

"Hey, kiddo—all the cows in? Listen, I hate to do this to you kids, but Sue's a nervous wreck. She's in no condition to drive herself to the hospital, so I'm going to have to take her."

"How is Mr. Kuerner? Is he going to be all right?"

"I think so. Looks like it was a heart attack. He'll probably be in the hospital for a few days for some tests, but the paramedics sounded positive."

"What should I do?" Charlie asked.

"You can come with me, or stay here until I get back—which will probably be an hour and a half, two hours—or you can row out to *Goblin* and ride it out with the rest of the gang." As he said those words, the sky opened up and began to drench them, so they moved under the barn's overhang.

"I'll wait here until the rain lets up," she said. "But if I take the dinghy, how will *you* get out to *Goblin?*"

"I'll go next door to the yellow house I told Nicholas about. Keep an eye out for me. I'm hoping this will all be blown over by the time I get back."

Charlie watched as the ambulance started down the drive, with Nick and Sue following in the Kuerners' tired Plymouth, and then went into the barn to wait out the storm.

It was a long wait. The final hour of daylight was completely obliterated by the dense clouds and unrelenting rain. Lightning knocked out the power all along the lake, so she sat with the cows in the dark, steamy barn, listening to the wind howling through the hayloft above her and wondering what Nicholas, Hetty, and Hayley were going through aboard *Goblin*.

"Maybe you'd better let out some more chain," Hayley said to Nicholas, for the third time in the last hour.

Nicholas stuck his head up out of the cabin, listening to the wind whistle through *Goblin*'s rigging. He looked to both sides of the cove, taking bearings as Nick had taught him to do, making certain that the anchor was holding them firmly in place.

"We haven't moved an inch," he reported. "It's not like in the book, when the tide came in and lifted the boat up. There's no tide here, I promise."

Unconvinced, the twins continued looking out the portholes until it was too dark to make out the shoreline.

"How much longer till Uncle Nick and Charlie get back?" Hetty asked. "It's been *hours*. What if something's wrong? I'm scared."

"Nothing's wrong," Nicholas replied. "And *we're* perfectly safe." His words were punctuated by a blinding flash of lightning and an earsplitting crack of thunder.

We're perfectly safe, Nicholas repeated to himself. On the terror scale, he was somewhere to the right of "slightly nervous," but was still well to the left of the twins, who were nearing "petrified with fright," and Pistol, who buried his head under a blanket. He did his best to seem cheerful as he lit the kerosene lantern on the bulkhead next to the mast.

The lamp filled the cramped cabin with golden light, immediately improving the twins' state of mind.

Hetty even reverted to her British accent. "That's *ever* so much nicer, Nicholas. Well done, old chap."

Nicholas slowly shook his head. "I think I liked it better when you were scared. Why don't you two take turns reading something out loud—to pass the time," said Nicholas. "But please, *not* in that stupid fake accent."

Another flash, another loud crack—from somewhere out on the lake—as Hayley retrieved her book from her duffel in the forepeak.

"Did you guys feel that?" she asked, diving under the blanket with Hetty and Pistol. "I think it hit *us*."

"It didn't hit us," said Nicholas. "Trust me, if lightning hits us, you'll *know* it."

Nevertheless, he climbed to the top step and stuck his head out of the cabin for a good look around. "At least the rain has stopped for now. I think the wind is picking up again, though. Uncle Nick is pretty smart; this cove is probably the calmest spot on this side of the lake. I don't know what we would have done if we were on the other side. It's nasty out there."

He flinched as lightning struck on the shore behind him, illuminating the lake for a tiny fraction of a second. Long enough, however, for Nicholas to see something—or at least *think* he saw something—he didn't expect to see: a sailboat, directly across the lake from him.

In the blackness that followed the flash, his eyes

detected nothing, and he couldn't help wondering if it was merely his imagination running wild, or perhaps a rare (according to Nick) second sighting of the "2:53," even though it was only a few minutes past ten. He stared in the direction of the boat, straining for another look, but the darkness was complete; it was impossible to distinguish the line separating sky from water. Rain began to fall again, but he didn't take his eyes off his spot, despite Hayley's pleas to close the hatch because the cabin was getting wet.

A burst of light directly in his line of sight blinded him momentarily, but the follow-up flashes confirmed his notion: there *was* a boat out there. A sailboat, and it was in trouble, its mast broken ten feet above the deck, sails and rigging hanging sadly from the stump.

Squinting through the rain, Nicholas noticed a dim light where the boat had disappeared again into the darkness that poured into the sky surrounding him. Someone, he was certain, was waving a flashlight back and forth.

Now what am I supposed to do?

Nicholas weighed his options as he continued to watch the barely visible light swing from side to side. The easiest solution was to simply ignore it—pretend he hadn't seen the light or the boat. After all, there was no reason to expect him, or anybody else, to see *anything* in those conditions, was there?

"Nicholas! Close the hatch! We're getting soaked!" Hetty cried.

But Nicholas had made up his mind. They had to help. Nick hadn't prepared him for a situation like this, but he was pretty sure there was a "sailors' code" that included helping a boat in trouble—no matter what.

He stepped into the cabin and closed the hatch. "Get your foul-weather gear on, girls. There's a sailboat out there, and it's in trouble. The mast is broken, and they're just drifting. Somebody might be hurt. They're waving a flashlight around, and we're the only ones who can help right now."

"Ha-ha, Nicholas. Very funny," said Hetty.

"No, I'm serious," he replied, taking their still-dripping rain gear from the hanging locker. "We have to help them."

"Wh-what about those patrol boats?" Hayley asked. "Uncle Nick says they're like the Coast Guard. Why can't *they* do it?"

"I doubt that they're even out there right now," said Nicholas. "They probably figure everybody's off the lake at this point."

"Why do *we* have to do anything? We're just kids," said Hetty. "And besides, didn't you promise Uncle Nick that we would wait for him here? What if he comes back and we're gone? Remember what he said about storms?"

Nicholas pulled on the yellow slicker that Nick had given him. "True, but we may be their only hope. We have to do it. Uncle Nick will understand."

Hayley and Hetty started to stir from the berth, but stopped when a brilliant flash illuminated the cabin through the portholes.

"Look, I need your help," Nicholas said to them. "We'll be okay—I promise. I know what I'm doing. Just like John did in the book. Didn't he take good care of his little brother and sisters?"

"We *did* want an adventure," Hayley admitted. "C'mon, Het. It's kind of exciting. Wait till we get back home and we can tell Jennifer and Katie. It'll be amazing. And Zoe Peterman. She will just *die* of jealousy."

Hetty's face brightened a little at the thought of having something special to brag about when school started back again in September.

"Great!" said Nicholas. "Get dressed, put your life jackets on, and come up on deck. And get Pistol into his life jacket, too. You know he's going to come up in the cockpit, and I don't want to lose him. You're all going to stay nice and safe in the cockpit. I need you to steer while I get the mainsail up."

Hayley's eyebrows shot up. "Mainsail? We're going to *sail*? Why don't we use the motor? Wouldn't that be a lot easier?"

Nicholas nodded. "Yep. It would. Unfortunately, the key must be in Uncle Nick's pocket. It's not in the ignition. Don't worry, I'm going to reef the main."

"What's that mean?" Hetty asked, zipping her several-sizes-too-big foul-weather gear.

"It means that I'll make the sail a lot smaller than usual, so it won't heel the boat as much. Theoretically."

Nicholas had never actually reefed, but Nick had explained the concept and the process to him, and he was certain it was the right thing to do.

Even though the wind and waves in the cove were nothing compared to what awaited them out on the lake, they were enough to make moving about on the deck difficult. Raising the mainsail and tying in the reefs took longer, and required more energy, than Nicholas had expected, but each time he stopped to catch his breath, that dim flashlight waving at him in the distance egged him on.

After what seemed an eternity, they were ready to cast off. Nicholas lifted the anchor aboard and quickly stowed it while Hayley and Hetty sat on opposite sides of the cockpit, all four hands glued to the curved wooden tiller. Hetty pushed, Hayley pulled, and *Goblin*'s bow spun away from the shore and headed out for the middle of the lake.

When Nicholas moved aft into the cockpit, the twins tried to hand him the tiller.

"No way," he said. "You guys are doing great. Just keep us headed in this direction."

The first taste of what lay ahead hit them—a gust of wind heeled them dramatically as Nicholas let out the mainsheet as fast as he could.

"Nich-o-las," cried Hetty, suddenly very close to the water racing past her.

"You're fine. You can move up to the high side, next to Hayley, if you want. Just remember what John's dad told him: one hand for yourself and one for the ship."

"Hey, I see the light now," said Hayley, looking forward. "I think the rain's slowing down, at least."

As the sturdy *Goblin* plunged forward into the waves, Nicholas explained his plan. They would make one pass by the disabled boat so he could talk to its captain and decide how to proceed.

"The most important thing for you two is not to get distracted. You have to listen to me, so if I tell you to turn hard to port, you do it right away."

"Wait. Which way is port again?" Hayley asked.

Nicholas's face fell as he glared at her. "Hayley! How can you not know—"

"Gotcha!" she screamed.

Hetty high-fived her. "*Nice*. Did you see the look on his face?"

"We're not *idiots*, Nicholas," said Hayley. "We know port and starboard."

"Just pay attention, okay?" he said with a shake of his head. "We're getting close."

Lightning, well off in the distance, provided enough light to see that it was a man standing and waving on the deck of the boat, which appeared to be sitting quite low in the water.

Nicholas aimed his flashlight up at the torn remnants of the mainsail to help the twins see where they were going as they surged closer and closer. As they swept past the stern, he saw the boat's name, *Maguffin II*, in gold letters.

"Hello! Is that *Goblin*? Nick? Boy, am I glad to see you!"

He was older than Nicholas had expected, with a scruffy gray beard, a long ponytail that stood straight out in the breeze, and a belly that no foul-weather gear could hide.

Hayley whispered to Hetty, "For a guy who's standing on a sinking boat, he sure seems pretty calm."

"*Quite,*" said Hetty. "I'd be screaming my bloomin' 'ead off."

Nicholas directed the twins to steer around the boat and point the bow into the wind so he could have a few extra seconds to talk to the man. He knew that they would have a hard time keeping her head to wind in those conditions, but it was necessary. For this first pass, *Goblin* kept her distance, getting no closer than thirty or forty feet to the hull of the sinking boat, which was low enough in the water that waves were breaking over her deck.

Pistol put his front paws up on the cockpit seat for a better view of the action. When he caught sight of a stranger so close to *Goblin,* he started howling.

"Hey, Pistol," said the man. "I'd recognize that old face anywhere."

Satisfied that the man wasn't a threat, Pistol quieted down, wagging his tail enthusiastically. Nicholas shouted across the water, "This is *Goblin*, but Nick's not on board. What happened?"

The man pointed at the broken mast that lay across the deck, sails dragging in the water. "Lightning. Took a direct hit. Blew out all the through-hulls, plus another big hole under the mast. She's going down. Fast."

"What can we do?" Nicholas asked. "Are you alone?"

"Yep—just me. No point in trying to save the boat— she's toast. But I could sure use a lift—if you've got room."

Nicholas couldn't help admiring the guy for maintaining his sense of humor after all that. "I think we can squeeze you in. We'll make another pass and try to get as close as we can."

"Sounds like a plan."

"Okay, Hayley," said Nicholas, sheeting in the main. "Hard to port!"

The twins pulled hard on the tiller, with Hetty letting out a scream as the wind filled the sail, heeling them over at a precarious angle.

Nicholas eased the sheet and *Goblin* leveled off a bit. "Get her moving, and we'll tack around and make another pass. But this time, you're going to have to get really close, so he can jump aboard. Think you can handle that?"

"Piece of cake," said Hayley.

"How do we know this guy isn't a pirate?" Hetty asked. "He could be faking this whole thing just to steal Uncle Nick's boat."

"He breaks his mast and sinks his own boat so he can

steal this one? Pretty good plan," marveled Nicholas. "You know, Hetty, I think you might be right. Maybe we should just go back to shore and wait for Uncle Nick. This guy looks kind of dangerous."

"Really?" Hetty's eyes grew wider and wider.

Nicholas counted to three. "Gotcha!"

CHAPTER FIFTEEN

Charlie checked her watch for the umpteenth time, her eyes straining to read the hands in the dark barn. Twenty minutes to eleven, and still no power, and no Nick. The rain had slowed considerably, but not the wind; its velocity had increased quite dramatically. The trees shook violently, littering the yard with small branches. When she thought about trying to row the inflatable dinghy around the point to the waiting *Goblin* in those conditions, she cringed.

"I have to see what's going on out there," she said aloud, half to herself and half to the cows. "I'll be back."

Her foul-weather gear zipped, tied, and Velcro-ed in every conceivable way, Charlie bolted out the barn door for the lake. She followed the shoreline, stumbling on rocks and tripping over pieces of driftwood in the blackness, until she reached the point of land that marked the start of the cove where *Goblin* was anchored. With the thick layer of low-flying clouds, the rain, and the power outage working against her, visibility was almost zero. Only the now-distant lightning provided her an occasional glimpse into the void.

Charlie stood perfectly still, letting her eyes adjust to the dark, and waited for the next opportunity. Finally, the sky before her flickered on and off like a dying fluorescent bulb. She saw the yellow house, a dock with a pontoon boat tied alongside, and an overturned dinghy on the shore.

She waited for the next three flashes to confirm her suspicions: *Goblin* simply wasn't there.

* * *

On the first rescue attempt, *Goblin* never got close enough for the stranded sailor to jump aboard, even with Nicholas standing on the deck—one hand on the shroud, the other reaching out to help.

"That's okay, Hayley," he said. "Take her around one more time, just like that. You're doing great. Don't be afraid to get close; I have all the bumpers out. The second he's on board, pull like mad on the tiller to get us away."

Hayley, growing more confident by the minute, brought *Goblin* around for her second run, and this time, she did her job perfectly, pointing the bow right at the stern of the floundering boat. Nicholas was ready to shout that they were *too* close when she turned just enough to slide by, *Goblin* passing within two feet of the other craft's hull. The sailor stepped aboard, taking Nicholas's hand and then glancing backward at his own boat, which sagged lower and lower in the water.

"Thank you. Would have been a long swim. She's going down fast. I'm Teddy, by the way."

"I'm Nicholas. And those two are Hayley and Hetty. And I guess you already know Pistol."

"Very nice job of handling this yacht, young lady," said Teddy.

"Thank you," Hayley said. "I just did what Nicholas told me."

"Well, I owe you kids."

Nicholas took one last look at Teddy's boat as they took a seat in the cockpit. "Are you sure you don't want to try to tow it in?"

"No—it's too dangerous. I don't want you taking any more chances with your own boat." He shook his head in disbelief. "I have to be the first person in history to sink two boats on this silly lake. Now, if you don't mind my asking, what in the world are you kids doing out on a night like this?"

As they circled the sinking *Maguffin*, Nicholas explained the sequence of events that had occurred since leaving Nick and Charlie at the Kuerners' farm.

"Well, I'll be. So Nick's your uncle. *Everybody* on Godforsaken Lake knows Nick Mettleson."

"What were *you* doing out there?" Hayley asked. "How do we know you're not a pirate or something?"

Teddy's head tilted back as he roared with laughter. "Fair enough, since you answered my question. I'm not a pirate, although I've been told I bear a certain resemblance to Blackbeard. No, it's nothing sinister, I promise. I was trying to make it up to the cove on the north side of Onion Island. It's pretty well protected. Figured I'd ride out the storm there."

"Look," cried Hetty, pointing at *Maguffin II*. "It's almost gone—kind of like the *Titanic*."

Once *Maguffin*'s decks were completely awash, the end came quickly. Her bow and stern lights continued to glow as the hull slipped beneath the angry waves. The stump of the mast tilted toward them, then away, and then was gone.

No one said anything for a long time.

Finally, Hayley turned to Hetty. "That was so sad— like watching somebody die. It seems like we ought to say a prayer or something."

Goblin dug her nose into wave after wave as the wind grew stronger by the minute. Hetty was taking a turn at the tiller, but the conditions were just too much for the twins. It was well past their bedtime, so Nicholas suggested that they go below and crawl into their sleeping bags.

"But do it fast," he warned. "Otherwise, you'll probably get seasick down there. Just get into bed and keep your eyes closed. And take Pistol with you. He'll be safer—and happier—down there."

Surprisingly, they didn't argue with him; Hetty handed him the tiller and followed Hayley into the cabin.

"Thanks again, girls. Great job," Teddy said before turning to Nicholas. "You want me to take her for a spell? You look like you could use a break yourself."

Nicholas gladly turned the tiller over to him and stood in the cockpit, his eyes scanning the distance for anything recognizable. There was nothing to see but more darkness, no matter what direction he turned. The power remained out all around the lake, and the lightning had passed them by, its distant flickering no longer helpful.

"What do you think we should do?" Nicholas asked. "I mean, with the wind blowing like this, and no lights onshore, I doubt if we could even find the house where we were anchored."

"Safest thing to do right now is stay out here in the middle, away from shore. We'll be able to see car headlights if anybody's crossing the causeway—that'll help us keep our bearings. The good news is, we can just reach back and forth until the wind dies down, or the power comes on, or the sun rises—whichever comes first. You wouldn't happen to have any coffee in the galley, would you?"

"Yeah, Uncle Nick had some this morning. It's funny, that seems like a *long* time ago. It's instant coffee—is that all right?" He knew his parents would rather have old motor oil than the instant stuff, but in the current circumstances, it was the best he could do.

Teddy nodded. "Good man. If it's hot and strong, I'll take it. And I'll keep *Goblin* here straight and true. Even I couldn't sink two boats in one night." He smiled, adding, "Maybe I shouldn't say that. Might be tempting fate a little too much."

Nicholas slid down the stairs to the galley, where he filled the kettle with water and lit the stove, bracing himself between the stairs and a bulkhead as *Goblin* rocked and rolled under his feet. Hayley and Hetty had wedged themselves into the port-side pilot berth, and were, to his surprise, actually sleeping. Pistol raised his head, his tail thumping against the floorboards in greeting. But as Nicholas waited in the bouncing, stuffy cabin for the water to boil, something unexpected occurred: he began to feel a little queasy. He had never been seasick before, and seemed to be suffering in equal proportions from nausea and shame. He was certain that *real* sailors didn't get seasick, especially in front of their ten-year-old twin sisters, who, he was equally certain, would *never* let him forget it. Climbing back up the companionway stairs, he stuck his head up out of the cabin, suddenly desperate for some fresh air.

"Duck!" cried Teddy as *Goblin* slammed into a wave, sending spray over the entire deck.

Nicholas had time only to spin his head around; rather than a full bucket of water hitting his face, a good half bucket ran down the back of his neck.

"Hooooo! That's cold!" he said, hopping up and down in an attempt to make the water run faster. The good news? The symptoms that had driven him out of the cabin in the first place had disappeared as quickly as they had arrived.

He wiped the water from his face with his sleeve and turned toward *Goblin*'s bow, happy that the queasiness was gone. Leaving his hood down, he leaned forward, watching the bow dive into wave after wave, and listening to the wind howling through the rigging above. Suddenly, he stiffened and turned his head; there was sound coming from somewhere other than *Goblin*, a sound that didn't quite belong. The source of the noise seemed to be off the starboard bow, but his vision in that direction was completely blocked by the staysail, which they had raised to make steering easier. When the bow rose on an especially large wave, he got a quick glimpse under the sail, but saw nothing out of the ordinary.

"Everything okay?" Teddy asked, noticing that Nicholas was looking around anxiously.

"Uh, yeah. I thought I heard something, but it must be the wind."

Teddy checked his bearings to port and then to starboard, making certain that *Goblin* was still basically in the middle of the lake.

"We're a good mile, mile and a half offshore," he said.

Nicholas, reassured, nodded at Teddy. "I'm sure it was the wind and the waves hitting the hull."

As he turned to face forward again, he gasped.

"Look out!" he screamed at Teddy as the sleek, pointy bow of another sailboat, slicing silently through the waves, suddenly appeared from behind the staysail.

As Teddy threw the tiller over, Nicholas braced himself against the side of the companionway, waiting for the inevitable collision, and immediately wondered how he was going to explain *this* to Uncle Nick.

But the collision never happened; the other boat glided past Goblin's bow with only inches to spare.

"Hey!" Teddy shouted at the other boat. "Who's there? Get some lights on!"

No response.

A break in the clouds let slip a sliver of moonlight, allowing Nicholas and Teddy—their hearts still pounding—to watch the other boat charge off into the distance, under full sail and still without running lights.

"Who *was* that?" Nicholas asked, finally able to breathe normally.

"No idea. Never seen the boat before. And I know *every* boat on the lake. Or thought I did."

"They were *flying*. What kind of boat was that, anyway?"

"Long and lean. Musta been thirty feet, maybe a little more. Narrow beam. And you're right—*fast*."

"You know, I only saw it for a second, and it's dark and everything, but I, uh . . ."

"Didn't see any people?" Teddy said. "I know. Very strange. I suppose it's possible that whoever it was just tied off the tiller for a minute so they could take care of something else, but you'd think they'd'a stuck their head up when I yelled. Well, what do you say we take down that stays'l so we have a little better visibility. One good thing about all that: I'm wide-awake now! But hot coffee still sounds good."

"The water should be boiling. I'll go make it."

After lowering and tying off the staysail on the bouncing foredeck, Nicholas went below and poured the hot water into two mugs, stirring two heaping spoonfuls of instant coffee into each.

His mind drifted back to that mysterious boat he'd seen from the tower room—the one that seemed to disappear into thin air. He was certain the boat that had nearly cut *Goblin* in two was the same boat. "That's twice," he said aloud.

"What's twice?" Hayley asked, poking her head out from under the covers.

"Nothing. Go back to sleep."

Climbing the stairs with two mugs of steaming coffee while being tossed this way and that by waves was no picnic, but he did it somehow—without spilling a drop.

Teddy took a mug, thanking him again for the rescue and the hospitality. "Hoo-boy!" he shouted into the wind after his first sip. "That'll put hair on your chest!"

"Did I make it too strong?" Nicholas asked.

"No such thing. It's perfect."

Between waves, Nicholas managed to bring his mug to his lips and take a big drink. He almost gagged. "Ugh. How can you drink this stuff?"

"Ah, you get used to it. Usually starts in college—all-night study sessions."

"The only time I ever drank it was at my grandmother's. She put in *lots* of milk and sugar, I think. It wasn't anything like this." If he hadn't been shivering from the cold, he would have tossed the rest of it overboard. Instead, he wrapped both hands around the mug, soaking up the warmth.

"Temperature's still dropping," Teddy noted, pulling his cap down over his ears. "And the wind's showing no sign of letting up. Nights like this always remind me of a salty old guy I used to sail with up on Lake Erie. The colder and wetter, the better he liked it. We'd be heading for Port Stanley, over on the Canadian side, slogging through a nor'easter, and he'd look me right in the eyes and say, in this gravelly voice of his, 'Teddy, my boy, it must be plain hell ashore on a night like this.' Used to crack me up."

Suddenly, the pieces of Teddy's story came together in Nicholas's mind like a jigsaw puzzle, and out of the blue, Nicholas asked him, "Are you Teddy *Bradford*, by any chance?"

Teddy tilted his head in surprise. "The one and only. How'd you guess?"

"Something you said—about that being the second boat you'd sunk. And you knew whose boat this was. Uncle Nick told us about . . . well, what happened down by the marina."

The howling of the wind drowned out Teddy's chuckle. "That was a long time ago. Back in my drinking days." He stared at Nicholas, struggling to make out details in the dim glow of the stern light. "Wait a second—I'll bet you're Will Mettleson's kids, aren't you? Well, this is just . . . a little *too* strange."

When Nicholas later told Charlie about that moment, he admitted that—for just a moment—he was afraid. His mind ran riot with images of Teddy Bradford taking his revenge by deliberately sailing poor old *Goblin* onto the nearest rocks.

That microsecond of panic passed quickly, though, when he realized that Teddy was laughing hysterically.

"I'm sorry, I shouldn't be laughing," he said. "But you

have to admit, it's quite a coincidence. You—of all the people in the world—saving my sorry butt from a sinking boat."

Nicholas prepared to defend his father's actions of that day, his mind replaying the film of the sinking that seemed to show Charlie's dad—who also happened to be Teddy's cousin—someplace he shouldn't have been.

But Teddy had a surprise for him.

"You know, it's about twenty-five years too late, but I owe your dad an apology. Big-time."

"What do you mean?"

"I don't know how much you know about what happened that day, but your dad kind of . . . took the fall, I guess, for somebody else. And I let it happen. It wasn't your dad's fault. Not even a little bit."

It wasn't your dad's fault.

Despite the noise and the spray, those five words hung above *Goblin* like a hot-air balloon.

"I know," said Nicholas. "I, er, *we*—me and my friends—did some snoop— er, *investigating*. We found the cut steering cable and backstay. There's no way my dad did those things. We found the camera they were using that day. You can see stuff on that film that just doesn't make sense. There was another kid. . . ."

"Jimmy Brennan. My cousin."

"Right. And while my dad was still up by the mast, you can see Jimmy coming out of the cabin—someplace he had no reason to go."

"No *good* reason, anyway," said Teddy. "Well, it sounds

like you've basically got it figured out. You're missing one important detail, though. What you don't know is that *I* was on the boat, too—totally by accident. Like I said, that was back in my drinking days. The night before, I had a few too many up at the Causeway Lounge, and I decided to sleep it off on my boat, which was docked at the marina. Completely forgot about telling your dad and Jimmy that they could use it the next morning. Well, next thing I know, I wake up and the boat's a-rockin' and a-rollin', and it feels like somebody's jackhammering away inside my head. I had no idea where I was. I look across the boat from where I'm stretched out, and lo and behold, there's my little cousin, Jimmy, messing around with something under the cockpit. I was wrapped up in a couple of sail bags and he didn't even see me."

"Did you say anything to him?"

"I remember *trying*. My head was pounding, my vision was still blurry—I think I was hoping it was a dream. And then he was gone. Meanwhile, I'm just layin' there, trying to muster the strength to get up on my feet, when—*bam!*—we hit something so hard I bounced off the ceiling." Teddy raised his mug to Nicholas. "And that was the end of *Maguffin*—Number One, that is. You just watched *Maguffin II* go down. You know, maybe it's time for a different name."

"So, what did you do?" Nicholas asked. "Didn't the people onshore see you?"

"If they did, nobody ever said anything. My guess is

that once that mast fell on that poor girl's head, *that* was where everyone was looking. While the boat was bouncing against the rocks and pilings, I tried to push her off, but I wasn't exactly steady on my feet, and I fell over the side. And that's when Jimmy found me. Let's just say he was surprised to see me."

"What did he say?"

"He begged me not to say anything. He didn't want to get into trouble. I told him I'd have to wait and see how things turned out. When I got up on dry land and saw the girl and the sheriff and then the ambulance, I thought, *Oh boy, here comes a lawsuit.* But next thing I know, everybody is pointing fingers at your dad and his secret plan to blow up my boat, and they're treating me like I'm just another victim of this horrible crime." Teddy wiped the rain from his face. "And I let them."

"B-but *why?* I mean, why did Jimmy do it?"

Teddy shrugged. "Don't know. He told me he wanted the movie they were making to be more realistic, but I always figured there was more to it than that. To tell you the honest-to-God truth, once I found out I was going to get a brand-new boat out of the deal, I didn't much care. Not something I'm proud of. It's easy for me to blame it on the booze, but the fact is, I should have spoken up. I'd like to think I would have if they'd arrested your dad or anything like that. When I heard that he'd gone back to New York, it was like my conscience was let off the hook."

"Can I ask you one more question? A few days after it happened, did you go looking for my dad's camera?"

A smile came to Teddy's face. "Mikey Bishop. When you said you'd found the camera, I immediately thought of him. Yep, I did go over there and ask him about it. I saw him talking to your dad. I was afraid of what that film might show—you know, if the police, or my insurance company, got ahold of it. So, was I right? Did Mikey have it all along?"

Nicholas nodded. "And he *still* didn't want to give it up to anyone except my dad—even to me. You never had a chance."

* * *

Nicholas and Teddy sailed on through the night, sharing steering duties, drinking foul-tasting coffee, and devouring an entire package of oatmeal cookies. When the rain finally let up, a little after two-thirty, and the last battalion of clouds had retreated to the east, the Big Dipper glistened in the black sky.

"Wow. And I thought the stars were bright *last* night," said Nicholas.

"It's nice with the power out," Teddy noted. "No lights onshore to interfere with them. The air is clear as can be, thanks to that storm. You know, they say that in Galileo's time—before air pollution and electric lights to mess things up—the Milky Way was so bright that it cast shadows on moonless nights. Can you imagine?"

Nicholas sat with his legs stretched out on the cockpit seat, his back pressed against the cabin house. Maybe it was because this shipwrecked sailor had been so honest with him, or maybe it was that he seemed so comfortable with a tiller in his hand, but Nicholas trusted Teddy completely—an idea that he would have found impossible to believe a few hours earlier. He closed his eyes—just for a second, he promised himself.

* * *

Nicholas threw his arm across the cockpit, grasping for the tiller. "I've got it!" he shouted as his eyes shot open and his body lurched up from the seat. A full second passed before the events of the night replayed in his mind and he remembered who that stranger at *Goblin*'s helm was. He rubbed the sleep out of his eyes, gazing with wonder at the stunning scene around him. The sun remained hidden behind the trees, but the sky to the east glowed in vivid shades of red, orange, and purple. Gone were the whitecaps of the long, stormy night, and in their place were sparkling ripples, each one seemingly dipped in gold.

As Teddy grinned at him, Nicholas got his first clear look at his sun- and windburned face and his laughing eyes, and he liked what he saw.

"Sorry," said Nicholas. "How long did I sleep? You must be ready for a break."

"Hey, no problem. I work the night shift over at the tool-and-die shop, so I'm a night owl anyway. And besides, I owe you. I'd still be swimming if it weren't for you."

"And *us*," added Hayley, suddenly appearing at the top of the companionway steps next to a very sleepy-looking Hetty.

"I stand corrected," said Teddy, laughing and doffing his cap at the twins. "I am forever in your debt, Your Highnesses. Now, if you look up ahead, you can see the yellow house where you left your friends behind. We'll be there in half an hour. So, how about you let me whip you up a nice breakfast. If there's any food left, that is."

"Oh, there's plenty of food," said Nicholas, sliding back to take the tiller from him. "Eggs, ham, cheese, bread—you name it, we've got it."

Teddy hoisted the twins into the cockpit and dropped down into the cabin. "Everybody like omelets?"

"Woof!" said Pistol.

* * *

At 4:30 a.m., Charlie was awakened by the sounds of twenty-eight cows, hungry and ready for their morning milking, which was already late getting started. She had slept next to the Kuerners' dog—whose name, appropriately enough, was Bear—a hulking, ninety-pound mutt with long black fur. As she lifted herself off the straw bales that had been her bed, she scratched her head and considered her options with the cows. They had to be milked, she knew that much. She also knew that she wasn't really qualified to do the entire job on her own. She'd *helped* her friends who lived on dairy farms milk plenty of times, but this was different. And calling somebody to come help at 4:36 wasn't really an option, she decided.

"What the heck happened to Nick?" she wondered aloud, deflecting answers she didn't want to contemplate—a car accident, a fallen tree blocking the road, or Mr. Kuerner's condition worsening.

When she turned on the lights inside the barn, the cows really came to life, clamoring for food, so she climbed into the hayloft and dropped a few bales through the opening. She then cut the strings and spread the loose hay throughout the mangers, hoping that by the time she finished, someone—anyone—would arrive to help her with the milking.

The sky outside was beginning to show signs of the coming day, but with no car headlights cutting through the mist hanging over the fields, Charlie turned into the pristine tiled milk house, where the milking equipment and the enormous refrigerated tank glistened. She breathed a sigh of relief when she saw that the milkers were the same type she was used to, so she prepared two and carried them to the far side of the barn to get the milking started.

At five-forty-five, Nick opened the barn door to the *tch-ka-tch-ka-tch-ka* of the milking machines, a sound he did not expect to hear.

"Charlie?" he called out.

On the opposite side of the barn, Charlie stood up from behind a cow, unplugged her milker, and lifted the heavy pail. "Over here!"

"What are you doing here? Why aren't you with the others on *Goblin*? Have you been here all night?" His eyes darted around the barn. "Are they here, too? Is everybody okay?"

"Yep. I slept over there on the straw bales with Bear," said Charlie. "I'm not sure where Nicholas and the twins are. I went looking for them once, but *Goblin* wasn't where she was supposed to be. They must have anchored somewhere else for the night. Where have you been, by the way? Is Mr. Kuerner okay?"

"I think so. When we got there last night, they sent him in for emergency surgery. Said his arteries were all blocked up. His wife was a wreck, so I had to stay with her, at least until they moved him into recovery. I called one of their neighbors—he said he'd come over and milk as soon as he finished his own cows." He looked around the barn admiringly. "But it looks like you've got things pretty much under control. Not that that surprises me— not one bit."

CHAPTER SIXTEEN

"There's Uncle Nick! And Charlie!" cried Hetty from *Goblin*'s foredeck, pointing at the dinghy inching toward them.

At the mention of Nick's name, Pistol raced to *Goblin*'s bow, where he watched the slow approach of the inflatable boat, howling all the while.

"Do you think he'll be mad, Nicholas?" Hayley asked.

"No, but we do have some explaining to do, I suppose. Maybe you should let me do the talking—especially since you two slept through most of it."

"He's going to be so relieved that you're all safe and relatively dry that I don't think you have to worry," said Teddy.

As the distance between *Goblin* and the dinghy dwindled, Hetty leaned out over the rail and cupped her hands to her mouth.

"We didn't mean to go to sea!" she shouted to Nick.

From his spot at the tiller, Nicholas scoffed. "You've been waiting all morning to say that, haven't you, Het?"

Teddy looked puzzled. "Inside joke?"

Nicholas nodded. "From this book Nick gave us." He turned *Goblin* into the wind, bringing her to a stop, and tapped Teddy on the shoulder. "Um, Teddy?"

"Yeah?"

"You see that girl in the dinghy? And remember when I told you that somebody was helping me figure out what happened with your old boat? Well, that's her. That's Charlie Brennan. Jimmy is her dad."

"I'll be darned. When you said the name Charlie before, it didn't even cross my mind that it might be Charlie Brennan. I should have known. Haven't seen her since she was yea high."

"Maybe we shouldn't say anything . . . you know, about what we talked about. I'll tell her later. It might be kind of weird for her, in front of everybody."

Teddy gestured zipping his lips shut and winked at Nicholas as Nick, who was rowing with his back to them, looked over his shoulder and got his second surprise of the day.

"We rescued a shipwrecked sailor!" Hayley announced.

"So I see," said Nick, not giving away his feelings on the matter.

For a moment, Nicholas feared that Nick was upset, but those fears were laid to rest when Nick looked up at Teddy and smiled.

"How are you, Teddy?"

"Better than I was a few hours ago. Took a direct hit—lightning—and was heading for Davy Jones's locker when this motley crew of yours came along. Just in the nick of time."

"Shouldn't that be the . . . *Nicholas* of time?" Hayley asked.

"Ha! Very clever, Hayley," said Teddy. "You have the brain of a writer, I think."

Hayley beamed. "You really think so?"

"Absolutely," Teddy answered, steadying the rope ladder and helping Nick and Charlie aboard. "These are some great kids, Nick. Handled *Goblin* like they've been doing it all their lives." He stuck out his hand to Charlie. "Hi there. I doubt if you remember me, but we're actually related. I'm Teddy Bradford."

Charlie's mouth dropped open. "No way."

"Ah, so you know who I am," Teddy said, grinning. "Let's see, your dad is my cousin, so that makes us second cousins, or first cousins once removed—I never really understood all that family-tree stuff."

Charlie's eyes met Nicholas's; he shrugged and smiled.

"It's been a long, strange night. It seems like we were out in that storm for a week."

"Well, take us home, Captain," said Nick, patting Nicholas on the back. "There's a nice breeze building, and it sounds like none of us got a decent night's sleep. I spent the night at the hospital—Mr. Kuerner had emergency bypass surgery, but it looks like he's going to be all right—and poor Charlie here milked a whole barnful of cows all by herself."

Nicholas aimed *Goblin*'s bow in the general direction of Nick's house. As her sails filled, she heeled a few degrees, and Nick, Charlie, and Teddy settled into the cockpit, trimming sails and sharing stories from their eventful night.

When they were alone in the cabin for a few minutes, Nicholas told Charlie about their near collision with the boat that he was certain he had seen once before, at 2:53 a.m. from his bedroom window.

"I can't believe you never told me about *that*," said Charlie. "What makes you so sure it was the same boat both times?"

"I'm not sure. I didn't get a really good look either time, but there was just something about it."

Charlie said nothing, but by the expression on her face, Nicholas knew she was skeptical.

"I know, I know," he said. "It doesn't make sense. I can't explain it, but the more I think about it, the more sure I am."

"So . . . assuming it was the same boat, who was it?"

Nicholas shrugged. "The *real* Seaweed Strangler, I guess."

* * *

An hour later, a very excited Hayley and Hetty, who had been stretched out on a beach towel on the foredeck, suddenly leaped to their feet and ran toward the stern.

"You guys won't believe this," Hayley started, "but you know how they say twins' brains are connected? Well, guess what—Hetty and I had the *exact* same dream last night."

"You're right," said Nicholas. "We don't believe you. In fact, I'm not sure I believe that you both even *have* brains."

Hayley stuck her tongue out at him. "Stop being a brat, Nicholas. It's true. And we think it was some kind of pre— . . . preno— . . . you know, when you see into the future."

"Premonition?" said Charlie.

"Yes! That's it," said Hayley. "In both of our dreams, the morning after the storm we were sailing back to Uncle Nick's—just like we're doing right now—and when we got there, guess who was waiting on the dock?"

"Daddy!" cried Hetty. "He was wearing that old red sweater that Mom tried to throw out. Remember, he was *so* mad? We both saw him. He must be back from Africa."

"He's going to be there, I just know it," said Hayley.

"Just because you had the same dream doesn't mean *anything*," said Nicholas. "Doesn't that story sound a little familiar?"

"What are you talking about?" Hayley asked.

"*We Didn't Mean to Go to Sea*," said Nicholas. "Remember? When they got to Holland, their father was standing on the deck of a ship about to leave for England."

Hetty waved off the coincidence. "That is *totally* different. Daddy's going to be there. I'll bet you anything."

"You're on," said Nicholas. "If Dad is waiting for us on the dock, I'll do the dinner dishes every night until we leave. If he's not, you two do them."

Hayley and Hetty scrunched up their faces, and moved back to the foredeck for a private discussion of the matter.

"One week," said Hayley, her arms crossed defiantly.

Nicholas nodded. "Deal. Uncle Nick, you heard that, right?"

Without opening his eyes, an exhausted Nick gave Nicholas the "okay" sign and then put his finger to his lips, signaling to everyone his desire for some much-needed sleep.

* * *

Goblin herself seemed eager to return to her mooring, and the rest of the journey down the length of the lake passed quickly, and quietly. As the sun rose higher and higher in the sky, and the band of explorers and their rescued shipmate got closer and closer to home, Hayley and Hetty kept their sharp young eyes peeled for signs of their father.

Hayley was about to admit defeat—to Hetty, but certainly *not* to Nicholas—when something caught her eye: a man in a red sweater, standing and waving at them from the end of Nick's dock.

"There he is!" Hayley yelled, leaping to her feet and raising Nick, Teddy, and poor Pistol from a deep sleep.

Nicholas squinted at the shoreline ahead. "No way."

"I see him, too," said Hetty. "And he's wearing the red sweater!"

"Hey, you're right—there *is* somebody there," Charlie said, joining the twins near the bow. "Sorry, Nicholas, but it looks like you've got some dishes to wash."

"I can't believe he's really here," said Hayley, waving wildly.

Charlie, with her better-than-perfect vision, zoomed in again on the man. "Wait a minute. That's not . . . Omigosh! That's not *your* dad—it's mine. What is *he* doing here?"

"Are you sure?" Hayley asked.

"Positive. Sorry, guys."

"I'm afraid she's right," added Teddy. "That's definitely Jimmy."

Nicholas pumped his fist. "Yes! I knew it couldn't be Dad. If he were back in the country, we would have heard from him—or Mom. Have fun washing those dishes!"

Jimmy Brennan waited patiently at the end of the dock as *Goblin*'s crew folded sails, coiled lines, and tidied up the sturdy little ship. Pistol, desperate to get ashore, started barking, so Nick gently lowered him into the water and let him dog-paddle in.

"How about lunch—and ice cream sundaes—at the diner? My treat," said Nick, not taking his eyes off Pistol until all four paws were on solid ground.

"That sounds so good," Charlie said, climbing into the dinghy. "I could really go for one of their cheeseburgers. And a big order of onion rings."

"Well, you're welcome to join us," said Nick. He clambered down the rope ladder. "Your dad might have other plans, though. He'd probably like to spend some time with just you."

Charlie shrugged. "Yeah, I suppose you're right."

"You don't sound very enthusiastic."

Another shrug. "My dad . . . doesn't always make it easy for me to get excited about seeing him. He's not exactly . . . reliable, if you know what I mean. He's always busy with his other kids."

"That doesn't mean he doesn't love you, too. Give the man a chance, Charlie. It takes some people a little longer than others to figure out what's important." He pulled hard on the oars, propelling the dinghy toward the dock.

Jimmy reached out to take the bowline as they came to a stop.

Charlie refused the hand he offered her and pulled herself up and onto the dock under her own power before giving her father an indifferent hug. "Hey, Dad. What are you doing here?"

"Nice to see you, too, kiddo. Hiya, Nick. It's been a while. I hope you were all anchored someplace quiet last night; that was some storm."

"Not exactly," said Nick. "But we all made it back. Even picked up a hitchhiker along the way. You recognize that guy standing in the cockpit?"

Jimmy shielded his eyes from the sun's glare with his hand and gazed out at *Goblin*. "Holy mackerel—is that my cousin Teddy? I haven't seen him in . . . years. You say you picked him up? What happened?"

"His boat got hit by lightning," said Charlie. "I didn't actually get to see it, but Nicholas said it sank like a stone. Pretty cool, huh?"

"Uh, yeah, I guess. Who's Nicholas?"

"That's him out there. And those are his sisters— they're twins. You used to know their dad."

"Oh yeah? Who's that?"

"Will Mettleson."

The color drained from Jimmy's face as his gaze shifted from Charlie to Nick, and then to Nicholas, who stood at *Goblin*'s stern, about to dive in.

"Will," he whispered.

"He's a doctor now," said Nick, climbing back into the dinghy to retrieve the twins. "He's in Africa for the summer on a humanitarian mission, and the kids are spending some time with old Uncle Nick—just like Will used to do. Funny, isn't it, how things work out in life."

"It *is* strange, isn't it?" Charlie pondered aloud. "I mean, you, Nicholas, me, Nick . . . this Teddy guy sinking *another* boat. Weird."

"So you know about the other boat, huh?" Jimmy asked. "I guess that makes sense, you spending time with Nick and all."

"I know *most* of the story. I do have a few questions for *you*, though."

Jimmy eyed his daughter suspiciously. "There's not much to tell. And it was a long time ago, so I doubt I remember many of the details. It was a shame about Will, though. I liked him." Anxious to change the subject, he awkwardly mussed her hair. "But listen, kiddo, the reason I came by—I thought you might like to stay with us at the farm for a few days. I talked to your mom and it's okay with her, but she says it's up to you. What do you think?"

"Right . . . n-n-now?" Charlie stammered.

"Sure, why not? The kids barely know you, and they're always asking about their big sister."

"*Step*sister. And why do they want to know me?"

Jimmy laughed. "That's a good question. I can't

imagine. I think they just like the idea of having a big sister to talk to about, you know, girl stuff. Come on—it'll be fun."

Charlie knew it was wrong, but she really didn't want to go. September, and Nicholas's inevitable return to New York, loomed ahead, a threatening cloud on the horizon speeding toward her. There was so much to do before Labor Day weekend! As she watched Nicholas swimming toward the dock, her father followed her eyes.

"Are you and Nicholas . . . you know—"

"No! Dad! We're just friends."

"Okay, okay. Sorry. I just thought maybe that's why you don't want—"

"Well, that's not it. Jeez. Hey, Nicholas, come on up here."

After a summer of swimming and sailing together, Nicholas had gotten over most of his self-consciousness about going shirtless around Charlie, but at that moment he still wished for a T-shirt to magically appear. When that didn't happen, he had no choice but to climb onto the dock, where he stood dripping, his arms folded across his chest.

After the introductions, Charlie pulled Nicholas aside and hit him with her news. "Dad wants me to come out to the farm with him for a few days."

Nicholas's heart sank; he, too, was all too aware of how fast the summer seemed to be zooming by. "A few *days?* Wow. Well, I guess that could be fun." He didn't really think so, but it seemed like the polite thing to say at that moment. "I've never seen an ostrich up close."

"It's no big deal, believe me," said Charlie. "They're like chickens, only bigger. I know I should *want* to go—he's my dad and all—but I really don't want to."

"It's only for a few days."

"Yeah, but what about the movie? We still have a *lot* of work to do. I've never edited a movie before. I have no idea how long it's going to take. And what if we have to—"

"Stop worrying. It'll be fine."

Charlie made a pouty face. "But summer's almost over. You'll be going back to New York, and I'll probably never see you again."

"That is not going to happen. I'm probably coming back next summer."

"*Probably?* So that means you might not."

"It just means I haven't even thought about it yet—that's all."

"Well, you'd better start. After all the work we did on *Imp*, and the movie, and . . . everything else. And you still haven't gotten a decent hit off me yet," she teased.

Nicholas winced. It was true; she still struck him out almost every time he faced her. Occasionally, he hit a weak grounder or a short pop-up, but he had yet to really "light one up"—to get a clear, undeniable hit. He knew that the law of averages was on his side, but sometimes he couldn't help wondering just how long his streak might go on. She was one tough pitcher, no doubt about it.

But there's more to life than baseball, Nicholas reasoned. And he knew that the way he had handled *Goblin* in that storm counted for *something*. He had seen the look of pride in Nick's eyes when Teddy told him the story of the rescue operation.

"I don't care if it takes until November, I'm not going back to New York until I knock something out of the infield, Brennan."

"November? I could keep you here through the winter if I wanted to, *Mettleson*. And winters are *long* here in Ohio."

"So, are you ready to go?" asked Jimmy, standing behind Charlie. "We'll make a quick stop at your mom's so you can pack and . . . shower, maybe."

"Dad! Are you saying I stink?"

Jimmy pinched his nose shut and grinned at Nicholas. "No, not at all."

"I can't help it. I spent the night in a barn."

"You can tell me the whole story on the way," said Jimmy. "After you shower." He put his arm around Charlie's shoulders and started to lead her away.

"Um, before you go, can I talk to you—for just one more second?" Nicholas asked.

Charlie broke away from Jimmy's grip. "Give me a minute, Dad. I'll meet you at the car—I promise."

Nicholas waited until Jimmy was a few steps away, and

spoke in a low voice. "Listen, Charlie, there's something I need to tell you. Last night, I found out a few things from Teddy . . . about what happened with his first boat. I wasn't sure I should tell you, but if it were the other way around, I would want to know. At least I think I would. You have to promise me you won't be mad."

"Nicholas! Just tell me!"

"You may not like it. Although I guess it shouldn't be a huge surprise. . . ."

"Nicholas!"

He breathed deeply and told her, in abbreviated form, Teddy's version of the events of that fateful morning at the marina.

"So, my dad is the villain of the story after all," Charlie said with a heavy sigh. "Not that I'm surprised. Ever since we saw that old film, I knew it was him. I just don't understand *why* he did it, or why he didn't stick up for *your* dad. Some friend."

"Maybe there's still something we don't know," said Nicholas. "You'd better get going. Call me tomorrow, okay?"

"I will. *After* I talk to my dad."

* * *

After long, and very welcome, hot showers, Nicholas and the twins called their mom in New York and shared the highlights—but not all the scary details—of their thrilling voyage around the lake. Then, with the exception of Pistol, who was ready for a little "alone time," the Mettlesons, old and young, piled into Betty for the trip into Deming. Over a celebratory lunch of burgers, chicken nuggets, fries, and Cokes, they toasted *Goblin* for getting them through the long, stormy night without so much as a scratch.

Three hot fudge sundaes later (Hayley and Hetty shared one), Nick raised his glass one more time. "I want to thank you kids. I'll be honest, when your dad first talked to me about your coming out for the summer, I wasn't sure. I didn't know you at all, and with your folks' divorce and all, well, I didn't know what to expect. But it's been one of the best summers ever, and I'm pretty sure you've added ten years to my life. So . . . toast yourselves. To the Mettlesons!"

"TO THE METTLESONS!" the kids screamed.

"Does this mean we can come back next summer?" Hetty asked.

Nick laughed. "We'll have to talk to your parents about that. I suspect that your mom is getting a little lonely about now. But if it's okay with them, it's okay with me."

"Yay!" shouted Hayley and Hetty.

Nicholas didn't say a word, but he couldn't help smiling.

* * *

Back at Uncle Nick's house!

August 9
Dear Dad,
    Well, our peaceful trip around the lake turned into kind of a crazy adventure. Now I really understand why they call it Godforsaken Lake! Sailed all night through a wild storm and saw some things I'll never forget. Funny how many of my questions got answered in one night—and how many new ones I have.

                                    Love,
                                    Nicholas

CHAPTER SEVENTEEN

When Charlie called Nicholas the next day, she had nothing to report. She admitted—reluctantly—that she was having fun at her dad's farm. Her stepsisters, Jenny and Cindy, just five and seven, were cute, and they practically *worshiped* her.

"What about your stepmom?" Nicholas asked. He knew that Charlie had resisted getting to know her, purely out of stubbornness.

"Linda? She's actually not so bad," Charlie confessed. "She's kind of funny. And she's nice. She's a lousy cook, though. No wonder my dad is still so skinny. We had this stuff for dinner; I'm not even sure what it was. Some kind of tuna casserole. Really bad."

"What about your dad? Did you . . . talk to him yet?"

"No. He was so happy that I came with him, I just couldn't bear to spoil it for him. Not yet, anyway. Maybe tomorrow."

But the next day, and the day after that, came and went, and Charlie still hadn't confronted her dad.

"I'll do it tomorrow," Charlie said. "Dad and I are taking the horses for a long ride. We'll have lots of time to talk, away from the kids. How's *The Seaweed Strangler* coming along?"

"Okay. At least I think so. I'm getting the hang of the editing program. I put a few scenes together, and it's actually starting to look like a movie. The old film is so scratchy and grainy compared to the new stuff that it's not that hard to believe it's been sitting out in the rain and sun on an island for a few years."

"Well, save some of the work for me. You have to teach me how to do it, too."

"Don't worry—there's still a ways to go. The twins are getting excited about it. They say we have to have a big premiere party, like they do in Hollywood. They asked Uncle Nick if he had a red carpet. Like he had one sitting up in the barn waiting for a special occasion. He told them they could paint a long sheet of paper red."

"That's a great idea—the party, I mean. We can invite everybody from the neighborhood. Maybe your mom can come out from New York. Too bad your dad's still in Africa. He's the one who really *ought* to see it.

It was his idea, after all. Do we have time to finish the movie?"

"Oh, sure. I mean, it's not going to win an Academy Award or anything, but it will be done. You're coming back the day after tomorrow, right? I can't wait . . . you know, so you can see what I've done so far. We can let the twins plan the party; it will make them feel important."

"Maybe we should have a theme. You know, like food made with seaweed or something."

"Or . . . not. How about hot dogs?"

"What does that have to do with anything?"

"Nothing. I just like hot dogs."

* * *

Charlie, who preferred to ride English rather than Western, sat high in her saddle aboard Patches, a four-year-old Appaloosa, following her dad down a trail that ran along the ostrich pasture. At the far end of the property, they continued on, crossing a creek and a dirt road, then climbing a slight grade to a neighbor's pasture, where they let themselves in through a wooden gate.

"Are we allowed to go in here?" Charlie asked. "Isn't this somebody's property?"

"It's okay," said Jimmy. "The owner's a friend. I let his kids ride across our pastures. There's a big oak tree up at the top of the hill—it's a perfect place to stop for a picnic lunch. Come on, I'll race you." He gave his horse a little

At the far end of the property, they continued on, crossing a creek and a
dirt road, then climbing a slight grade to a neighbor's pasture, where they let
themselves in through a wooden gate.

nudge with his heel and cantered up the trail. Charlie, never one to turn away from a contest of any kind, pressed her heels down in the stirrups, leaned out over the horse's neck, and urged her into a canter. She caught and passed Jimmy easily, opening up into a gallop as their destination came into view.

As Charlie pulled back on the reins to slow Patches to a walk, she couldn't help marveling at the picturesque scene before her. "Big" didn't do the oak tree justice; it was *enormous*, its trunk the size of her bedroom, its branches creating enough shade to protect a small army from the sun. It stood alone at the summit, the winner of a game of king of the hill, after which all the other trees fled in embarrassment.

Her dad brought his horse to a stop beside her a few seconds later and dropped out of his saddle. "Not a bad view, huh?"

"It's like something out of a movie," said Charlie.

"Believe it or not, I first found this place when I was just a little bit older than you. This farm used to be a stable where you could rent horses. When we were in high school, your mom and I used to come out here to ride all the time. I think we imagined that we were the only people who knew about it. It was *our* tree, our special little place."

For the first time in her life, Charlie felt sorry for her dad. He seemed sad, looking back on that part of his life, knowing that it was gone forever.

Jimmy led the two horses into the shade, where he loosely tied the reins to an iron ring nailed into the trunk of the oak and set his backpack on the ground. After spreading out a fleece blanket, he pulled out two sandwiches, a bag of carrot sticks, and a thermos filled with homemade lemonade. He handed a sandwich to Charlie. "Egg salad okay?"

She raised a single eyebrow. "Ostrich eggs?"

"Ha! No, just ordinary chickens. You're a funny kid, Charlie. You get that from your mom."

"Really? I don't think we're that much alike."

"You're not exactly like her, but sometimes you say something, or get this look on your face, that just . . . well, it kind of freaks me out, to be honest."

"You know, it's funny," said Charlie. "Mom had the same reaction when she met Nicholas the first time."

Jimmy chewed his sandwich slowly as his sad smile returned.

"Dad?"

"Mmm."

"Back when you and Mom were kids, and—"

"You want to know about me and Will, don't you?"

"Well, I do have some questions." She told him about Nicholas finding the movie in the tower room, their discovery of the tampered-with steering cables, and the film that was shot the day Teddy's boat sank. "And in that horrible storm, when Nicholas rescued Teddy, the final pieces of the puzzle came together."

Jimmy listened silently as the realization that the time had come for him to clear his conscience once and for all sank in.

"The other day, when I saw Teddy standing out there on Nick's boat, and then you introduced me to Will's kid, I was actually relieved. I don't know how—maybe it was the way you looked at me—but I *knew* you had figured out that I had something to do with Will leaving."

"But . . . why?" Charlie asked. "You guys were friends."

"That's easy. Love. Jealousy. A combination of those two will make people do all kinds of crazy things. I fell in love with your mom in the third grade. I was just a kid, but she was all I ever thought about. And even though Will was only around in the summers, he was my best friend. But then . . ."

"He and Mom."

"Exactly. Watching the two of them spend more and more time together, the way she looked at him—it just ate away at me. I had to do *something* to break them apart. So, at fourteen, I sacrificed the best friend I ever had so I could have her to myself. It was the worst thing I ever did, and even though I ended up married to her, and got you as part of the bargain, I have felt guilty every day of my life since. I know that I can never make up for what happened, and it can't change what's already happened, but I am sorry—you have to believe that, Charlie."

Charlie threw her arms around him. "It's okay, Dad, really. It was all a long time ago. Nicholas and I have already agreed—we're not going to say anything to Mom or his dad. Like you said, it won't change anything. And who knows, even though you and Mom didn't last forever, you two must have been meant to get together. I mean, if you hadn't, *I* wouldn't be here, right?"

Blinking back tears—the first Charlie had ever seen in his eyes—Jimmy smiled. "Thanks, Charlie. You're the best."

"And you know, Dad, you have a *great* family, and we all love you . . . and your stupid ostriches."

He nodded. "How did you get to be so smart, anyway?"

"Simple. I got my brains from Mom," Charlie said, grinning mischievously. "Now come on—I'll race you back to the barn."

* * *

The days following Charlie's return from her dad's farm were a blur of activity in and around Nick's house. Finishing *The Seaweed Strangler* became the top priority for Nicholas and Charlie, but they were also determined to spend as much time as possible sailing *Imp* and *Goblin* before the three Mettleson kids boarded the train to New York. And so, days were spent sailing, biking, swimming, playing baseball, and shooting the final scenes, while evenings were devoted to editing and adding the sound track and other final details to the movie, and planning the "world premiere" extravaganza that Hetty and Hayley had dreamt up. No one argued about bedtimes; by nine-thirty, they were all exhausted, and when the lights went out, sleep came instantly.

Hayley and Hetty, the official co-hostesses for the movie's premiere, created and printed invitations using Charlie's computer, and then addressed, stamped, and mailed them to everyone on the guest list for the party, which had morphed into an end-of-summer barbecue *and* movie premiere. As the days rushed past, that list somehow grew from a few names to more than thirty as Nick reached out to friends and neighbors, and Charlie invited Little League teammates and a handful of friends from school.

Franny, obviously, would be there, and even volunteered to help Nick with the food. On the way back from the ostrich farm, Charlie had tried to persuade her dad to come, too, but he admitted that, under the circumstances, it would just be too uncomfortable. Instead, he made Charlie promise to bring a copy of the movie the next time she came to stay at the farm.

And then, just two days before the party, Jo Mettleson called to tell Nicholas that she wouldn't be able to make it, either. She was swamped at work, and even a quick trip to Ohio was out of the question at the moment.

"Besides, you three will be back here in no time at all," she reminded him.

The twins were very disappointed, but her promise of a surprise that would arrive the day of the party—which kept them busy guessing for several hours that afternoon—seemed to take away some of the sting of disappointment.

"I'll bet it's a cake," said Nicholas, in an attempt to end the debate. "She has that friend who makes those crazy cakes—you know, the ones that look really cool, but don't taste very good."

"Do you really think so?" Charlie asked. "We already have dessert. Mom just bought a million blueberries—she knows how much you and Nick love her blueberry pies."

"No such thing as too much dessert," said Nicholas.

Nick looked at him like a proud father. "Amen," he said with a pat on the back.

* * *

The day of the party finally arrived.

Charlie and Nicholas had declared the movie complete the night before and burned the final copy onto a DVD, toasting their achievement with ginger ale.

"We did it," said Nicholas. "Hard to believe it was only a few weeks ago that I found that old can of film in Dad's hiding place."

"I know—it seems like I've been striking you out forever," Charlie said, giving him a good-natured punch on the upper arm.

"The summer's not over yet."

"That's what I like best about you, Nicholas—you're an optimist, even when you have no reason to be."

"I don't know; I think today might be the day."

"Are you serious? Let's go. Right now. I'll get my glove. Hey, Nick!" she shouted down the stairs. "Meet us out at the barn in five minutes. Nicholas wants me to strike him out. *Again*."

Nicholas couldn't help laughing at her confidence as he grabbed his bat and followed her out into the yard. "One of these days, Brennan."

But not *this* day. She caught him off guard with a first-pitch curve for a called strike, and then, after fouling off the next two pitches, he struck out on a knee-high fast-ball.

"Hang in there, Nicholas," said Nick. "You're getting good looks at the ball. You're going to make good contact. Just a matter of time."

* * *

At noon, the local florist delivered a huge bouquet of daisies with a card addressed to Hayley and Hetty.

To my favorite movie stars, Hayley and Hetty, and their talented director, Nicholas: So sorry I can't be there with you tonight. Break a leg!

Love, Mom

PS There's one more BIG surprise on the way.

"They're lovely," said Hetty, reverting to her British accent.

"Quite," Hayley agreed. "*Another* surprise? Maybe that will be the cake. I hope it's not chocolate."

The first guests—Zack, Joey, and Kirk, also known as the Three Stooges—arrived a few minutes after five, followed by Ryan Crenshaw, another of Charlie's teammates. Nicholas smiled to himself as he remembered the first time he saw Ryan flail wildly at one of Charlie's curveballs and end up in a heap on the ground. He, at least, had never looked *that* bad against Charlie. Meanwhile, Pistol barked his own greetings, and Hayley and Hetty stuck name tags on the boys and pointed them all toward the enormous bowls of Franny's secret-recipe guacamole and chips waiting on the folding tables that lined the shore in front of Nick's house.

Next to arrive were Mrs. Bishop and her son, Mikey.

"Is Will here?" he asked, over and over. "Will is my friend."

"Sorry, Mikey," said Nicholas. "He couldn't be here today. But I'm sure he'll come soon to thank you for what you did."

As the party got under way, Charlie and Nicholas took on bartending duties, while Nick, wearing a pristine white apron, built two fires—one in a stone-lined pit on the narrow beach, to be used for marshmallow roasting and s'more making after the movie, and the other in a large grill that he'd constructed out of an old fifty-five-gallon steel drum. When the coals were ready, he set to work, cooking rows and rows of hamburgers, hot dogs, and chicken to accompany the potato salad, sweet corn, and fresh-picked green beans that Franny had prepared.

As the sun dropped lower and lower in the sky and the screening time drew close, the twins, fueled by too much soda, could barely contain their excitement and actually started cleaning up—without being asked! Nicholas and Charlie, growing more anxious by the minute, set up the big-screen TV and DVD player (on loan from the owner of Deming Appliance, yet another friend of Nick's) in the living room, checking and double-checking that everything was just perfect.

At seven-forty-five, Hetty made her way through the crowd, ringing a little bell as Pistol helped herd the crowd toward the house. Once they were inside, they sat wherever they could—squeezing onto the couch, the matching wing chairs, and the dining-room chairs that had been moved for the occasion—with the younger audience members sitting Indian-style on the floor. The twins stood before everyone, and at the stroke of eight, Hetty rang her bell once again.

Hayley stepped forward and read from a yellow index card. "Ladies and gentlemen! Welcome to the *world* premiere of *The Seaweed Strangler*!" She waited for the cheering and applause to die down before continuing. "Before I introduce the directors, let's all thank my uncle Nick and Charlie's mom, Franny Brennan, for cooking all that food."

More applause and cheering, followed by Hetty, reading from her index card. "And we want to thank our dad, who started this movie a *long* time ago." She added, proudly, "He's not here today because he's a doctor, and right now he's in Africa, helping people."

Nicholas cleared his throat. "C'mon, Hetty. Hurry up."

"Oh, fine," she said, sighing dramatically. "And now it is our pleasure to introduce the people who *finished* the movie, Miss Charlie Brennan and Mr. Nicholas Mettleson!"

Charlie spoke first, blushing at the attention. From her baseball career, she was used to people cheering her, but not from *inches* away. "Hey, everybody—thanks again for coming. Especially you, Mom—you're the best. I just hope you all like the movie. It was a lot of fun working with Nicholas. We both . . . learned a lot this summer, I think. Um, that's all. Your turn, Nicholas."

Nicholas forced himself to look up from his shoelaces. Desperate to avoid making eye contact with anyone, he focused on the wall behind the audience. "Um, hi, everybody. I really don't have anything to—" He stopped midsentence, his mouth hanging open in utter disbelief. "*Dad?*"

Thirty heads spun around to see Will Mettleson leaning against the door frame, a wry smile on his face.

"Daddy!" screamed the twins as they raced to him

and launched themselves into his arms. He lifted them, squeezing tightly as they buried their faces in his chest.

Nicholas, momentarily forgetting his personal rule against public displays of affection, rushed to this thinner, tanner, and bearded version of his father and threw his arms around him.

"What are you doing here? I thought you were going to be in Africa for two more weeks."

"Got a reprieve. Things weren't as bad as we'd feared, and on top of that, my replacement showed up a couple of weeks early. Besides, I heard that Hayley and Hetty were throwing a party." He winked at Nicholas.

"How *did* you know about the party?" Nicholas asked. "Oh. Mom."

Will nodded. "I was able to get ahold of her from Amsterdam the day before yesterday. But look, I'm interrupting—you were right in the middle of a speech."

"Under the circumstances, I think they'll understand if we're a few minutes late getting started," said Nick, reaching out to shake his nephew's hand. "Good to see you, Will. Been a while."

Will glanced around the room, taking it all in. "Too long. The house still looks exactly the way I remembered it. Just perfect."

"There's someone else here who's probably a little surprised to see you," said Nick as he gently nudged Nicholas aside.

Will's eyes met Franny's in a moment right out of a

1940s movie. She smiled up at him from her spot on the couch, her eyes sparkling.

His lips formed her name, but no sound came out.

"Hi, Will," she said.

With every eye in the room on them, Will and Franny glided silently across the room toward one another, coming to a stop just a few feet apart.

"Franny," Will repeated, his voice still barely a whisper.

She moved in close, her arms held wide, and hugged him; it was the hug of two old friends—heartfelt, but colored by a thin glaze of regret.

"I always knew you'd come back," she whispered.

When they pulled apart, Charlie was at her mother's side. Franny put her arm around Charlie's shoulders and pulled her close. "This is Charlie. She's my baby. She has a sister, Natalie, who's in her second year at Hiram. Charlie and your Nicholas here are quite a team."

Will stood openmouthed, first looking at Charlie, then turning to Nicholas. "Wait. *This* is the Charlie you've been writing about all summer? You know, you never mentioned that Charlie is a girl, Nicholas. I'm sorry to stare, Charlie. I just assumed you were . . ."

"Nope—sorry," said Charlie. "I'm a girl."

"No, no, don't apologize. I didn't mean . . . It just never occurred to me that Nicholas was spending so much time with . . . Look, I'm pleased to meet you, Charlie. Thanks for showing Nicholas around this summer. Sounds like he was in very good hands. And I can't wait to see this movie," he added, pointing to the banner that the twins had hung over the fireplace.

"I can't believe you never told him about me," said Charlie, poking Nicholas in the side. "Actually, Nicholas did most of the work on the movie. Almost all the ideas—the good ones, anyway—were his."

"It was a team effort," said Nicholas, struggling not to blush. "Charlie—and the twins—everybody helped."

Suddenly, Mikey appeared at Will's side, tugging on his shirt. "Hi, Will."

Will recognized him immediately, and his eyes lit up. "Mikey Bishop. My gosh. You haven't changed a bit." He held out his hand, which Mikey shook and shook, stopping only when Mrs. Bishop put her hand on her son's shoulder.

"Let him go, Mikey," she said. "You can talk to him later. Right now I think he wants to talk to his own children."

Will smiled, grateful for her intervention, and then held up a hand. "Look here—everybody—we can all catch up later. I've disrupted things long enough. The show must go on, as they say. I'm pretty sure I'm not the only one who wants to see this movie." The audience cheered in agreement, so he playfully shoved Nicholas to the front of the room and then joined Franny on the couch.

Nicholas took a few seconds to collect himself before starting over. "Ummm . . . so, before we get started, I was just going to say that my dad started this movie when he was fourteen, but never got to finish it because he had some, um, 'equipment problems.' When I found it, I didn't know any of that, but over the past few weeks, well, Charlie and I learned a *lot* of stuff about what happened back then, and that made us even more determined to finish it. Dad, I know it's not exactly the movie you were making, but I hope you like it anyway."

Charlie turned off the lights and hit PLAY on the DVD player. The crowd clapped and cheered as Will's original footage, announcing the title of the movie in enormous seaweed letters, flickered on the screen:

The Seaweed Strangler

CHAPTER EIGHTEEN

The first scene, in which the man in the rowboat shoots and injures the poor creature, appeared exactly as Will had remembered it, but from that point forward, *The Seaweed Strangler* was Nicholas's film. Will was astonished by what he saw. His son had incorporated the grainy 8 mm film into an entirely new story, artfully intercutting the original scenes with crisp, clear video starring the twins, Charlie, Nick, and himself.

Instead of watching the movie for the umpteenth time, Nicholas watched his father's reactions. Out of the corner of his eye, he saw Will smile at the scene in which the (improbably young) twin archaeologists discover a long-lost reel of film in the tower room at Nick's house—in

Will's old hiding place behind the paneling. And, as the "missing scene" (from the camera that Mikey had cared for all those years) began to unfold, Will cringed when he saw himself aboard Teddy's boat, helpless as it plowed onto the rocks. It was the first time he, or anyone else in the room besides Nicholas and Charlie, had seen those images, and the look on his face was one of utter confusion. He turned to see Nicholas grinning slyly at him.

"How on earth did you . . . ?" Will asked, palms facing the ceiling.

Nicholas gave him a little shrug and a smile.

The audience oohed and aahed when the action moved aboard *Goblin* for the voyage into "the perilous, uncharted waters of the north," as Charlie's character described it. Nicholas, who did the filming, revealed an artistic side that even he didn't know he had. He captured the beauty of the little ship silhouetted against an evening sky of purple and orange, sails slicing through the growing darkness until all was black and only the sound of water rushing by the hull remained.

Hetty was unable to contain her excitement any longer. "Omigosh—we're coming to the best part. This is so cool."

"Shhh!" said Hayley. "Don't ruin the surprise."

As morning breaks over *Goblin* and nearby Onion Island, the young archaeologists row ashore, with filmmaker Charlie tagging along, determined to be the first to actually film the Seaweed Strangler—and survive. After searching the island for several days, they finally find signs of their old friend, the professor who was obsessed with the creature—and who had disappeared on his most recent expedition. First, they find a pocketknife bearing the professor's initials, and a little later, they notice something hanging from a tree branch. It is his backpack—the one that he *always* carried with him. With sad faces, they pull out his journal and a small camera.

Hayley reads the journal entry in which the professor described the creature eating the raw fish and wrote about going deeper into the woods, and then hands the journal to Hetty.

"I'm afraid this may be all that's left of the professor," Hetty adds, looking directly into Charlie's camera. "What do we do now?"

"We owe it to him to continue his work," says Hayley.

Hetty, meanwhile, flips through the professor's journal. "Wait! Listen. This is his *final* entry: *As a scientist, I am compelled to carry on with my research—to learn all I can about these strange and wonderful human beings (and they are human, let there be no mistake about that) and to tell the world about them. But after spending two weeks observing them, I have arrived at a very different conclusion: they deserve to be left alone. They are peaceful and resourceful and have lived on this remote island for hundreds, if not thousands, of years. Yes, they have acted violently on occasion,* but ONLY *when provoked by other humans. Therefore, I have made the decision to return to the university and announce that my expedition was a failure—that the creatures do NOT exist—with the sincere hope that my announcement will bring an end to any further investigation of the mystery.*"

Hetty looks into the camera. "Blimey. Well, that settles it. We're going home."

Cue the ominous music.

"Not so fast," says Charlie, holding a pistol on the two young adventurers. "Nobody's going anywhere. Now, if you don't mind, I'll take that journal and the backpack."

Hetty takes a step toward her. "Have you lost your bloody mind? Put that gun down."

"I don't think so," Charlie says, pointing it at Hetty's chest. "I killed the professor, and I'm willing to kill you."

Hayley explodes. "*You* killed the professor? But . . . why? When?"

"Because he went soft on me. We could have made millions, taking the Seaweed Strangler—alive—back to civilization. I was with your precious professor on his last expedition, and everything was going great. Then one morning he tells me we're going back, and we're going to tell the world— Well, you read the stupid journal."

"But why did you have to *kill* him?" Hayley asks. "He was a good man. A *great* man."

"He knew things about me that no one else knew.

Things that would ruin me. And he threatened to reveal them if I didn't go along with his story. My career would have been ruined. But when I was chasing him, he tossed his backpack into the woods and I couldn't find it. It wasn't just the camera that I wanted. His journal contained all his notes, including how to find this place. I'm no sailor; I knew I could never find it again on my own, even though I somehow managed to find my way back to civilization without him the last time."

"I think I get it now," says Hetty. "You knew *we* would find it. Hayley and Hetty Mettleson *always* find what they're looking for, right?"

"Precisely," says Charlie with an evil grin. "When I heard you were on the trail of the professor, I pretended to work for that cable channel so I could tag along. And now here we are. These are enough to make me rich." She holds up the camera and journal.

"What about . . . us?" Hayley asks.

"Two more missing adventurers. The world will hardly notice."

As Charlie aims her gun at Hayley, her finger on the trigger, a twig snaps in the thick brush behind her. She spins around and finds herself face to face with the Seaweed Strangler, played by a glaring, snarling, sort of terrifying-looking Nicholas. Before she can pull the trigger, however, he snatches the gun from her hand and throws it deep into the woods. Hayley and Hetty watch in horror as the creature wraps a coil of seaweed around her neck. Charlie's body slowly goes limp and drops to the ground in a heap.

"Uh-oh," says Hayley as the Seaweed Strangler slowly turns to face her.

"Should we run for it?" Hetty asks.

"No! No sudden moves. Keep your hands up where he can see them."

The Strangler stands perfectly still, only his eyes moving—from Hayley to Hetty and then back again to Hayley. After twenty seconds of staring down the two girls, he reaches out and ever so gently touches Hayley's cheek. She resists the urge to scream and looks him directly in the eyes. He takes one small step back, touches his chest with his open palm, and then disappears into the woods.

In the movie's final scene, the twins are back home, where they place the professor's journal, his camera, and Charlie's camera in a large iron safe. (Nick just happened to have an old one in his barn.)

"Are you sure about this?" Hetty asks.

"We're doing the right thing," says Hayley. "When I looked deep into the eyes of the Seaweed Strangler, I saw kindness and gentleness—not the monster that everyone assumes his kind to be. He deserves to be left alone. The professor was right. We owe it to him to honor his final wish."

Hetty nods in agreement. "But what will we tell everyone?"

"We'll think of something," Hayley says. "We always do."

She closes the safe, and the screen goes black, followed by:

The End?

* * *

"Bravo!" shouted Nick as the final credits came to a stop. Everyone else joined in, and much cheering, hand shaking, back patting, hair mussing, and picture taking followed.

Nicholas was hailed as the next Steven Spielberg, while Charlie and the twins were assured by all that their performances were worthy of Academy Awards and, quite possibly, Nobel Prizes.

"Dad deserves at least half the credit," said Nicholas. "I mean, it was his idea in the first place."

"He's just being modest," said Charlie. "Seriously, I think he's some kind of genius or something. I was at my dad's for a few days, and when I came back, he almost had the whole thing put together."

"Like father, like son," Franny said, with a nod in Will's direction.

Will chuckled, pulling Nicholas close to him. "I'm even in the same league with this guy."

Hetty reminded everyone that it was time for dessert—blueberry pie and s'mores down at the beach. "C'mon, Daddy, I'll show you how to make s'mores."

The party moved down to the shore, where Nick stoked the beach fire with new wood. In minutes, it was perfect for roasting marshmallows. Not a single cloud obstructed the stars as the adults settled into beach chairs and the kids sat on towels on the warm sand.

"Touch of fall in the air tonight," Nick said to Will and Franny, who had decades of catching up to do. "But you couldn't ask for a prettier night."

The three of them clinked glasses.

"No place like the lake," said Will. "I've missed this place."

A few feet away, Nicholas and Charlie set up an assembly line to manufacture s'mores for the younger kids. As Nicholas pressed the graham crackers down on the last bunch, Charlie nudged him in the ribs.

"So, my mom and your dad seem pretty happy to see each other, don't you think?"

"Oh jeez. I *knew* you were going to say something."

"Yeah, but I'm right, aren't I? Look at them. It's like they were never apart. Do you think she told him about the letter yet?"

Nicholas shook his head. "I doubt it. They're probably just talking about us. Parents love to brag about their kids."

Charlie's mouth suddenly dropped open as she

looked out at Nick's dock. "Oh no! Nicholas! Where's *Imp?*" She was about to start for the dock when he grabbed her arm.

"Shhh! She's safe. I moved her—so my dad wouldn't see her until tomorrow. When I remembered that we would be coming back down here, I snuck out for a minute after the movie was over and moved her over to the far side of Mr. Jensen's dock. I want it to be a surprise tomorrow."

Charlie put her hand over her heart. "Whew! I was scared there for a second. Good thinking! You remember what Mom's letter said?"

"I remember. So you have to get your mom to come back here in the morning. Say, ten o'clock. We can surprise them both."

* * *

An hour later, Will tucked the twins into their bed, said good night to Nick, and rejoined Nicholas on the beach in the glow of the slowly dwindling fire.

"I'm really proud of you, Nicholas, and not just because of the movie, which really was amazing, by the way. It's hard for me to believe I was only away for two months. You seem two *years* older. And I have a feeling I haven't even scratched the surface of what you've been up to. Am I right?"

Nicholas smiled. "There's a little more, I guess. You'll see."

Will leaned back in his chair and looked up at the moon, which was peeking around the edge of a line of fast-moving clouds. "I was thinking about you the other night," he said. "It was a couple of weeks ago, I suppose. The days all run together after a while. I'd been up all night with a boy—a little younger than you, no family. He had malaria and was in pretty rough shape. He finally fell asleep at about three in the morning, and I walked outside to get some fresh air. Remember those phone calls we used to have, when I made you stand by the window and look at the moon? Well, when I got outside, that's the first thing I saw, and at that moment, I wanted to talk to you more than anything in the world. It just wasn't possible right then."

"I know this sounds kind of hard to believe, but I think I know the night you're talking about," said Nicholas. "We were sitting up in *Goblin*'s cockpit—just me and Charlie—staring up at the moon and stars, and talking about how you can't really see the stars in New York. I was telling her about those old phone calls, and then . . . I don't know, I just got this weird feeling—like you were *there* somehow. . . . I told you it was hard to believe."

Will touched Nicholas on his arm. "No, not at all."

"Whatever happened with that boy—the one with malaria?" Nicholas asked, afraid of what the answer might be.

"A rare happy ending," said Will. "An aunt showed up and took him home. He'll be fine."

"That's good."

They sat quietly for a few minutes before Will spoke again. "I shouldn't have waited so long to bring you kids out here. I'm sorry. I should have been the one to teach you to sail. And I understand you can ride a bike, too."

"It's all right, Dad. Really. I learned a lot this summer—about a million different things. Even about *you*. But now that I have a few answers, it's like I have more questions than ever."

Will tilted his head back and laughed. "Welcome to *my* world, Nicholas."

* * *

Nicholas sprang out of bed at seven-fifteen, dressed, and ran down the spiral staircase. Nick, who had taken his newspaper and mug of coffee onto the porch, peered at him over his reading glasses.

"Where's the fire? Thought for sure you'd be sleeping in. Big day yesterday. And a late night. Can I get you some breakfast?"

"No thanks, I'll get something later. If Dad wakes up, you don't know where I ran off to."

Nick nodded. "Got it. I don't know where you are. Just out of curiosity, where *are* you running off to—with dish soap and sponges?"

"Me and Charlie have a little work to do. Oh, and one more thing. If Dad asks about his old Heron, it's still up in the hayloft, buried under a bunch of other stuff."

"Heron. Buried. Got it. Anything else I don't know?"

"Nope, that's it," said Nicholas, grinning. "Thanks, Uncle Nick. Oh, wait—one more thing. Could you bring Dad down to the dock at ten o'clock sharp?"

He ran out the door and down to Mr. Jensen's dock, where he climbed aboard *Imp*. In a matter of seconds, the mainsail was up and he was under way, confidently guiding her to a spot out of sight of Nick's house. He anchored her in knee-deep water to the left of the launching ramp and nibbled on a leftover chocolate bar while waiting for Charlie. She flew down the dirt road on her bike, skidding to a stop just as her front tire hit the water.

"Hey, I brought you a cinnamon roll," she said, wading out to him.

"Cool."

"Are you eating a chocolate bar?"

"Um . . . yeah," he admitted.

"For breakfast? Yuck."

"Excuse me, but I was in a hurry. My dad is still on Africa time, and there's no telling when he's going to wake up. I had to get *Imp* farther away from the house. Here's the soap and sponges."

As they rehashed the highlights of the party and the after-party conversations with parents, they scrubbed every square inch—inside and out—of the pretty little

Imp, until she looked exactly as she had on the day they launched her.

"Do you think your dad will be surprised?" Charlie asked.

"Definitely. He never mentioned her last night. I'm not sure he even remembered she was here. Either that, or he figures Uncle Nick got rid of her a long time ago." Nicholas checked his watch. "We still have a bunch of time. And the breeze is picking up. Feel like a sail?"

Charlie shrugged. "Why not? Now that your dad's here, I don't know how many more chances we'll have. You could be leaving tomorrow. Or today," she added sadly.

Giving the main halyard a mighty tug, Nicholas insisted, "We're not leaving today. Or tomorrow. Dad totally loves this place, and he even told me he's not ready to go back to work in the city. He seems more burned-out than usual. We may *never* go back." He handed the tiller to Charlie and hauled in the anchor.

"Somehow, I doubt that," said Charlie, sheeting in the mainsail. They scooted away on a beam reach, hugging the shoreline.

"So," they said simultaneously, followed by laughter.

"We're as bad as the twins," said Nicholas. "You go first."

"I was just going to ask if you think we should say anything about, you know, my dad's part in everything."

Nicholas pondered the question for a few seconds, and then answered with a definite "No."

"That's it? No?"

"Uh-huh. Look, maybe it was a pretty crappy thing to do to somebody, but your dad *was* only fourteen at the time. And from what you said, he's already paid the price. I just don't see any point in dragging it up again. I think it's enough for us to be able to tell Dad about the cut steering cables, and that we *know* he didn't wreck Teddy's boat on purpose. We don't have to tell him about everything we found out."

"You're right," said Charlie.

"As usual," Nicholas added. "So, *I* was going to say that today is the day I'm going to get a hit off of you."

"No way. What makes you think that, city boy?"

"I'm on a roll."

"Correction. You *were* on a roll."

"Meet you at the barn. High noon. And bring your best stuff, Brennan."

"You can count on it, Mettleson."

CHAPTER NINETEEN

Franny walked around to the front of Nick's house, where she found Nick and Will on the porch, chatting away, and well into their second pot of coffee.

"Look who's here," said Nick, opening the screen door to let her in. "Can I get you a cup of coffee? Will and I are trying to keep those coffee-bean pickers busy."

"Good morning, you two," she said. "No coffee for me, thanks."

"So, what brings you out this fine morning?" Will asked.

"Charlie told me to meet her here at ten. Have you seen her?"

"No sign of her," said Nick. "I saw Nicholas for about ten seconds before he ran out the—" He stopped, remembering his promise to Nicholas. "What time is it?"

"One minute to ten," said Will.

"I made Nicholas a promise this morning. Follow me, both of you." He led them past the remains of the still-smoldering bonfire and out on the dock.

"What are we doing here?" Will asked.

"Some kind of surprise, I suppose," answered Nick, who had noticed the missing *Imp* and guessed at the rest.

Will shielded his eyes from the sun and squinted at a small sailboat coming around the Beach End point. A smile spread across his face as he realized what—and who—it was.

"Is that what I think it is, Nick?"

It took a few more seconds for Franny to get there. "Omigosh. That's the boat you built, isn't it?"

"But never finished," said Will. "Kind of like *The Seaweed Strangler*."

Franny nudged Nick with her elbow, recalling the conversation in the diner about an old canoe. "And just how long have you known about this?"

"I may have helped them out a little," Nick said. "A little advice here and there. A dollar or two for some paint and hardware. But other than that . . . not much."

Will pointed at Charlie and Nicholas, who were smiling and waving at him and Franny. "Those two have had *some* summer. I'm sorry I missed it."

"If it's any consolation, it sounds like I missed a big chunk of it, and I was here all along," mused Franny.

Charlie expertly brought *Imp* alongside the dock and smiled up at her mom. Nicholas hopped up next to Will and handed him the short line attached to the bow. "She's all yours, Dad. Sorry, we put a few miles on her this summer, but she's still good as new. We polished her up special for you this morning."

Will's eyes turned watery as he pulled Nicholas to his chest, squeezing him tightly. "Please tell me that this is the last of your surprises, Nicholas. I don't think I can take much more."

Nicholas broke loose from his father's grip and started to point out all the work he and Charlie had done. "Uncle Nick made us sand for *days* before he would even buy the paint and varnish."

"Well, you did an amazing job. She looks just how I imagined she would. Even the color is right. I always wanted a bright red boat. How does she sail?"

"Awesome. But take her for a spin and see for yourself."

"Will you be my crew?"

Behind Will, Franny cleared her throat. "*Ahem!* Mister, er, excuse me, *Doctor* Mettleson, I believe you promised *me* the first sail in your new boat."

Will smiled, remembering his long-ago vow. "You're absolutely right, Miss Sherbrooke. I did." He stepped gingerly down into the tiny craft. "Oh my. It's smaller than

I remember. Shall we?" He held a hand out to guide her aboard.

"Why, thank you." She sat on the narrow seat and located the jib sheets. "I hope I still remember how to do this. I'd rather not capsize."

"Don't worry, Mom—it's like riding a bike. Once you learn how, you never forget. Right, Nicholas?" she added with a friendly nudge.

As her sails caught the warm late-summer breeze, *Imp* heeled gently, accelerating away from the dock—from the past—and into a bright future.

* * *

The grandfather clock in Nick's living room struck noon. Will and Franny had sailed by the dock at eleven-fifteen, ordering a couple of sandwiches and drinks, which the twins were more than happy to prepare and toss aboard *Imp* on her next pass. Nicholas waited, bat in hand, outside the barn, a few feet in front of the wall with the painted-on strike zone. The hundred-year-old siding was marked by thousands of baseball-sized dents where Charlie's pitches had struck. For the first time, Nicholas noticed how few were in the middle of the rectangle; they were concentrated around the edges, exactly where the great pitchers try to keep the ball. He took a couple of practice swings and smiled to himself. *Yep. She's good. But today's the day. I can feel it.*

Nick and Charlie came out the kitchen door, pausing when they saw Nicholas swinging at imaginary fastballs.

Nick whistled. "He looks pretty serious. How's your arm?"

Charlie made a muscle with her pitching arm. "Great."

"I thought maybe you chickened out," said Nicholas.

"*Ha!* That'll be the day," said Charlie, tossing the ball into her glove again and again as she strolled to the pitcher's mound. "Give me three warm-up pitches, and I'll be ready."

Nicholas stood next to Nick and watched the first pitch, a fastball, hit the rectangle dead center with a loud thud and bounce straight back to the mound. The next two were curveballs that caught the low inside corner.

"Her curve is sharp today," whispered Nick. "Wait for a fastball."

"What are you whispering over there, you two?" Charlie asked.

"Never mind," said Nicholas. "Are you ready?"

"The better question is, Are *you?*"

Nicholas dug his heels into the batter's box and looked out at her. "Ready."

Nick, the umpire, stood behind Charlie. "Play ball!" he shouted.

Charlie wound up and let loose with a fastball that sailed away from Nicholas and the strike zone, hitting the barn so hard that it actually broke through the siding and

Nick and Charlie came out the kitchen door, pausing when they saw Nicholas swinging at imaginary fastballs.

fell inside the barn. Nicholas fished it out and tossed it back to Charlie.

"Ball one!"

Pitch number two was a waist-high fastball—a slugger's dream pitch. Nicholas swung mightily, but missed completely.

"Strike one!"

Nicholas stepped out of the batter's box and breathed deeply, composing himself. *You can do this.*

He fouled off the next pitch, another fastball, into the barn wall behind him.

"Strike two! The count is one and two."

He knew what was coming: a curveball. The strikeout pitch. It had tormented him all summer. Charlie smiled at him from the pitcher's mound. She knew that he knew, but it didn't matter. He bent over and rubbed some dirt on his hands and closed his eyes for a few seconds, visualizing the pitch before she even threw it. Then he took his place in the batter's box, held his bat high, and waited.

Charlie rubbed the baseball in her hands and then gripped it tightly inside the pocket of her glove. She wound up and let it fly.

Nicholas followed the ball like a hawk eyeing its prey. It appeared to be heading right for him, but he fought off the instinct to back away. His muscles tensed, and his bat began its descent, slicing violently through the air until . . .

Crack!

The ball rocketed off his bat, over Charlie's head, and past the barbwire fence that marked the edge of the pasture, a good two hundred and fifty feet away.

It would be hard to say who was most surprised. Charlie, Nick, and Nicholas all stood openmouthed, watching the ball finally land in a cloud of dust.

Nick raised his arm and made a circling motion over his head. "Home run!" he announced.

Falling to his knees, Nicholas threw his arms into the air. "Yes! Finally!"

Nick and Charlie jogged over and lifted him back to his feet. "No question about that one!" Nick declared. "Dead center field. Congratulations."

"Yeah—nice going, Mettleson," admitted Charlie with a grin and a hearty pat on the back. "It's about time. You could have done it the very first day we met, but you didn't *believe* you could."

"What do you think about that, Uncle Nick?"

"I think you can do *anything* you set your mind to, Nicholas."

* * *

Nicholas stood at the tower-room window a few minutes after midnight, staring at the moon through the brass telescope, trying to absorb as much of his surroundings as possible, and hoping for one last glimpse of the mystery sailboat. A chilly wind blew through the room—yet another reminder that summer really was over. It had been three days since the party—and his dad's arrival—and the day he and the twins had been dreading for weeks had finally come. The Mettlesons were leaving for New York in the morning: back to the city, back to school, back to reality.

As he spun the telescope in *Goblin*'s direction, something flew in through the open window beside him, hitting him squarely on the side of his head.

"Oww! Hey!" he shouted, turning and looking for a bat, or perhaps a confused seagull. Then he saw the tennis ball that had come to rest on the bed. *Charlie!*

One floor below, Pistol barked, and Nick called up to him, "Nicholas? You all right up there?"

"Yeah, I'm fine. Just a dream."

"All right—see you in the morning."

" 'Night, Uncle Nick."

He looked down at the yard, and Charlie waved up at him. "Sorry! Where'd I hit you?"

"In the head," Nicholas hissed.

Charlie pumped her fist. "Yesss! I've still got it."

"What are you *doing* out there?"

"Come on down. I couldn't sleep. Let's go sit on *Goblin*."

"Okay, I'll be down in a minute." Nicholas reached his hand under his mattress, feeling around until he was able to wrap his fingers around the object he was searching for.

He dropped it in his pocket and slipped quietly down the stairs and out the front door.

"You know, next time, instead of nailing me in the head with a tennis ball, you could try calling my name."

"I know, but the tennis ball is more fun."

Nicholas pointed at the plastic grocery bag that Charlie carried. "What's in the bag?"

"Couple of pops—sorry, *sodas*—and some surprises. C'mon!" She pulled him by the arm down to the beach, where they set the dinghy in the water and rowed out to the waiting *Goblin*.

They opened cans of icy root beer and leaned back against the wooden coamings, gazing up at the stars and shivering.

"Blimey, it's cold," said Nicholas, crossing his arms over his chest.

"What did you just say?"

"I said it's cold."

"No, you said, '*Blimey*, it's cold,'" Charlie corrected.

"No I didn't. I've never said 'blimey' in my life."

"Well, you just said it."

"Are you sure?"

"Positive."

"Oh man. Do you see what the twins are doing to me? I'm going to have to go away to boarding school; I'm starting to talk like them."

Charlie's laugh seemed to linger in the still air before

slowly drifting away, leaving the two friends in silence for a few moments.

"This is the last time I'll see anything like *this* for a while," said Nicholas. "Not many stars to see in the city."

"You can always call me. I'll describe them to you."

"Not exactly the same."

"Hey, remember the first time we took *Goblin* by ourselves and we got stuck on that sandbar?"

Nicholas laughed. "The look on our faces when she started sailing away without us."

"Almost as funny as the look on Pistol's face! And Nick saw the whole thing," said Charlie. "He really is a good guy."

Another few moments passed silently between them.

"So . . . you really think you'll come back next summer?"

"Yeah, especially now that Dad and Uncle Nick have reconnected. I wouldn't be surprised if Dad decided to skip Africa next summer and come out here for a while. He loves the whole Doctors Without Borders thing, but I overheard him talking to Nick about how hard it is on him. He said that next year he needs to take some time off."

"Well, I got you a little going-away present, but I'm only going to give it to you if you promise to come back."

"I promise, I promise."

"Are you just saying that to get the present?"

"Maybe."

"Nicholas!"

"I'm kidding. And how do I know that *you'll* be here next summer? You might decide that you want to be an ostrich farmer."

"That's *not* going to happen. Here, take it before I change my mind." She handed him a paperback-sized package, wrapped in the Sunday comics.

"I like the paper," said Nicholas as he tore it away, revealing a stack of postcards with pictures of the lake and the town of Deming. "Wow. Where did you get all these? Is every one different?"

"Yep. There's *eighty* of them. I've been collecting them for a while. Every year, they come out with new ones. Notice anything else about them?"

"They already have stamps on them. That must have cost a fortune."

"And my address."

"Hmmm. You know, I'm not *sure*, but I'm starting to get the idea that you want me to write to you."

"Two postcards a week. And you're already in the habit, thanks to your dad. It's forty weeks, maybe a little less, until you come back. *If* you come back."

"Can't I just call? Wouldn't that be better?"

"Not the same. We can talk on the phone, too, but the postcards are . . . real. I'm going to do the same for you. So, when you get back to New York, you have to send me a bunch with pictures of different parts of the city. I've never been there, so it'll be almost like I'm visiting."

"You're crazy, you know."

"Yep."

Nicholas reached into his pocket. "Um, I have something for you, too. It's really your mom's, but she wants you to have it. I found it up in the tower room a few weeks ago. I didn't tell anybody, especially the twins, but there *is* another secret compartment in the tower room. If you push on this one piece of the floor, it slides under the wall, and there's a little hiding place underneath. And *this* was in it. Hold out your hand and close your eyes."

She did as he said, and he placed a silver ID bracelet in her palm, with the engraved letters—FRANNY—facing her.

Her face brightened when she opened her eyes. "Mom's bracelet! How did—"

"Remember, she told us that she lost it that day at the marina? It must have fallen off her arm when she got hit in the head. I guess Dad picked it up, figuring he'd give it back to her later."

"But there was no later," said Charlie.

"I gave it to Dad the other day, and then last night, when they were sitting out on the porch swing, he gave it back to her. But she . . ."

Charlie laughed. "It all makes sense now." She held her closed fist out to Nicholas. She slowly turned her hand over, uncovering a gold pocket watch on a short chain.

"What's that?"

Charlie handed it to him. "Believe it or not, it's your dad's watch. Which was originally his grandfather's watch. A few days ago, before your dad got here, Mom showed it to me, and told me that she took it from your dad's hiding place the same day she left him that letter. She said she wanted to have something of his to hold on to, until he came back. She's kept it hidden away in her jewelry chest all this time."

"Wait a minute. And she . . . *they*, on the porch swing . . . decided—"

"Exactly. To give them to us."

Nicholas turned the watch over and over in his hand. "What do you think will happen next? I mean, to my dad and your mom—do you think they'll ever . . ."

Charlie looked up at the moon and shrugged. "Stranger things have happened."

* * *

A blast of cold air rattled the tower-room windows and ruffled the pages of the book Nicholas had left on the sill, waking him. He sat up halfway in bed, groping for the blanket that had fallen to the floor. As he reached down to pick it up, the red numbers of his alarm clock read:

2:53

He made it to the window just in time to see a sailboat— sleek and fast—glide past the cove and out of sight.

"Someday, somehow, I'm going to find you, whoever you are," he said.

Suddenly wide-awake, he sat on the edge of the bed, his mind brimming with ideas. He smiled as he reached for his notebook and a pen.

* * *

Sheets of rain pelted the windows of Nick's house as Will loaded the last duffel bags into the family station wagon. Drenched, he stepped into the kitchen, where Nicholas, the twins, Pistol, and Nick waited.

Nick cleared off the kitchen table and unrolled a faded blueprint, weighing down the ends with salt and pepper shakers. "Hayley, Hetty, come here a second. You're not leaving here with those frowns on your faces. That's not how I want to remember you. I have one more little surprise. These are the plans that your dad used to build *Imp*. On your way back to New York, you two need to start thinking about a name for *your* boat."

"*Our* boat?" Hayley asked.

"That's right. I'm starting work on a sister ship to *Imp* this afternoon. She'll be ready for you in June."

They ran to Nick, screaming and hugging him for dear life.

"You really mean it?" asked Hetty.

"I really do," said Nick. "I ordered the lumber yesterday."

Will started to squeeze Nick's hand, and then reconsidered, pulling him into a quick hug. "Thanks, Nick. For *everything*."

"My pleasure. You're always welcome, you know. Now let's get you on the road. You've got a long drive ahead of you." He tapped his finger on the blueprint. "And I have work to do."

Will went out the door, followed by the twins. Squealing, they ran through the rain and into the backseat of the car, where they would spend most of the next seven hours asleep, dreaming about the voyages on which they would embark the next summer—in their very own boat.

Nicholas and Nick stood face to face in the kitchen, each determined to maintain his composure. They moved toward each other without a word, and Nicholas buried his head in Nick's shoulder.

"See you in a few months," said Nick, holding him at arm's length.

Nicholas, forcing himself to smile, nodded and stepped out into the cold, rainy morning.

"Hey, Nicholas," said Charlie, startling him. She stood in the gravel driveway, straddling her bicycle. "I know we said goodbye last night and all, but Mom wanted me to bring these for you guys." As she held out a plastic bag full of chocolate chip cookies, he noticed that she was wearing the ID bracelet.

"Thanks. Look at you—you're getting soaked."

"No, I *am* soaked."

"Well, your lips are turning blue. You should go in-side."

"I'll be all right. I just wanted to see . . ."

Nicholas nodded, blinking away the rain and smiling through the bleak, damp air at the best friend he'd ever had. "I started working on something last night." He held up a small notebook so she could see what he'd written on the cover.

Charlie's face broke into a jubilant smile as she read the words aloud: *"The Return of the Seaweed Strangler."*

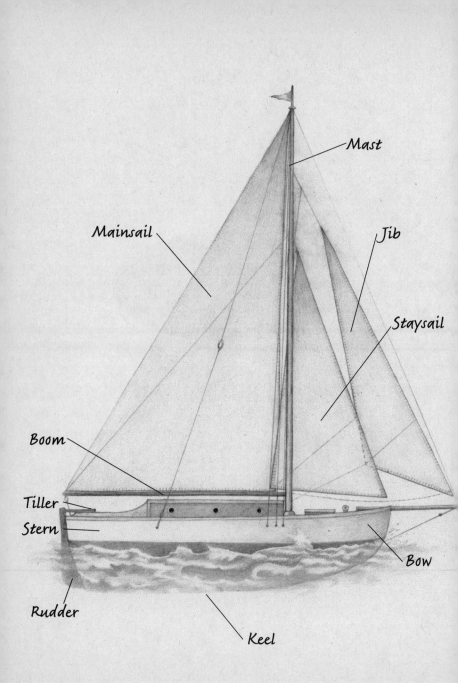

Mast

Jib

Staysail

Mainsail

Boom

Tiller

Stern

Bow

Rudder

Keel

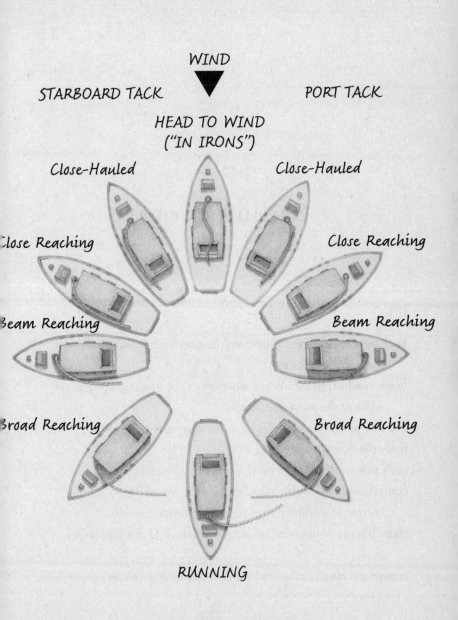

WIND

STARBOARD TACK

PORT TACK

HEAD TO WIND
("IN IRONS")

Close-Hauled

Close-Hauled

Close Reaching

Close Reaching

Beam Reaching

Beam Reaching

Broad Reaching

Broad Reaching

RUNNING

Sailing Terms

backstay: a cable stretching from the masthead to the stern on most larger sailboats

beam reach: the point of sail where the boat is sailing at a right angle to the wind direction

boom: a wood or metal pole attached at a right angle to the mast

bow: the front part of a boat

cat's paws: small ripples on the water that resemble cat footprints

centerboard: a movable board that can be lowered through the bottom of a sailboat to reduce sideways movement

cleat: a piece of hardware used to tie off the end of a line (rope) or sheet

coaming: a raised rim around the cockpit, designed to keep water out

cockpit: the area near the stern of the boat where the tiller is located

dinghy: a small rowboat, often used to reach a moored sailboat

forestay: a cable stretching from the masthead to the bow

gunwale (pronounced "gunn'l"): the upper edge of a boat, where the deck meets the hull

halyard: a line used to raise or lower a sail

heel: to lean over because of the force of the wind on the sails

jib: a triangular sail that attaches to the forestay

knot: a nautical mile

mainsail: a sail attached to both mast and boom; it is usually the largest sail

mainsheet: the line used to control the mainsail

mast: a tall wood or metal post on a sailboat to which sails are attached

masthead: the top part of a mast

mooring: a place for keeping a boat secure; it includes a heavy anchor and a float of some kind to which the boat is attached

port: the left-hand side of a boat

reef: to reduce the size of a sail by tucking in a part of it and tying it off

rudder: a hinged plate below the waterline used to steer a boat

sandbar: a shallow, sandy spot in a lake or ocean, also known as a shoal

sheet: a line used to control sails

shroud: a cable that stretches from the top of the mast to the sides of a boat, supporting the mast

starboard: the right-hand side of a boat

staysail: a triangular sail similar to a jib but attached to a stay between the mast and the forestay.

stern: the rear part of a boat

tack: to follow a zigzag course (because sailboats cannot sail directly into the wind)

tiller: a wooden handle attached to the rudder used to steer a sailboat

topsides: the surface of a boat's hull that is above the waterline

Acknowledgments

I would like to thank the following people:

First and foremost, my parents, who went to the 1962 Cleveland Boat Show and, despite having no real knowledge of sailing, bought a Wayfarer 608 because it was "the prettiest boat there"—a decision that changed all our lives.

My aunt Dot and uncle Jim, for the amazing memories and inspiration that you provided.

And, in no particular order:

Rosemary Stimola, superstar agent and BFF of the RBGs.

Nancy Hinkel, editor extraordinaire, sounding board, critic, and tireless advocate of middle-grade fiction.

Everyone at Knopf Books for Young Readers, Random House Children's Books, and Listening Library, for their continued support and efforts on my behalf.

My brother Steve, for starring in the original 8 mm version of *The Seaweed Strangler*, and for buying a worn copy of *We Didn't Mean to Go to Sea* at a school-library sale for a quarter.

Sister Gail Morgan, OP (a fellow Buckeye!), and everyone at SVF, for the continued support and friendship.

Friends and family may recognize certain similarities as well as some striking differences between Forsaken Lake and Pymatuning Lake, on the Ohio-Pennsylvania border. Pymatuning Lake is a wonderful and most certainly *not* forsaken place, nor is it home to a creature with a penchant for strangling his victims with a length of seaweed. As far as I know, that is.

And Laura, for everything.